Traditional Iranian Music

Orality, Physicality and Improvisation

Traditional Iranian Music

Orality, Physicality and Improvisation

Masato Tani

TRANS
PACIFIC
PRESS

Traditional Iranian Music: Orality, Physicality and Improvisation
© 2024 by Masato Tani
Published in 2024 by Trans Pacific Press Co., Ltd.

Trans Pacific Press Co., Ltd.
PO Box 8547
#19682
Boston, MA, 02114, United States
Telephone: +1-6178610545
Email: info@transpacificpress.com
Web: http://www.transpacificpress.com

Copyedited by Dr. Karl E. Smith, Melbourne, Australia
Designed and set by Ryo Kuroda, Tsukuba-city, Ibaraki, Japan

Most scores, figures and tables in this book have been reproduced or modified based on the originals.

The publication of this book was supported by a Grant-in-Aid for Publication of Scientific Research Results (Grant Number 22HP6001), provided by the Japan Society for the Promotion of Science, to which we express our sincere appreciation.

Library of Congress Cataloging-in-Publication Data

Names: Tani, Masato, author.
Title: Traditional Iranian music : orality, physicality and improvisation / Masato Tani.
Description: Tokyo, Japan : Trans Pacific Press, 2024. | Includes bibliographical references and index. | Summary: "Improvisation is a defining characteristic of traditional Iranian music. Iranian musicians describe their music as 'impossible to play in the same way twice' or 'able to be performed in many ways,' emphasizing that they do not perform prepared compositions. What exactly do musicians play and how do they play it? How does the musician's individuality and originality come into play? What norms are acquired during the learning process that make improvisation possible? What is the concept of "improvisation" in Iranian culture? The author, a researcher as well as a santūr player, explores these various points based on field studies and personal experiences from studying and playing traditional Iranian music over many years. This auto-ethnography is an attempt to academically elucidate the senses, physicality, and mentality of musicians by engaging with the subject through first-hand participation"-- Provided by publisher.
Identifiers: LCCN 2024002506 (print) | LCCN 2024002507 (ebook) | ISBN 9781920850357 (paperback) | ISBN 9781920850364 (epub)
Subjects: LCSH: Music--Iran--History and criticism. | Music--Iran--Analysis, appreciation. | Music--Performance--Iran. | Improvisation (Music) | Dastgāh.
Classification: LCC ML3756 .T36 2024 (print) | LCC ML3756 (ebook) | DDC 780.955--dc23/eng/20240402
LC record available at https://lccn.loc.gov/2024002506
LC ebook record available at https://lccn.loc.gov/2024002507

Contents

List of Figures vi
List of Photos vii
List of Tables vii
List of Scores viii
Introduction: Locating the problem 1

Part I 17

   1. What is *radīf*: Toward a redefinition of the word 19

   2. The vocal image underlying notation reading 35

   3. Improvisation, mental state and memory 45

   4. *Charkh*: The circulatory paradigm in performance form
      and musical structure 61

   5. Analysis of *gūshes* 73

   6. Change in the context for learning improvisation:
      The influence of writing on Iranian music 115

Part II 129

   7. How can individuality be described and explained? 131

   8. Verbal rhythm and musical rhythm 143

   9. Trial and error on hammered dulcimers:
      Iranian and Indian *santūr* 153

   10. Perceiving and understanding through the fingers:
       Toward a comparative study of instrumental somatic sensibilities 163

   11. The *santūr's* new physicality:
       Toward a geopolitics on the board of the instrument 173

   12. What we learn from the *radīf* 183

Notes 209
Bibliography 223
Index 231

List of Figures

3.1 Relationship among *gūshes* 50
3.2 Index of the *radīf* passed on by Mirzā Abdollāh 57
3.3 Index of the *radīf* passed on by Mūsā Ma'rūfī 57
4.1 Examples of performance in the *shūr* mode by three musicians 63
4.1-a Examples of performance in the *shūr* mode by three musicians 68
4.2 The structure of *charkh* 64
4.3 Multi-layered *charkh* 67
6.1 Liner notes of the *radīf* passed on by Abdollāh Davāmī 125
9.1 Iranian *santūr* string arrangement 157
10.1 String arrangement on a *santūr* 166
10.2 Fretting positions on a *setār* 167
10.3 Four tetrachords by Talā'ī 168
10.4 Fingering positions on *'ūd* neck 170
10.5 Basic idea behind *modgardi* 171
11.1 Relative positions of low-register and middle-/high-register strings 177
12.1 Temporal structure of *shūr* mode 184
12.2 Temporal structure of *homāyun* mode 185
12.3 Temporal structure of *māhūr* mode 186
12.4 Tetrachord structure of *hoseini gūshe* in *shūr* mode 188
12.5 Tetrachord structure of *darāmad* in *dashtī* mode 188
12.6 A typical form of *modgardi* 189
12.7 Tetrachord structure of *'Erāq* in *afshārī* mode 190
12.8 Tetrachord structure of *darāmad* in *bayāt-e tork* mode
   (example shows a version on B♭, a perfect fifth below) 191

List of Photos

9.1 An Iranian *santūr* 153
9.2 Kashmiri *santūr* 156
9.3 Shiv Kumar Sharma (right) and the author at Sharma's home
    in Mumbai, August 2016 156
9.4 Kashmiri *santūr* (right) on a wooden stand 156
9.5 Placing the *santūr* on the player's lap. Player: Takahiro Arai,
    a pupil of Shiv Kumar Sharma 156
9.6 Kashmiri *santūr* with four strings per course 156
9.7 A contemporary *santūr* played in Hindustani music
    with three strings per course 156
9.8 An Iranian *santūr* from above 157
9.9 *Chikari* course on a *santūr* played in Hindustani music .. 158
9.10 *Santūr* mallets in India (left), showing grooves in the striking face (right) .. 160
9.11 Iranian *santūr* mallets 160
9.12 Lesson with Ardavān Kāmkār, a master of contemporary Iranian *santūr*,
     who is known for his virtuosic techniques 161
11.1 Strike zones for each register of *santūr* 177
11.2 Sābet and Pāyvar's striking points (connected to form lines) ... 179
11.3 Ardavān's recommended strike lines 180

List of Tables

2.1 Persian alphabet 39
2.2 Rhythmic patterns of the eight feet 41
5.1 The *gūshes* and corresponding scores analyzed in this chapter ... 75
8.1 The original meter of *Sāqīnāme* by *Hāfez* 146
8.2 *Sāqīnāme* in *zarbi* 146
8.3 Metrical structure in the original meter of *Chahārpāre* by *Hātef Esfahānī* . 148
8.4 Metrical structure in *tasnīf-e dogāh* 149
8.5 Metrical structure in "*Mehrabānī* in five-eight time" 149
8.5.1 The location of the *shāhed* in "*Mehrabānī* in five-eight time" ... 150
8.6 Metrical structure in "*Mehrabānī* in two-four time" 150
8.6.1 The location of the *shāhed* in "*Mehrabānī* in two-four time" ... 150
8.7 Metrical structure in "*Mehrabānī* in six-eight time" 151
12.1 Metrical analysis of Hāfez's poetry 199

List of Scores

1.1 *Darāmad* (E *koron*) 24
    1.1a *Darāmad* (E *koron*) 26
1.2 *Kereshme* 24
1.3 *Zābol* (G) 24
    1.3a *Zābol* (G) 27
1.4 *Mūye* (G–B flat) 24
    1.4a *Mūye* (G–B flat) 27
1.5 *Mokhālef* (C) 25
    1.5a *Mokhālef* (C) 27
1.6 *Kereshme* 25
1.7 *Forūd* (C → E *koron*) 25
    1.7a *Forūd* (C → E *koron*) 27
2.1 *Chahārbāgh* passed on by A. Sabā 38
2.2 *Chahārbāgh* passed on by Mahmūd-Karīmī (1927–1984) 39
2.3 *Mansūrī* passed on by A. Sabā 42
2.4 Notation of descending figure with slur 42
2.5 Actual performance with *rīz* 42
3.1 The *radīf* passed on by Abolhasan Sabā (1902–1958) 52
3.2 The *radīf* passed on by Mizrā Abdollāh (1843?–1918) 53
3.3 The *radīf* passed on by Mūsā Ma'rūfī (1889–1965) 53
3.4 The *radīf* passed on by Farāmarz Pāyvar (1933–2009) 53
4.1 Small *charkh* in *Chahārmezrāb* 66
4.2 *Darāmad* in the *segāh* mode from the *radīf* by Davāmī 70
5.1 *Radīf* passed on by Mirzā Abdollāh (A *koron*) 76
5.2 *Radīf* passed on by Abdollāh Davāmī (B *koron*) ... 76
5.3 *Radīf* passed on by Mahmūd Karīmī (E *koron*) 76
5.4 *Radīf* passed on by Abolhasan Sabā (A *koron*) 78
5.5 "Another kind of *darāmad*" from *radīf* passed on by Mahmūd Karīmī (E *koron*) 78
5.6 *Radīf* passed on by Farāmarz Pāyvar (A *koron*) ... 79
5.7 *Radīf* passed on by Mūsā Ma'rūfī (E *koron*) 80
5.8 *Radīf* passed on by Mirzā Abdollāh (A *koron*) 80
5.9 *Radīf* passed on by Mūsā Ma'rūfī (E *koron*) 80
5.10 *Radīf* passed on by Mirzā Abdollāh (A *koron*) ... 82

5.11 *Radīf* passed on by Mūsā Ma'rūfī (E *koron*) 82

5.12 *Radīf* passed on by Mirzā Abdollāh (A *koron*) 82

5.13 *Radīf* passed on by Mūsā Ma'rūfī (E *koron*) 82

5.14 *Radīf* passed on by Mirzā Abdollāh (A *koron*) 84

5.15 *Radīf* passed on by Mūsā Ma'rūfī (E *koron*) 84

5.16 *Kereshme* in the *homāyun* mode from the *radīf* passed on
  by Abolhasan Sabā 84

5.17 *Radīf* passed on by Mirzā Abdollāh (A *koron*) 85

5.18 *Radīf* passed on by Mūsā Ma'rūfī (E *koron*) 85

5.19 *Radīf* passed on by Mirzā Abdollāh (C) 86

5.20 *Radīf* passed on by Abolhasan Sabā (C) 86

5.21 *Radīf* passed on by Farāmarz Pāyvar (C) 86

5.22 *Radīf* passed on by Mūsā Ma'rūfī (G) 87

5.23 *Radīf* passed on by Mahmūd Karīmī (G) 87

5.24 *Radīf* passed on by Abdollāh Davāmī (D) 87

5.25 *Radīf* passed on by Mirzā Abdollāh (C) 89

5.26 *Radīf* passed on by Mūsā Ma'rūfī (G) 89

5.27 *Baste negār* in another pitch range (C),
  from the *radīf* passed on by Mūsā Ma'rūfī 89

5.28 *Radīf* passed on by Mūsā Ma'rūfī (G–B flat) 91

5.29 *Radīf* passed on by Mahmūd Karīmī (G–B flat) 91

5.30 *Radīf* passed on by Abdollāh Davāmī (D–F) 91

5.31 *Radīf* passed on by Mirzā Abdollāh (C–E flat) 92

5.32 *Radīf* passed on by Abolhasan Sabā (C–E flat) 92

5.33 *Darāmad* in *shūr* from the *radīf* passed on by Mirzā Abdollāh 93

5.34 *Āvāz* in the *afshārī* mode taken from *radīf* by Sabā 94

5.35 *Radīf* passed on by Mahmūd Karīmī (A *koron*) 95

5.36 *Radīf* passed on by Abdollāh Davāmī (E *koron*) 95

5.37 *Radīf* passed on by Mirzā Abdollāh (F) 97

5.38 *Radīf* passed on by Abolhasan Sabā (F) 97

5.39 *Radīf* passed on by Farāmarz Pāyvar (F) 97

5.40 *Radīf* passed on by Mūsā Ma'rūfī (C) 98

5.41 *Radīf* passed on by Mahmūd Karīmī (C) 98

5.42 *Radīf* passed on by Abdollāh Davāmī (G) 98

5.43 *Kereshme* in *darāmad* (top) and *kereshme* in *mokhālef* (bottom),
  from *radīf* passed on by Mūsā Ma'rūfī 99

5.44 *Radīf* passed on by Abolhasan Sabā (F) 100

5.45 *Radīf* passed on by Abdollāh Davāmī (G) 100
5.46 *Radīf* passed on by Mirzā Abdollāh (F) 100
5.47 *Radīf* passed on by Mūsā Ma'rūfī (C) 101
5.48 *Radīf* passed on by Mirzā Abdollāh (F) 101
5.49 *Radīf* passed on by Mirzā Abdollāh (F) 102
5.50 *Radīf* passed on by Mūsā Ma'rūfī (C) 102
5.51 *Radīf* passed on by Mahmūd Karīmī (E *koron*) 103
5.52 *Radīf* passed on by Mūsā Ma'rūfī (E *koron*) 103
5.53 *Radīf* passed on by Abolhasan Sabā (A *koron*) 103
5.54 *Radīf* passed on by Mirzā Abdollāh (A *koron*) 104
5.55 *Radīf* passed on by Abdollāh Davāmī (B *koron*) 104
5.56 *Radīf* passed on by Mirzā Abdollāh (F) 105
5.57 *Radīf* passed on by Mūsā Ma'rūfī (C) 105
5.58 *Forūd* presented in the latter half of *gūshe* "*mokhālef be maghlūb*"
   excerpted from the *radīf* by Mahmūd Karīmī 106
5.59 *Forūd* presented in *gūshes* "*hazin*" through "*hozān*"
   excerpted from the *radīf* by Mūsā Ma'rūfī 106
5.60 *Forūd* presented in the latter half of *gūshe* "*hazin*"
   excerpted from the *radīf* by Mirzā Abdollāh 107
5.61 *Forūd* presented in the latter half of *gūshe* "*masnavī-ye mokhālef*"
   excerpted from the *radīf* by Abolhasan Sabā 107
5.62 *Forūd* presented in the latter half of *gūshe* "*maghlūb*"
   excerpted from the *radīf* by Farāmarz Pāyvar 108
5.63 *Forūd* presented in the latter half of *gūshe* "*masnavī-ye mokhālef*"
   excerpted from the *radīf* by Abdollāh Davāmī 108
5.64 Another kind of *mūye* excerpted from the *radīf* by Mirzā Abdollāh 108
5.65 *Radīf* passed on by Abolhasan Sabā (A *koron*) 110
5.66 *Radīf* passed on by Mahmūd Karīmī (E *koron*) 110
5.67 *Radīf* passed on by Abolhasan Sabā (The melody
   descends from F to A *koron*. In *forūd*, E *koron* returns to E flat) 110
5.68 *Radīf* passed on by Mahmūd Karīmī. (The melody descends
   from C to E *koron*. In *forūd*, B *koron* returns to B flat) 110
5.69-a Beginning of *reng* in the *radīf* passed on by Mirzā Abdollāh (A *koron*) ... 112
5.69-b The part of *darāmad* (A *koron*) 112
5.69-c The part of *zābol* (C) 112
5.69-d The part of *mūye* (C–E flat) 113
5.69-e The part of *mokhālef* (F) 113
5.69-f The part of *forūd* (movement down from F to A *koron*) 113

List of Scores

6.1 Etude for *Takie* imitating *Tahrīr* 120
6.2 Transcription of Mirzā Abdollāh's *radīf* by Kiyāni 121
6.3 Excerpt from "Khazān" composed by Meshkātian 121
6.4 Transcription example by Jean During 126
6.5 Transcription example by Dāryūsh Talā'ī 126
7.1 *Darāmad* passed on by Abolhasan Sabā 134
7.2 *Darāmad* passed on by Mirzā Abdollāh 134
7.3 *Radīf* for *āvāz* passed on by Mahmūd Karīmī 137
7.4 *Radīf* arranged for *santūr* by Arfa'e Atrā'ī 137
7.5 Tuning system of *santūr* 139
7.6 Excerpt from "Rāz o Niyāz" by Pashang Kāmkār 139
7.7 Excerpt of "Khātere" by Ardavān Kāmkār 140
8.1 *Kereshme* in *homāyun* mode, from the *radīf* passed down
    by Abolhasan Sabā (1902–1958) 145
8.2 *Sāqināme* in *māhūr* mode, from the *radīf* passed down
    by Mahmūd Karīmī (1927–1984) 146
8.3 *Chahārbāgh (Chahārpāre)* in *abū'atā* mode, from the *radīf*
    passed down by Mahmūd Karīmī (1927–1984) 148
8.4 *Tasnīf-e dogāh* in *bayāt-e tork* mode 149
8.5 "*Mehrabānī* in five-eight time" in *bayāt-e tork* mode 149
8.6 "*Mehrabānī* in two-four time" in *bayāt-e tork* mode 150
8.7 "*Mehrabānī* in six-eight time" in *bayāt-e tork* mode 151
9.1 Etude for *Takie* imitating *Tahrīr* 160
11.1 Etude from *santūr* tutor *Dastūr-e Santūr* 174
11.2 Ardavān's mallet technique, in which D and E♭ are both played
    with the right hand 175
11.3 Dyad mallet assignment 176
11.4 Two dyads 176
11.5 Conventional dyad mallet assignment 176
11.6 Dyad mallet assignment by Ardavān 176
12.1 The four tetrachords 185
12.2 *Hoseini* in *shūr* mode, from Sabā's *radīf* 189
12.3 *Darāmad* in *dashtī* mode, from Sabā's *radīf* 189
12.4 *Darāmad* in *afshārī* mode (followed by *Qarā'ī*)
    (transcribed by Masato Tani) 190
12.5 '*Erāq* in *afshārī* mode (transcribed by Masato Tani) 190

12.6 *Darāmad* in *bayāt-e tork* mode (transcribed by Masato Tani) 191
12.7 *'Erāq* and returning to original component pitch of *Darāmad* (from E *koron* to E♭) in *afshārī* mode (transcribed by Masato Tani) 193
12.8 *Rohāb* (line 1) and return to *darāmad* in *afshārī* mode (line 2) (transcribed by Masato Tani) 193
12.9 Internal structure of a *gūshe* 194
12.10 The *gūshe darāmad* in *shūr* mode (taken from Mirzā Abdollāh's *radīf*) ... 196
12.11 Examples of musical development based on *motafā'elon* foot 197
12.12 *Chahārbāgh* composed by repetition of *motafā'elon* foot 197
12.13 Correspondence between the letters and staff notation 201
12.14 Numbers beneath letters to indicate note length 201
12.15 Demonstration by Rāhati (transcribed by Masato Tani) 201
12.16 Analysis of Rāhati's demonstration (transcribed by Masato Tani) 202
12.17 *Rohāb* in *shūr* mode, from *radīf* of Mirzā Abdollāh 203
12.18 *Baste negār* 204
12.19 *Baste negār* in *segāh* mode 205
12.20 *Ouj* in *shūr* mode, from *radīf* of Mahmūd Karīmī 207

Introduction: Locating the problem

What images do the words "Iranian music" (or "Persian music") elicit? What kind of sounds or musical instruments do we imagine? The late Japanese ethnomusicologist Fumio Koizumi (1927–1983) stated:

> When I die, if someone tells me I can listen to whatever music I like for the last five minutes, I would no doubt ask him to play a Persian song for me. Among the songs of the world's many ethnic groups, there is no song so beautiful as Persian songs... Those glamorous melodies take listeners to the dream world, as do the tiles of mosques in Isfahan. (Koizumi 1978: 358–59)

Iranian music is an extremely rich form, not only the traditional music of the so-called "center," which is based on the modal system called *dastgāh* and is closely connected to classical Persian poetry, but also the folk music reflecting ethnic, linguistic, and cultural diversity of the various regions of Iran, including Kordestān in the west, Khorāsān in the northeast, Balūchestān in the southeast, and Āzarbāyjān in the northwest. The term "folk music" refers to religious and popular musical traditions enjoyed and supported by a broad range of everyday people. Religious musical traditions include not only the recitation of the Qor'ān, but also the music accompanying various events such as *ta'ziye* (passion plays), *rouze khāni* (recitations of the tragedy of Karbalā), *sīne zadan* (breast-beating marches), which are based on the theme of the suffering and martyrdom of religious leaders. Popular music traditions have included traditions of spoken recitation, perhaps exemplified by the epic poetry recited during the ritualized exercises of traditional Iranian wrestling in domed venues called *zūrkhāne*. They also include the outdoor music played at wedding ceremonies and festivals, chiefly on the *sornā* (a reed instrument) and *dohol* (a large drum); lullabies and lyrical folk songs nurtured by the peoples of different regions; and the music played by itinerant entertainers called *motreb* at small local communities – the diversity is very broad. Furthermore, there is no strict separation between these folk music traditions and the traditional music of the "center": each influences the other.

Iranian music has long been regarded as significant for its profound relationship with the musical cultures of India and the Arab world, and it has become commonplace that when people talk about Iranian music, they cite its improvisational performance as one of its appealing characteristics. The present work was occasioned by problematizing the improvisational nature of Iranian music, raising the questions, "what and how do musicians play, and – in the course of learning traditional Iranian music – what are the norms instilled that enable improvisation?"

Traditional Iranian music – especially the form known as *āvāz*, which has no definite meter – has generally been described as being "improvisational," even in academic accounts. Iranian musicians describe their music as "impossible to play in the same way twice" or "able to be performed in many ways," emphasizing that they do not perform what is composed in advance.

The nature of improvisation, however, differs greatly across the world's various musical genres, which makes it difficult to describe in concise or comprehensive terms. Hence, we must clarify what specifically characterizes the improvisation of traditional Iranian music. To this end, let us take a quick survey of the definitions of the word "improvisation," considering them from the perspective of their usefulness in the study of Iranian music, and thereby define our problem.

Bruno Nettl's "improvisation model"

The entry for "Improvisation" in *The New Grove Dictionary of Music and Musicians*, 2nd ed., defines improvisational performance as "The creation of a musical work, or the final form of a musical work, as it is being performed" (Nettl 2001: 94). This definition recognizes several aspects of improvisation. On one hand, "the creation of a musical work ... as it is being performed," indicates that the musical piece does not exist until the moment of its performance. That is, in view of the brevity or absence of time spent for composition prior to the performance, improvisation is seen as antithetical to the composition, itself a time-consuming act of creativity that tends to be as prescriptive in detail as possible.

On the other hand, the definition of improvisation as "the creation of ... the final form of a musical work, as it is being performed," offers a much broader conception of improvisation, inclusive of the claim that

"All performances have improvisational elements more or less." There is no doubt that various unpredictable factors affect the performance of even highly-prescribed compositions in both positive and negative ways, such that it is impossible to perform the piece in exactly the same way twice. In this sense, all performances are improvised to some degree, and the final form of a composition is determined by improvisation during the performance. However, as this conception of improvisation is applicable to all musical phenomena, it is unhelpful in the quest to identify the improvisation that characterizes particular musical cultures. If so, can the broader definition above, then, be interpreted as signaling other aspects of improvisation, which would be missed if we defined improvisation only in the narrow sense of opposite to the act of "composition"?

Considering this question, ethnomusicologist Bruno Nettl, in his "Thoughts on improvisation: A comparative approach" (1974), posits that the border between composition and improvisation is ambiguous and culture-dependent, citing various examples of musical creation around the world. The practice of improvisation that Nettl may have in mind is described by Jairazbhoy, for example, in the following statement.

> An Asian musician usually spends many years memorizing and absorbing traditional models before he improvises, and his final rendering may well include fragments composed earlier. Improvisation may also imply the giving way to natural impulse, without premeditation; but this impulse is highly schooled and usually guided by an underlying scheme of development. (Jairazbhoy 1980: 52)

That is to say, musicians do not create music *ex nihilo*, but are furnished in advance with a basis for improvisational performance. Nettl calls those bases "models" or "points of departure" (Nettl 2001: 96). Improvisational performance based on a modal system, such as *dastgāh* in Iranian music, is an example of improvisation based on such a "model."

According to Nettl (1998), improvisation has always been discussed in contrast to composition, and portrayed as a "natural impulse," a "lack of planning," or a "vague structure," but there are in fact a number of restrictions on improvisation. Having established that a contrastive view of improvisation and composition does not hold true in all cases, Nettl's discussion of "model" can be seen as presenting his most comprehensive insight into improvisation.

To date, there have been studies which have had as their primary goal elucidating those "models" and "points of departure" which differ greatly from one musical culture to the next. The components (Nettl calls them "building blocks") comprising the model of traditional Iranian music – that is, the modal system called *dastgāh*[1] – are shown to be the various "traditional melody types," the "core note" of those melody types, "the particular melody types which lead to the final section," etc. (Nettl 1974: 13).

Is "freedom" contrary to restriction?

Studies of improvisation which have focused on explicating "models" share a certain paradigm: a view that performers improvise by establishing a balance between "sticking to rules" and "doing your own thing" (Nettl 1998: 16). Such a perspective sounds plausible, but it is necessary to consider whether "freedom" truly exists in opposition to constraint for performers in various genres of improvisation throughout the world in the first place.

To this end, traditional oral narrative, which is improvisatory and not based on fixed texts, can provide us with some clues. As Walter Ong pointed out (1982), orally-transmitted stories exhibit different characteristics from those stories which lead to a certain closure through a logical development, consciously created in a mindset of fixed texts.

Improvisation in orally-transmitted stories displays a certain fundamental characteristic, beyond the level of freedom typified as "left up to the performer." Improvisation, in this case, does not mean, for example, that new elements are added to the episodes depending on the narrator's abilities, but instead refers to the style in which the narrator paraphrases fragments of an oft-repeated story as he "recalls" them. There is, in other words, little need for a logical development of the entire story, so the narration suffices as a "fragmental recall." Consequently, the narrator's paraphrasing has, in a strict sense, the strong characteristic of a "repetition" of fragments that were told in the past rather than a voluntary creative act.

Toward a reexamination of "arbitrariness"

The implications of the word "repetition" will be discussed in more detail in the main chapters, but for now, the above example aptly reveals that the performer's "freedom" does not necessarily exist in direct opposition to constraint. The word "freedom" here becomes difficult to define in a literal sense.

In previous studies of "models" and "points of departure" in various musical cultures, divergent characteristics were pointed out only in terms of "constraint" and few discussed the divergent quality of "arbitrary choice" which is inextricably linked to the characteristics of constraint. The reason for this is that constraint is recognized as unique to each culture and its characteristics tend to be the focus of examination, whereas "selectivity" has tended to be interpreted in a literal sense as a behavior shared by all human beings, and has therefore seldom been an object of investigation.

The paradigm at work in the preceding studies suggests that there cannot be "absolute freedom" or "absolute constraint" in employing expression "balancing freedom and rules." But the studies are incomplete in the sense that they do not inspect "freedom" *per se*, and grasp freedom only as a concept opposing "constraint." Such perspective is little different from viewing freedom as "absolute freedom." If we take it literally, our view would essentially be no different from the Western view of improvisation – as "natural impulse," or "lack of planning" – which Nettl criticized.

What is needed here is an explication of how performers understand and use models. A model must be examined not only in terms of constraint but also over the entire system of operation, including how freedom is executed. No matter how detailed one's explication of the model itself, it would be difficult to uncover the principle of improvisation in question if one's perspective is limited by the researcher's own bias. For this reason, based on fieldwork conducted in the 1990s, Part I (Chapters 1–6) of the present work aims to explicate the mental state and memory of musicians with which they confront their models, rather than to examine the models (constraint) *per se*. Thus, the discussion will be organized in the following fashion.

Organization of Part I (Chapters 1–6)

As an introductory discussion, the first chapter, "What is *radīf*: Toward a redefinition of the word," focuses on a body of traditional melody types, called *radīf*,[2] which beginning students of Iranian traditional music must learn. Until recently, *radīf* had been defined as a "collection of small musical pieces which comprise the repertory of traditional Persian music," a "collection of canonical melodies," etc. However, such definitions barely reflect the mechanism of the learners' motivation toward improvisational performance inspired by learning *radīf*. They lack, in other words, reference to and consideration of the function of *radīf* itself for the students, or of the mechanism which instills the "norm" enabling them to perform improvisation.

The chapter first examines what *radīf* means for the novices and then examines how this meaning changes for advanced students and musicians performing improvisationally. In so doing, this chapter will focus on the issue of "function" or "mechanism" and attempt to redefine *radīf*.

The second chapter, "The vocal image underlying notation reading," re-examines the relationship between Iranian music and the rhythm of poetry – which has been repeatedly identified as one of the principles of Iranian music – in the act of reading scores. It has been stated many times that the essence of Iranian music resides in song. However, an automatic acceptance of this axiom would run contrary to the stance of the present work, which places its emphasis on the performers' reality. Therefore, this chapter considers the act of score reading, which Iranian music performers routinely do, as a case study revealing how musicians comprehend the link between music and poetry.

The third chapter, "Improvisation, mental state and memory," investigates the idea of improvisation in Iranian music. Based on the view that musicians who improvise do not create music out of the void but are equipped in advance with a basis for improvisation, ethnomusicology has, as a central subject, attempted to explicate the basis for improvisational performance in the world's various musical cultures. At the same time, it has held that, although improvisation is based on such models (obligatory elements) acquired in advance, it is created by the performers' free expression at the very moment of the performance. In other words, earlier studies sought to understand improvisational performance fundamentally within the realm of artists' creativity.

The chapter explores the extent to which the notion of "individual creativity" is appropriate in considering the concept of improvisation in traditional Iranian music from the perspective of pan-West Asian psychology. Here, the dichotomy of the "orality-centered mentality" and the "text-centered mentality," proposed by Walter Ong (1982), will be explicitly introduced, by which I will reassess whether "freedom" or the "exertion of individual uniqueness" truly exists for the performers in a modern Western sense, that is, as a literal sense of freedom which is in contrast to obligatory elements, and address the concepts of "author" and "opus" in Iranian music.

The fourth chapter, "*Charkh*: The circulatory paradigm in performance form and musical structure," inquires into the term, *charkh* (that which circulates), which is one of the key words for understanding Iranian culture. It demonstrates that the improvisational performance, which appears to be merely redundant and lengthy, as might originate from an "orality-centered mentality" discussed in the previous chapter, actually bears an overall temporal structure consistent with the concept of *charkh*. Furthermore, it considers the point that, for the performers of improvisational music, "norms" denote "relationships" such as *charkh* between melody types, rather than specific melody types themselves.

The fifth chapter, "Analysis of *gūshes* (melody types)," analyzes the *radīfs* passed on by six musicians according to the themes discussed in the third and fourth chapters, and shows how musicians share the traditional melody types to create music – more specifically, how they treat the models and paraphrase them – by looking at a variety of examples. In the process, the chapter illustrates the point that all the musicians establish the flow of the *charkh* as a whole, without exception.

The sixth chapter, "Change in the context for learning improvisation: The influence of writing on Iranian music," will discuss the influence of the "mental structure of writing," introduced by the notation system and the concept of "étude," which gradually took root beginning in the first half of the twentieth century, with a focus on the shift in views on knowledge and education. It points out that in learning traditional music, the standard (heretofore customary) relational view of knowledge – as expressed in the statement that "knowledge refers to a dynamic process of cognizance by the learner who relationally grasps events which arise infinitely in his work and living sites" (Ikuta 2001: 244) – is gradually shifting toward a pragmatic view of knowledge which holds that what is taught is itself useful as knowledge. The discussion goes on to suggest that an appreciation of *charkh*, which is indispensable for learning improvisational performance, is becoming obscure in the current learning process, and that the traditional view of improvisation as paraphrastic (and the associated notion of originality, as well as of identity and difference based upon it) has been changing.

Part II (Chapters 7–12)

Part II of this book records a variety of discoveries I have made as a researcher and a player of the traditional Iranian instrument called the *santūr*[3] during my trial-and-error approach to improvisation. Below I offer an overview of the background to these efforts.

As noted above, improvisatory performance in Iranian music is based on the modal system called *dastgāh*. I was not born or raised in Iran; I first encountered and began to learn this music as part of a foreign culture at around the age of 20. Understanding and elucidating the *dastgāh* "canon" was my highest priority. Some of the results of these efforts are found in the first part of this book, in which I consider how learners conceive of improvising with *dastgāh*, while focusing on the mentality of not grasping music visually (i.e., without written notation). I have found the themes for my research – including the research found in the first part of this book – through the experience of performance, and over time my "performing self" became increasingly important to me. This is because, as I put it at the end of Chapter 1, the "uninterrupted activity of generating one's own *radīf* from those of predecessors in traditional Iranian music" made me more determined year by year to master the *dastgāh* canon and use it "freely" in my own musical improvisations. As a researcher, I also wanted to articulate in words the experience of acquiring this mastery.

Generally speaking, researchers who take themselves as their subject are susceptible to criticism. Reasons for this include the impossibility of adopting an "objective" distance from the self-as-subject, the risk of overgeneralization, and the inadequacy of the sample size. However, there are concrete questions that arise precisely because I am in this position of sincerely longing to master *dastgāh*.

"When improvising, how multilayered are the musician's resources, and how specific are the hints and choices available to them?" "How much do those resources and hints differ depending on the instrument being played?" "What, indeed, is the Iranian music world like when experienced through an instrument you have never played, and which therefore has a physicality different from the instruments you know?" "How are the meters of classical poetry connected to the moment of actual performance?"

Questions like these have seldom been apparent from the perspective of most researchers, and the insights of musicians themselves have not been sufficiently verbalized for the outside world. Here lies the value of taking myself, as a *santūr* player and Iranian music researcher, as a "sample population." To go further, taking myself as standpoint as I attempt to enter an unknown world or struggle to improve my performance imparts to these questions an additional sense of reality.

Adopting this "first-person" perspective, I had some suspicions about the factors that prevented my improvisation from improving as much as I hoped. One was that, as extensive as my experience with the *santūr* was, it was nevertheless the only experience I had. As this book will explore, taking lessons only in a single instrument is entirely inadequate for improvisation and performance of Iranian music.

For example, the intimate connection between Iranian music and classical Persian poetry means that the learner must find separate opportunities to gain an understanding of the meters and worldview of this poetic tradition. To have some degree of experience and skill at singing that poetry as an *āvāz* (vocal performance) is, even for an instrumentalist, preferable from the standpoint of musical expression.

Similarly, to understand the *dastgāh* modal system, it is necessary to study the *radīf*. The *radīf* transmitted by Mirzā Abdollāh (1843–1918),[4] said to be the root of other *radīf-hā* (*hā* denotes plural noun forms) today, was systematized for plucked instruments like the *tār*[5] and *setār*.[6] *Radīfs* arranged for the *santūr*, however, are necessarily simplified compared to the original for *tār* and *setār* due to the limitations of the *santūr*'s tuning. *Gūshe-ha* that should be learned are left out, concealing major options during improvisation at times of *modgardi* (modulation between modes). Furthermore, as I will explain in detail in Chapter 10, practicing the *radīf* on the *tār* or *setār*, or the bowed instrument called the *kamānche*, helps the player learn to recognize the tetrachords (groups of four notes spanning a perfect fourth; *dāng* in Farsi) that make up the *dastgāh* system not only aurally but also through finger position. In that sense, the experience of performing the *radīf* on *tār* or *setār* is an utterly different world from the experience of a *santūr* player – and yet, if anything, it is the experience of *tār* and *setār* that is vital for understanding the mainstream of Iranian music.

Even within the world of the *santūr*, which I have continued to play, studying under teachers from other traditions – rather than staying within a specific "school" – broadens a player's horizons. For example, as described in Chapter 11, the traditional grammar of *santūr* performance is completely different from the grammar seen in recent years, which derives from a new physicality of the instrument and incorporates virtuoso technique. Insight into the repertoire that incorporates that new grammar, as well as the physicality and mallet technique that makes it possible, opens new possibilities for improvisation.

With the above in my mind, my approach toward fieldwork from 2014 onward has been completely different from the approach I adopted during my 1990s fieldwork, on which the first part of this book is based. I took lessons not only in my main instrument, the *santūr*, but in as many different types of instruments as I could, along with vocal music, classical Persian poetry, and even improvisation and songwriting. I also conducted participatory observations at Alexander Technique lessons in Japan and the United States. This has helped me accumulate hints and choices for improvisation in a more concrete form than before. In other words, the second part of this book is a kind of reconstruction of the wide range of realizations that I obtained with these lessons around various themes.

Organization of Part II (Chapters 7–12)

Chapter 7, "How can individuality be described and explained?", serves as an introduction to the second part of this book. Instead of viewing individuality as something complete and integral, it argues for "breaking down the phenomenon into the various elements from which individual characteristics emerge" – carefully considering and describing the range of elements involved and how they can become choices for musicians. Through this process, it comes to argue that many of these elements (at least many of those discussed in this book's second part) are involved in improvisation.

Chapter 8, "Verbal rhythm and musical rhythm," considers the influence of classical Persian poetic meter on the rhythm of Iranian music, as noted by many previous researchers. One observation made is that, in performance, the influence of poetic meter extends beyond "long versus short" to a wider range of elements, including "weight" and "stability."

Chapter 9, "Trial and error on hammered dulcimers: Iranian and Indian *santūr*," discusses the "disadvantages" faced by hammered dulcimers seeking to imitate the human voice and compares efforts to overcome these disadvantages on the Indian and Iranian *santūr*.

Chapter 10, "Perceiving and understanding through the fingers: Toward a comparative study of instrumental somatic sensibilities," inquires into the differences in somatic perception in various musicians specializing in different instruments with Iranian music as "common ground." In particular, it compares players of the *setār* and *'ūd'* to *santūr* players, arguing that the former understand the tetrachords of the *dastgāh* system not only aurally but also through finger position, and exploring how this is useful for improvisation.

Chapter 11, "The *santūr*'s new physicality: Toward a geopolitics on the board of the instrument," is also about the physicality of musicians, but unlike Chapter 10 the focus here is on differences in physicality between players of the same instrument, specifically the *santūr*. After describing the "generic" physicality associated with the *santūr*, the chapter offers an account of the new physicality based on participatory fieldwork in lessons given by *santūr* player Ardavān Kāmkār.[8] Finally, it considers the relationship between instrument construction (string arrangement and mallet "strike zones") and the player's body.

Chapter 12, "What we learn from the *radīf*," is based on fieldwork I conducted beginning in 2014, particularly during my sabbatical during the second half of 2019. It elucidates a more concrete understanding of the *radīf*, exploring the multilayered hints and opportunities for improvisation contained therein.

As developmental content, the second section of the chapter reports and analyzes in detail how the modal system of *dastgāh*, which has been discussed from many angles, is employed by experienced players. This discussion is based on a detailed analysis of an advanced performance involving modulation (*modgardi*). Based on the insights into tetrachords from Chapter 10, this section reports on how *modgardi* is performed during improvised performance, considering the elements and opportunities that facilitate it. It also explores the possibility that *modgardi* is not, in Iranian music, as special as its name might suggest.

The third section of the chapter shifts the focus to how improvisation and musicmaking – which were not taught in the past – are taught and learned today, with reference to specific procedures. Based on fieldwork at *setār* and *tār* player Bābak Rāhati's lessons about performing in *shūr* mode, I report and analyze a method for assembling an improvised performance based on a classical poem by Hāfez that was chosen at random on the spot. This offers concrete proof that the various unconscious processes around improvisation are unobtrusively present in the *radīf*'s "ground" (the parts of the *radīf* other than the parts where the mode's character is clearly evident), and that musicians cultivate these internally through the process of playing, mastering, and memorizing many *radīfs*.

The titles of these chapters may seem unrelated at first glance, but on closer inspection, they reflect the "mutually interactive," "interdisciplinary" character of Iranian music. These chapters explore relationships between different instruments or modes, relationships between instruments and the voice or body, and the relationship with Western music. In that sense, the second part of this book could be viewed as research into the interpermeative characteristics of Iranian music in terms of voice, body, mode, and instrument, establishing the necessity for improvisation of this kind of cross-disciplinary understanding.

The aims of the present work

If I may state as a general trend, commentary on Iranian music, especially in music dictionaries, tends to be written in ways that only those who have been trained in Iranian music can understand, as is discussed later. Therefore, in this book, I organized each chapter with a single theme; each, except the fifth chapter, can be read as an independent study, and I endeavored to employ a writing style that would accommodate a learner's perspective in unraveling each theme, step-by-step, from the start.

In pursuit of such intentions, I must note at the outset that this work is not meant to be a comprehensive textbook about Iranian music. So, it does not, for example, introduce all the musical instruments and modes (*dastgāh*) used in Iranian music, or cover every historical event. As mentioned earlier, the questions addressed by the present work are, simply put, "what and how does the learner learn, and what and how does the musician play?" In other words, the interest of this study resides in clarifying how the student of music learns the "norms" which enable improvisational performance – one of the characteristics of Iranian music – by focusing on the learning process. As such, the success of this attempt depends on how realistically I can convey to the reader the various "events" which occur in the process of learning and the actions comprising "improvisation," at which the process aims in the end, as seen through the eyes of learners and performers. Therefore, in this work, I consciously avoided dictionary-like explanations – as are often seen in introductory writings – as much as possible. Let me state it more specifically.

Most guides to Iranian music have explained concepts such as *dastgāh* and *radīf* at the start. These terms are no doubt extremely important key words that are central to understanding Iranian music, which is why quite a few pages are devoted to the annotation of those terms in works such as *The New Grove Dictionary of Music and Musicians*.

However, it is rare that reading those descriptions leads us to a clear understanding. Dictionary-like definitions or textbook overviews of technical terms tend to give the reader an arid impression without an understanding of the context behind it; the concepts of *dastgāh* and *radīf* have multi-layered meanings in the experience of the performers, and as a result, some meanings are invariably overlooked by an encyclopedic style of writing which seeks to provide general definitions.

For this reason, I would rather not attempt to answer questions like "what is *radīf*?" or "what is 'norm' or 'improvisation'?" in a comprehensive and concise way at the beginning in this work. Instead, I wish to employ a writing style in which I touch upon the above questions along the way, as I describe the student's process of learning step-by-step, so that the reader can gradually acquire a more thorough understanding of the multi-layered meanings of the terms.

Parts of this book were previously published as indicated below.

First half of Introduction

"Kōsokusei no kaimei kara nin'isei no kentō e: Sokkyō moderu no aratana rikai o megutte" ["From a clarification of "restraint" to an examination of "arbitrariness": Towards a new understanding of an improvisation model"], *Tōyō Ongaku Kenkyū* [Journal of the Society for Research in Asiatic Music], Vol. 70, pp. 93–99, 2005.

Chapter 1

"Iran dentō ongaku no radīfu: Sono saiteigi ni mukete" [Towards a redefinition of "radīf" in Iranian traditional music], *Ongakugaku* [Journal of the Musicological Society of Japan], Vol. 48–3, pp. 193–206, 2003.

Chapter 2

"Imēji jyo de narihibiku oto: Iran dentō ongaku ni okeru gakufu no sonzai o sasaerumono" [The image of the sound that supports the existence of musical scores in Iranian traditional music], *Tōyō Ongaku Kenkyū* [Journal of the Society for Research in Asiatic Music], Vol. 68, pp. 1–12, 2003.

Chapter 3

"Iran dentō ongaku no sokkyō gainen: Sokkyō moderu to taiji suru ensōsha no seishin to kioku no arikata" [The concept of improvisation in Iranian traditional music: The performer's mental state and memory when confronting the improvisational model], *Ongakugaku* [Journal of the Musicological Society of Japan], Vol. 51–1, pp. 28–40, 2005.

Chapter 4

"Iran ongaku no charufu: Ensō keishiki to gakkyoku kozō ni miru meguri no paradaimu" [Charkh in Iranian music: A paradigm of "circulation" in its performance type and musical structure], *Tōyō Ongaku Kenkyū* [Journal of the Society for Research in Asiatic Music], Vol. 70, pp. 19–33, 2005.

Chapter 7

"Kosei wa ikani kenkyū kanō ka (kijyutsu kanō ka): Iran ongaku o jirei to shita ichishiron" [How can individuality be described and explained? A Case Study of Iranian Music], *Arabu no oto bunka: Gurōbaru komyunikēshon eno izanai*" [Arabic Sound Culture: An Invitation to Global Communication], Nishio, Tetsuo, Mizuno, Nobuo and Horiuchi, Masaki (eds.), Tokyo: Stylenote, pp. 216–229, 2010.

Chapter 8

"Verbal Rhythm and Musical Rhythm: A Case Study of Iranian traditional Music" *Indian and Persian prosody and recitation.* Nagasaki, Hiroko (ed.), Delhi: Saujanya Publishers. pp. 59–69, 2012.

Chapter 9

"Dagen gakki o meguru shikō sakugo: Indo, Iran no santūru" [Trial and error on hammered dulcimers: Indian and Iranian *Santūr*], *Kikan Minzokugaku* [Ethnology Quarterly], Vol. 116, pp. 43–50, 2018, Senri Cultural Foundation.

Chapter 10

"Yubi de kanji rikai suru koto: Gakki kan de kotonaru shintai kankaku no kenkyū ni mukete" [Sensing and Understanding from Fingers: Toward Comparative Studies of Different Physical Senses among Various Instrument Players], *Iran kenkyū* [Journal of Iranian Studies], Vol. 13, pp. 136–149, 2017, Graduate School of Language and Culture, Osaka University.

Chapter 11

"Santūru ensō no atarashii shintaisei: 'Gakki banmen no chiseigaku' e mukete" [The new physicality of *santūr* performance: Toward a "geo-politics on the board of the instrument"]. *Chūtō sekai no ongaku bunka: Umarekawaru dentō* [Music cultures of the Middle Eastern world: Traditions reborn], Nishio, Tetsuo and Mizuno, Nobuo (eds.), Tokyo: Stylenote, pp. 98–115. 2016.

Part I (chapters 1–6) was published in 2007 as *Iran ongaku: Koe no bunka to sokkyō* [Iranian Music: Oral Culture and Improvisation] by Seidosha, and Part II (chapters 7–11 and part of chapter 12) was published in 2021 as *Iran dentō ongaku no sokkyō ensō: Koe, gakki, shintai, senpō taikei o meguru sōgo sayō* [Improvisation in Traditional Iranian Music: Interactions among Voice, Instrument, Body, and Modal System] by Stylenote.

PART I

Chapter 1
What is *radīf*: Toward a redefinition of the word

1.1 Introduction

In Iranian traditional music, there is a body of melodies which have been passed on among musicians. These are called *radīf* and each school has transmitted them as canon. This chapter aims at providing a new insight to the conventional definition of the term by scrutinizing the traditional learning process for *radīf*.

Radīf each comprises smaller melodic units called *gūshe* (pl. *gūshe-hā; hā* denotes plural noun forms). *Gūshe* means a "corner," and their scale ranges from that of a brief melody to one almost like a small musical piece. In contrast, *radīf* means "a row," or "things in a line." As these definitions suggest, *gūshes* are arranged sequentially in a fixed order by *dastgāh*, creating "corners" that together comprise the sequence of melodies called *radīf*. Thus, to inherit a *radīf* specifically implies the task of memorizing each *gūshe* along with its order in the sequence by *dastgāh*.

Instruction in *radīf* at the transmission site, or more specifically, the actual teaching of *gūshes*, has been reported on in previous studies of Iranian music. Gen'ichi Tsuge, for example, writes, "In each lesson, students were required to memorize one *gūshe* and to reproduce it on their particular instrument... In tests, each student played an assigned *gūshe* learned, of course, by rote" (Tsuge 1989: 279).[1] Since he was reporting on a class at the Music Department of the University of Tehran, which was newly established at that time, we cannot assume it is a description of traditional musical instruction, but at least it is clear that students were required to memorize the *gūshes* their teacher taught and to play them without change. In the *radīf* lessons I took during my fieldwork – which used staff notation – primary importance was placed on playing precisely as written and performing it from memory. Once students memorized one *gūshe*, they could move on to another, and they learned a new *dastgāh* upon finishing their current one; thus, there were plenty of materials to learn, but there was no variation in the order of learning.

Chapter 1

However, the *radīf* which are thus precisely memorized are not necessarily used in exactly the same manner in actual musical performance. Between having us memorize *gūshes*, my teacher would at times pick out the names of some *gūshes* and tell us to play them. Once, as soon as an Iranian student who had memorized the *gūshe* he was asked to play began to perform it, the teacher stopped him and said, "Don't play from the *radīf*. Play your own." Initially, I could not fathom whether he meant a kind of variation or something else, but in the end, the student played a melody imitating the one he had memorized, being perhaps not able to rid his head of that melody. Another student began to play something upon the same request, but it too did not seem to please the teacher. The names of *gūshes* are shared by schools to some degree; in fact, the melody which the second student played highly resembled that of a *radīf* belonging to another school.

The anecdote is an apt illustration of Tsuge's statement that the *radīf* "is learned and memorized as a canon, but there is almost no occasion in which it is performed as was learned" (Tsuge 1989: 282). If such is the case, then, in what way is *radīf* performed? Are there any rules that operate in the way it is altered? Tsuge does not discuss this in depth, and they were never explicitly demonstrated during my lessons. In fact, such questions were met only with vague answers, like "as you feel" or "you will get it in the course of playing a lot of *radīfs*."

When performing, I was told, musicians play their own music which differs from *radīf*. Also, people say that musicians would never repeat a performance, playing in the same way. How then are the *radīfs*, which are memorized with precision, utilized in performance? What principle determines the relationship between the fixity of *radīf* as taught and the "non-fixity" observed in actual musical performance? This question is a focal point in this chapter.

If the non-fixity of *radīf* can be understood by playing a vast number of *radīfs*, as Iranians say, the key to understanding should be learning several *radīfs*. As we have seen, even an Iranian disciple ended up playing a *radīf* as he memorized it, so the student's comprehension of this non-fixity of *radīf* seems to be gradually formed over the course of learning many *radīfs*. I therefore decided to conduct fieldwork learning several *radīfs* along with Iranian students, so that I would be able to expcerience the process of learning. In that setting, I should be able to feel a marked difference between what is presented as material for the student to learn and what the student distills from it, coupled with a variety of musical experiences contingent to the transmission of a musical tradition. Thus, this chapter aims to elicit an answer to the question of how a *radīf* is used in actual performance in a more specific manner, based on the performer's process of cognitive change, and thereby redefine the *radīf*.

1.2 Definitions of *radīf* in previous studies and a statement of the problem

In previous studies, the interpretation of the term *radīf* varies slightly from one scholar to another, since *radīf* can denote a multiplicity of meanings, depending on one's standpoint, although the differences between them can be subtle. Perhaps because of this variability in meaning, it is rather hard to find a full statement that suffices as a definition of *radīf*. What follows is an overview of the *radīf* we see today.

Speaking of *radīf*, Tsuge writes, "A frame of the melody to be performed is laid out here as one archetype," "a collection of canonical melodies," and "a fundamental form on which actual performances (which are often the playing of variations or improvisations) and compositions depend" (Tsuge 1989: 272–73). About *gūshe*, he states, "it is not a finished piece of music or of a song, but is a kind of a melody type," and "the music unfolds melodically based on this" (Tsuge 1998: 29).

Hormoz Farhat defines *radīf* as:

> The pieces that constitute the repertoire of Persian traditional music are collectively called the *radif*. To be sure, these are not clearly defined pieces but melody models upon which extemporization takes place. (Farhat 1965: 21)

About *gūshe*, Ella Zonis notes that, "the *gusheh-ha* are the musical materials used as models for improvised composition," and "[f]or a performance of traditional music, a performer selects a number of *gusheh-ha*, not from the entire *radif*, but from one *dastgah*, to use as a framework for his improvisation" (Zonis 1973: 46, 62).

Since the *gūshe* melodies are often expressed as "flexible melodies" (e.g., Talā'ī 2002: 867), such general explanations reveal an inclination to highlight the non-fixity of *radīf* and *gūshe* in actual musical performance, indicating that the concepts of *radīf* and *gūshe* have been largely captured in the terms "norm" or "model."

Certainly, the classic keyword "norm" might be able to elucidate the non-fixed characteristics of *radīf*. The *radīf*s – which are not used as learned, but loosely mold performances in various ways – regulate a wide spectrum of things, ranging from concrete elements such as melodies and rhythms, to something more sensory like melodic direction or musical atmosphere and feeling. Considering this, norm is a convenient term to express them all collectively.

Here, however, we must note that "norm" and "model" are frequently conceptualized as keywords which presuppose concrete substance, such as "material," "basic form," or "frame." Indeed, these terms may work effectively for concrete aspects of *radīf* like specific melodies or rhythms, but can we fathom the norms at the perceptual (sensory) level as well, in such things as melodic direction, or even atmosphere and feeling, using those same words?

During my fieldwork, I was able to observe a number of students closely, ranging from beginners who had just begun to study *radīf*, to students who were ready to leave behind the canonic *radīf* to create their own musical expression, and others in between who were in the process of transformation. it was clear that, save for definite rhythms or specific melodies, it is difficult even for Iranians to convey melodic direction, musical atmosphere, or feelings as their own expression while still novices in the study of *radīf*. Like the case of the Iranian disciples mentioned earlier, I witnessed a number of players who more or less repeated the melodies of the *gūshes* they memorized, not being able to get them out of their heads.

The term "norm" used in previous studies indeed shows us a certain vision for the understanding of the non-fixed characteristics of *radīf*, when considered solely from the listener's perspective. The above-mentioned examples, however, reveal that the content of that very "norm" is never uniform as seen by the creator of the music, and that the term is, in fact, ambiguous, conveying a range of meanings. My point is that oft-used terms such as "material," "basic form," and "frame" might only be able to express one aspect of the norm of *radīf* and that the popular usage of those terms may have resulted in emphasizing that aspect alone. Perhaps the reason that beginners have difficulty in maneuvering melodic direction or conveying musical atmosphere and sentiment as fully their own is because these elements involve a different kind of norm which cannot be grasped using those terms. There must be multiple layers to that which the norm signifies, and I suspect that there is another type of norm, almost invisible to the audience but which reveals itself to the performers, calling upon their ability to comprehend it. Thus, an effort to identify the characteristics of this norm is central to this study, since that disclosure, *per se*, may be critical to explicate the non-fixity of *radīf*. With that examination, *radīf* will be redefined by finding new, more appropriate terms to describe the characteristics of that norm in a concrete manner.

The reason *radīf* carries a variety of meanings according to our level of involvement is precisely because the norms are not static. We can only grasp the full spectrum of its meaning by examining how *radīf* is perceived at each stage of learning. In the next section, therefore, I will describe how students sense the norm of *radīf* at each stage, from their first exposure to *radīf* to the advanced level of studying multiple *radīfs*, by citing actual *radīfs*, thereby attempting to discover how the characteristics of the norm vary in different stages. This way, I hope to focus on the learners' process in reaching a systemic understanding.

1.3 Various levels of "norm"

1.3.1 The first *radīf*

As stated earlier, students learn *radīf* by memorizing each *gūshe*. These *gūshes* are not passed on randomly but are taught by the modal system called *dastgāh*. This way, the characteristics of each *gūshe* are understood, not as independent of others, but as elements which support the sentiment and atmosphere of the *dastgāh* to which the particular *gūshe* belongs. Scores 1.1–1.7, given here as an example of the *radīf* learned first (excerpted from the *radīf* for *tār* passed on by Mūsā Ma'rūfī (1889–1965)) present several *gūshes* in the *segāh* mode, in the order that they are performed.

What, then, does the first-learned *radīf* signify to the student? If we consider the traditional learning method for *radīf* – to memorize each *gūshe* and its place in sequence – the learner at this stage most likely finds fixity in all the *gūshe* melodies. As a result, the name of the *gūshe* is understood as akin to the title of a particular musical piece, and the order of the *gūshes* is not given particular attention, except as an object to be memorized.

Chapter 1

Score 1.1[2] *Darāmad* (E *koron*)[3]

Score 1.2 *Kereshme*

Score 1.3 *Zābol* (G)

Score 1.4 *Mūye* (G–B flat)[4]

What is *radīf*: Toward a redefinition of the word

Score 1.5 *Mokhālef* (C)

Score 1.6 *Kereshme*

Score 1.7 *Forūd* (C → E *koron*)[5]
(see Score 5.59 and Chapter 5, note 10)

1.3.2 The second *radīf*

When students begin to study their second *radīf*, they instantly realize one thing: now, there is a *gūshe* with the same name as the one previously memorized, but the melody is somewhat different. For comparison, let us look at the *radīf* for vocal music (Scores 1.1a–1.7a) passed on by Maḥmūd Karīmī (1927–1984) in the same *segāh* mode.

As is clear from those examples, the *gūshe darāmad* by Maʿrūfī (Score 1.1) and by Karīmī (Score 1.1a) have different melodies. The same applies to the *gūshe zābol* (Scores 1.3 and 1.3a), *mūye* (Scores 1.4 and 1.4a), *mokhālef* (Scores 1.5 and 1.5a), and *forūd* (Scores 1.7 and 1.7a). In other words, at this point, students discover for the first time that a *gūshe* with a specific name does not correspond to one specific, unique melody, but that its melody varies depending on the inheritor of the *radīf* and on the instrument. Furthermore, the number and order of *gūshes* that are taught also vary in detail.

These differences emerge from the idiosyncrasies of each musician or school; thus, the term *radīf* refers to an aggregate of a number of *gūshes* that are transmitted uniquely within each school. In other words, a *radīf* exists as an assemblage of concrete examples for each school, showing the *gūshes* that are included, the order in which they are arranged, and the details of each *gūshe* melody. Each *radīf* is identified by the name of the musician credited with originating, compiling, or transmitting it (thus, for example, "musician so-and-so's *radīf*") and serves as the canon of its school.

Score 1.1a[6] *Darāmad* (E *koron*[7])

Hence, there are multiple *radīfs*, each of which demonstrates the musician's school and pedigree, and, as we have compared two kinds of *radīfs* in this chapter, it is not that the students study only one *radīf*. In the case of my teacher,[8] for example, students were taught two *radīfs* by Farāmarz Pāyvar (1933–2009) and another *radīf* by Abolhasan Sabā (1902–1958); thus, they learn three *radīfs* in total. Also, in reality, the

What is *radīf*: Toward a redefinition of the word

Score 1.3a *Zābol* (G)

Score 1.4a *Mūye* (G–B flat)

Score 1.5a *Mokhālef* (C)

Score 1.7a *Forūd* (C → E *koron*)

more well-known, transcribed, and published *radīfs* are taught widely beyond lineage and instrumental difference. This very environment of learning multiple *radīfs* brings the revelation to students that a *gūshe* is manifested in varied melodies depending on the teacher (that is, the *radīf* taught by him) and the instrument. With this realization, the sense of fixity which the student felt in *gūshe* when studying only one *radīf* begins to lose ground, albeit only slightly.

However, it is worth noting here that even though the students are exposed to the difference between *radīfs*, it is rather the affinities of which they become gradually aware. In other words, they begin to feel a vague sense of the "norm," which previous studies attempted to demonstrate in their definitions of *radīf* and *gūshe*.

From the perspective of the concept of norm, students first recognize the distinctive features of the *gūshe* (such as *kereshme* presented in Scores 1.2 and 1.6) in terms of their melodic and rhythmic characteristics. These characteristics represent the norm which we can grasp via the terms adopted by previous studies, such as "material," "basic form," and "framework." But then, students further begin to feel a perceptual quality to the norm as well, in such things as melodic direction or even in the atmosphere and sentiment of the *gūshe*.

At this point, it is worth repeating that the *gūshes*, in which we felt only a vague sense of norm, are taught in a fixed order; both *radīfs* we have seen above share a sequential order – from *darāmad* to *zābol*, and from *mūye* to *mokhālef* to *forūd*.

Thus, at this stage, the students' attention, which had been directed at *gūshe* sharing the same name in different *radīf* (for example, *darāmad* in different *radīf*), now broadens to include the temporal sequence of *gūshes* as well which, in turn, brings recognition of the norm in the order of *gūshes*.

1.3.3 The third *radīf*, or a variety of traditional music that is heard

Students may have opportunities to hear a variety of *radīfs* and actual musical performances in addition to the scores shown above. Such listening activity has two principal functions for the students. One is that it helps them recognize the permissible range of musical variation in a concrete manner through their exposure to various examples of *gūshes* with the same name. Another is that listening provides the students with an opportunity to think about what the norm of each *gūshe* is, such that it can be maintained even in those musical variations. This reminds us of the norm observed in the temporal arrangement of *gūshe*, discussed above. At this stage, the attention of the students begins to shift to the temporal sequence of *gūshes*. Here, the students start to predict the order of the *gūshes* as something having a logical necessity which is not limited to the two specific cases of *radīfs* mentioned earlier.

When we review *radīf* with this in mind, it is easy to find another case that supports such prediction. Both *forūd* in Scores 1.7 and 1.7a have a descending movement from higher C to E *koron*. As shown in Score 1.7, this movement can be also accomplished by crossing another *gūshe*. Thus, the students learn that the temporal structure of the *gūshes* clearly exists as a model, even if it is not necessarily delineated by the name of a *gūshe*. The systematic knowledge about the temporal sequence of *gūshes* which the learner acquires through those experiences can be roughly summarized as follows.

Dastgāh of Iranian music are not merely musical scales but always incorporate short melody types or small musical pieces. Those short melodies or musical pieces are called *gūshe(s)*, each of which has unique melodic and rhythmic characteristics in its own narrow register (range of notes). More specifically, these *gūshes* are arranged sequentially in such a way that the tessitura gradually ascends within the tonal range of the *dastgāh* to which those *gūshes* belong. When the music reaches the highest tessitura of that particular *dastgāh*, the melody quickly descends to the original tessitura by way of a certain melody type (*forūd*, literally meaning "*descent*"). In this manner, a *dastgāh* in Iranian music is expressed as an aggregate of musical characteristics of several *gūshes* which constitute such temporal sequences.[9] Let us turn now to exploring the significance of understanding the temporal arrangement of the *gūshe*, obtained by learning a number of *radīfs*, in relation to the ways *radīf* regulate the actual performance.

1.4 Norm as "function"

Since a *dastgāh* in Iranian music is expressed as an aggregate of the characteristics of a series of *gūshes*, each *gūshe* – particularly ones like those we have just seen, which in their temporal sequence show unique pitch-range frameworks with core tones at their center, from the lower to the higher tessituras within their *dastgāh* – is recognized by students as an indispensable component of that *dastgāh*, together with its order in the sequence.[10]

Here, the pitch-range framework incorporates a melodic vector to the core tone, and it serves a function for the progression of *gūshes*. The function of the framework of each *gūshe* is not grasped independently but is always understood in relation to the framework of other *gūshes*. If we view the norm in performance in this light, we can see what might be called a relational norm – in which the activity of a *gūshe* is somewhat restrained by the parallel forces of the *gūshes* of other pitch ranges, as a result of their function to carry the music forward – as seen in the *gūshes* in the previous section. This contrasts with the norm discussed in prior studies that suggests strongly centripetal characteristics, as explained by using the terms "material," "basic form," or "frame." The relational norm, however, emerges from the functionality of *gūshes*. In other words, it is the overall motive function of the *gūshes* – the ascending tessitura – that regulates the melodic movement within each individual *gūshe*.

Indeed, in my own performance experience, I feel the tessituras and characteristics of the *gūshes* before and after the *gūshe* I am playing. When I play *zābol*, for example, I feel on a subconscious level the presence of the prior *gūshe*, *darāmad*, and *mūye* (or *mokhālef*) which comes immediately after *zābol*. In fact, performers of traditional Iranian music play each *gūshe* under the broader scheme of a *dastgāh* as a whole, anticipating as far as *forūd*. It is this consciousness that regulates the performance of each *gūshe*.

Furthermore, the characteristics of the *kereshme* type of *gūshe* (Scores 1.2 and 1.6, for instance) are learned by repeated listening to that section, whereas the attributes of the type of *gūshe* whose function is to carry forward the music are gradually understood in relation to the comprehension of *gūshes* in other pitch ranges. Here we can find the fundamental reason that students always learn and memorize *gūshes* in a particular order. Perhaps this kind of norm can be defined as a norm operating on a functional level, without substance. This norm manifests itself only after we achieve a comprehensive understanding of the progression of *gūshes*.

1.5 *Radīf* as an example of norm

If we consider the norm of *gūshe* from the perspective of its function to carry the music forward, it is no mystery that there is no melodic or rhythmic uniformity in the music. Although there is typical movement, as long as the *gūshes* serve their function to advance the music, it is possible to deviate from that, too. As a matter of fact, melodic difference and variants between *radīf* are attributed to this propensity of *gūshe*. This provides an immediate answer to the question regarding the non-fixed nature of *radīf*, and reveals how Iranians view the *radīf*.

To Iranians whose attention is drawn to the functional aspect of *gūshe*, the melodic difference between *radīfs* is no longer perceived as a difference (this will be discussed in Chapter 3 in detail). From this perspective, a player may give various performances, all under the same *gūshe* name. The "difference" here is perceived as only a paraphrase which follows the functional norm.

Furthermore, from this perspective, the notation of *radīf* is not viewed negatively due to its inflexible aspect, since no one takes the "fixity" of the transcribed *radīf* at face value. This principle also applies to the fixity observed in orally transmitted lessons which require students to precisely memorize the *radīf*. When students have completed the stage of memorizing given *radīf* and have reached the level of realizing their own music, the *radīf* is understood as one sample of the norm while nevertheless remaining somewhat canonical. This point of view toward *radīf* is further applied to all the traditional Iranian music to which the students listen.

When we contemplate this, however, we notice that each example, including *radīf*, exists as a manifestation of the idiosyncrasy of the performers. In this sense, what was initially described as the melodic difference or variants between *radīfs* is actually the divergence arising from each performer's idiosyncrasy. For instance, in the Karīmī *radīf* presented in the examples above, one can see his unique musical perception, distinct from that in the *radīf* by Ma'rūfī. In other words, the students gradually renew their understanding of *radīf* – which was up to that point presented as a canon with an absolute value – as an example of the interpretation of a norm which develops within each musician, rather than the norm itself. As *radīf* is always referred to as "so-and-so's *radīf*," affixing a musician's name to it, *radīf* carries the notion of an individual person. As such, *radīf* itself is multi-layered. Bruno Nettl and Hafez

Modir use the term "version" when referring to *radīf* (Nettl and Foltin 1972; Modir 1986). While we need a clear explanation of the meaning of the word "version" and the reasoning behind its usage, we can certainly appreciate the suggestion that *radīf* is "one example of interpretation" and that there are many of those.

We can clearly see that the students understand *radīf* as one sample interpretation of the norm in the fact that the *radīf* is always subject to evaluation. If *radīf* shows one example of a musician's interpretation of the norm, then it is natural that the evaluation of that interpretation emerges within the learners. Actually, it is not uncommon for students who have learned several *radīfs* to form some opinions about them and at times to become severe critics. Such critique is only possible by viewing a *radīf* against the totality of their own musical experience, including that of other *radīf*. Thus, their criticism highlights the fact that at this point, distinct interpretations of the norm are already developing within the students which will serve as foundations for their own expressions of musicality.

1.6 *Radīf* as the compass of interpretation of the norm and as the totality of individual musicality

By now, we slowly begin to see, if vaguely, the system of musical learning based on *radīf*. As the teacher said "you'll understand when you play a lot," the students start to recognize *radīf* as an interpretation of the norm once they understand the functional norm of the *gūshe*, and have accumulated sufficient experiences in it. This accumulated experience is not only of learning *radīfs*, but also from a variety of listening activities in daily life. As a result, each student should have uniquely formed what one might call a compass for interpreting the norm. This compass, *per se,* manifests the individual's musicality from which concrete examples are drawn.

The word "compass" (or "range" or "territory") may suggest the idea of boundaries which might suggest that the compass is concrete and visible, but the musicians are not necessarily conscious of this in the beginning. They start to partially recognize it only when evaluating a piece of music. One cannot grasp a complete picture of any individual's compass, although it may be glimpsed in the music drawn from it. The territory we are discussing here is, thus, ostensibly concrete, yet flexible and invisible as well.

The Iranian student mentioned earlier could play only by reproducing the melody of the *gūshe* he had learned because he had not yet established a perspective for viewing *radīfs* as an interpretation of the norm. Thus, we can see that explaining the difference between *radīfs* and performed music using terms such as "to vary or develop a *radīf*," as previous studies have done, is superficial at best. So, too, describing the melody of *gūshe* using terms like "basic form," or "prototype" which suggest that variation is necessary, and "frame" which, again, sounds like it needs fleshing out. Even if there may appear to be a direct linkage between the *radīf* and the performance on a phenomenal level, a performance is not reducible to varying or developing a certain *radīf*. *Radīf*, therefore, should not be defined in terms that suggest a direct correspondence. Furthermore, responses such as "Then in what way is *radīf* performed?" or "Are there any principles for this change?" to learning that *radīf* is not performed as memorized – typical questions among beginning students who posit such a relationship between a *radīf* and an actual performance – only dissipate with accumulated experience.

A *radīf per se* is not a model to be shared among the students. Such a model – the norm itself – is never even presented. What is presentable is an *interpretation* of the norm, and in the act of interpreting it, Iranians share the norm as a universal model. Its concrete realization is only through the form of *radīf* as the result of interpretation.

If we find a true musicality in the learner's unique and distinct compass of interpretation which is established through accumulating examples of interpretation of the norm, that compass will be called the *radīf* of that musician, along with the music born from it. Thus, *radīf* not only signifies what is presented externally in the form of transcription and performance, but is also present as a term that respectfully expresses the totality of the inner musicality that produces the art. This uninterrupted activity of generating one's own *radīf* from those of predecessors in traditional Iranian music is evidence that the character of the *radīf* – an example of the interpretation of norms initially presented as material for memorization – continues to function to stimulate students to produce new *radīf*.

Chapter 2
The vocal image underlying notation reading

2.1 Introduction

In Iran, as elsewhere in Western Asia, music was traditionally passed on orally. Within the field of art music, established during the Qajar Dynasty (1796–1925), a large number of melody types, called *gūshe*, were passed from master to disciple through the students' imitation of the teachers' performance.

However, following the introduction of Western music in the mid-nineteenth century, staff notation has become established in contemporary Iran as effectively the only system for musical notation and instruction, while teaching through oral transmission or by similar means is still employed to some degree. Published staff notation of various *radīfs* and lesson books are commercially available at bookstores, and it has become commonplace that students purchase those scores in order to practice for lessons.

That does not mean, however, that staff notation is by nature suited to transcribing the characteristics of Iranian music, however widely it has spread into the Iranian population. As I will discuss shortly, Iranian musicians have independently established their relationship with staff notation by inventing devices for describing pitches and note values and by incorporating unique Iranian perspectives in the score reading.

This chapter observes people's interaction with their notation – that is, transcribing and reading it – with the aim of uncovering a universal principle underlying those activities. Ultimately, it demonstrates that this principle is active not only in working with staff notation but also in the background of all musical behavior.

2.2 The foundations of notation

The introduction of Western musical notation in Iran began during the time of the Qajar Dynasty, when a French music advisor was sent to Iran around 1868 to train the military band. Of course, Iranian music was not easily transcribed into staff notation, and attempts at notating Iranian music on staves since that time have encountered various problems, such as the notation of microtones and note values.

In Iranian music scores published today, the notation of microtones is systematized by the use of two kinds of accidentals: *koron* (for lowering a note approximately a quarter tone) and *sori* (raising a note about a quarter tone). This system was invented by 'Alīnaqī Vazīrī (1887–1979). Vazīrī was a *tār* player who established the Higher Institute of Music, Madrese-ye 'Ālī-ye Mūsīqī, in Tehran in 1923. Besides being accomplished in Iranian music, he was also well-versed in Western music due to his study in France, and sought to introduce Western music's technical approach into Iranian music pedagogy. In his lesson book for the *tār*, *Dastūr-e Tār*, which he wrote in 1921, the two accidentals above, *koron* and *sori*, appear for the first time, and have since become established as the most standard symbols for indicating microtones.

There is, however, a more subtle and complex problem than that concerning pitches; the issue of note values. Anyone who has heard Iranian music will have noticed that its sound flows as if it were drifting without a fixed rhythm. This free, elastic rhythm without a definite sense of meter is called *āvāz*[1] and is characteristic of Iranian music.

Indeterminate and elastic note values cannot be fully expressed through staff notation which indicates exact note values. To solve this problem, the notation of *āvāz* does not use bar lines, attempting to express the characteristics of *āvāz* that cannot be divided into measures by a fixed meter.[2] But this device is intrinsically different from that used for microtonal notation, mentioned above, in that the durational value of notes in this notation largely depends on the interpretation of the person reading the music, whereas transcribers use the symbols for microtones in an agreed-upon, consistent manner.[3]

In fact, people who read the music of *āvāz* know that fundamental principles regarding durational values in ordinary Western notation – such as "a quarter note has a durational value of two eighth notes and the durational value of two quarter notes corresponds to a half note" – can only have relative meanings in *āvāz*, such as, to put it in an exaggerated way, "a quarter note is longer than an eighth note and shorter than a half note." A long note may be stretched far beyond the indicated note value. The same thing applies to rests: the length or brevity of a rest is determined in relation to the notes surrounding it and in the overall context of the music. In this way, the notation does require the reader to fill in information which is otherwise lacking.

For that matter, this requirement applies not only in Iran but more broadly to the use of the Arabic letter-based music notation system used in the Arab world since antiquity; in it, only pitches were designated by the letters; note durations were not specified (see Scores 12.13 and 12.14). In this sense, even in staff notation, the readers' interpretation is not necessarily in complete accord with the transcriber's intent, no matter how carefully the transcriber notates or infuses significance into his note values. This seems to have much to do with the fact that improvisational performance is a predominant characteristic of Iranian music and that musicians typically do not play music exactly as it is passed on (in notation). Whatever the case, in Iranian music there is no uniform way of transcribing note values nor any clear-cut consensus on those values even among transcribers.

Nevertheless, people who know Iranian music can interpret it and recreate it from notation because something in the activities involving notation – transcribing and reading music –supports their efforts, as a universal element of Iranian music. To put it another way, their ambition to rigidly standardize transcription methods has not risen significantly, due to the existence of that particular element.

It is, of course, a truism beyond Iranian music that musical experience is of great significance in reading any notation. To better understand the role of that experience in Iranian music, let us consider classical Persian poetry sung in *āvāz*. Music and poetry were long inseparable in the Islamic world. The recitation of classical Persian poetry has a power to move even listeners who do not understand the language. This is perhaps largely due to its rhythmic characteristics, that is, the meter of the poetry.

2.3 The meter of classical Persian poetry: Iambic (short-long) pattern

Score 2.1 presents the *gūshe* called *chahārbāgh* in the *abū'atā* mode, as contained in the *radīf* passed on by Abolhasan Sabā.[4] When we listen to this *gūshe*, we are immediately able to identify a characteristic rhythm in it, a sequence of "short-short-long-short-long" notes; listening to the poetry sung with an instrumental accompaniment, we then notice that the rhythm is precisely in the meter of classical Persian poetry. In the

Chapter 2

Score 2.1 *Chahārbāgh* passed on by A. Sabā (Sabā 1992: 16)

vocal *radīf*, such as the one in Score 2.2, we can hear that the poetry and music become one, by which the dynamic feeling of the rhythm increases further.

che shavad be chehre-ye zard-man nazarī barāye khodā konī

ke agar konī hame dard-e man be yekī nazāre davā konī

(Poetry by Hātef Esfahānī)

چه شود به چهرۀ زرد من نظری برای خدا کنی

که اگر کنی همه درد من به یکی نظاره دوا کنی

What would happen if, for heaven's sake, you give one look at my pallid face;

For if you do, all my pain with one glance you cure. (Miller 1999:189)

Now, let us examine the meter used in the above poem. According to Tsuge, classical Persian poetry has two principles of versification. One is called *taqtī'-e hejā'ī*, a classical Persian versification principle which concerns the number of syllables. The other is *'arūzī*, an ancient Arabic metric principle that recognizes the short and long syllables and concerns the combination of them.[5] Poetry based on *taqtī'-e hejā'ī* is mainly used for metric songs, but the poetry sung in non-metric *āvāz*, like the example above, is based primarily on *'arūzī* (Tsuge 1985: 60–61).

As illustrated in Table 2.1 (Kuroyanagi 1998: III), the Persian alphabet has 32 letters, of which four (*p, ch, zh, g*) are unique to the Persian language while the rest are borrowed from Arabic. This writing system based on Arabic letters is the foundation for generating the long and short syllables which comprise *'arūzī*. Allow me to explain the

38

The vocal image underlying notation reading

Score 2.2 *Chahārbāgh* passed on by Mahmūd-Karīmī (1927–1984) (Mas'ūdie 1995: 44)

Table 2.1 Persian alphabet[6]

Letter name	Transliteration	Letter name	Transliteration
ا (alef)	a, e, o, ā	ص (sād)	s
ب (be)	b	ض (zād)	z
پ (pe)	p	ط (tā)	t
ت (te)	t	ظ (zā)	z
ث (se)	s	ع ('ein)	'a, 'e, 'o
ج (jīm)	j	غ (ghein)	gh
چ (che)	ch	ف (fe)	f
ح (he)	h	ق (qāf)	q
خ (khe)	kh	ک (kāf)	k
د (dāl)	d	گ (gāf)	g
ذ (zāl)	z	ل (lām)	l
ر (re)	r	م (mīm)	m
ز (ze)	z	ن (nūn)	n
ژ (zhe)	zh	و (vāv)	v, ū, ou
س (sīn)	s	ه (he)	h
ش (shīn)	sh	ی (ye)	y, ī, ei

39

Chapter 2

generation of long and short syllables in the Persian language further in the following, based on the discussion by Tsuge (1990: 149–50).

1. In Persian, all letters except *alef* become consonants when used alone (for example, *t*). This is called *harf-e sāken* (literally, "quiescent sound"). *Alef* by itself becomes a short syllable.
2. Next, the sound in which a short vowel is added to the *harf-e sāken* is called *harf-e motaharrek* ("moving sound"), and this becomes a short syllable (for example, *ta*). In principle, these short vowels are limited to *a*, *e*, and *o*, and are not notated in the Persian language.
3. a. The above short syllable plus another *harf-e sāken* forms a long syllable (for example, *tan*).
   b. A long syllable is also formed by the combination of *harf-e sāken* with a long vowel (*ā, ī, ū*) (e.g., *tā*), or with a diphthong (*ei, ou*). Unlike the short vowels, these long vowels and diphthongs are notated in Persian, and form long syllables by themselves.
4. The extra-long syllable is formed by adding a further *harf-e sāken* to a long syllable (for example, *tant*). In the poetry itself, other than at the end of a line, a consonant at the end of a word (*harf-e sāken*) may be treated like a short syllable linking to the next word (this half-vocalization is called *nīm fathe*), which results in a long + short syllable compound.

Depending on the case, some syllables can be treated as short or long, but as we have seen, it is understood that the generative principle of long and short syllables in Persian depends on the existence or absence of vowels and on which vowels are used. According to this principle, based on the short syllables and the long syllables that are said to have double the length of the short syllables, eight rhythmic patterns are established, as shown in Table 2.2.[7] These patterns correspond to poetic feet.

These rhythmic patterns are given names using conjugations of the Arabic verb *fa'ala* (meaning "to do"), as shown in 1 through 8 in the table, and are practiced using mnemonics which emphasize their rhythmic aspect. *Bahr* (meaning "meter"), which comprises the core of *'arūzī*, is created by repeating the same pattern alone or by combining different patterns. This *bahr* is purported to have been systematized by an eighth-century scholar in Basra, al-khalīl Ibn Ahmad (718–786). It included a

Table 2.2 Rhythmic patterns of the eight feet

Name	Syllables	Mnemonic
1. *fa'ūlon*	short-long-long	*tanantan*
2. *fā'elon*	long-short-long	*tantanan*
3. *mafā'īlon*	short-long-long-long	*tanantantan*
4. *fā'elāton*	long-short-long-long	*tantanantan*
5. *mostaf'alon*	long-long-short-long	*tantantanan*
6. *maf'ūlāt*	long-long-long-short	*tantantant*
7. *motafā'elon*	short-short-long-short-long	*tananantanan*
8. *mafā'elāton*	short-long-short-short-long	*tanantananan*

total of 16 basic combinations, which were described by Khalīl using five circular figures.[8]

According to Khalīl's figures, the meter (*bahr*) of the poetry quoted above is called *kāmel*, which consists of the repetition of *motafā'elon*, (short-short-long-short-long syllables). Naturally, these *bahr* are not always used in their original form (*sālem*; lit. "intact"). On the contrary, it is far more common for *bahr* to be altered in various ways from their original forms or to be combinations of different patterns.

However, I wonder if we can find a common metric element among those variations. Is there a latent rhythm when classical Persian poetry is sung in *āvāz*, or further, when *āvāz* is performed as an instrumental on the *santūr* or *tār* alone?

As is understood from Score 2.2, the student learns a close relationship between the rhythm of *āvāz* and the poetic meter more somatically through exposure to the classical poetry sung. In contrast, Score 2.1 is taken from the *radīf* arranged for *santūr*, where the poetry is not sung continuously throughout the performance. Except where the poetry is sung, the music is basically performed by the instrument alone. There, the language unique to musical instruments appears freely, as if the instrument had liberated itself from the poetic meter. Nevertheless, viewed from a larger perspective, in the performance and ornamental techniques which appear to be unique to instruments, we can still find the latent rhythm of the poetry even though it may not be exact poetic meter.

Score 2.3 is a *gūshe* called *mansūrī* in the *chahārgāh* mode, contained in the *radīf* of A. Sabā. In this excerpt, the poetry is not yet sung, and the *santūr* passage continues. The rhythm pattern "16th note–8th note–16th

Chapter 2

Score 2.3 *Mansūrī* passed on by A. Sabā (Sabā 1990: 37)

Score 2.4 Notation of descending figure with slur

Score 2.5 Actual performance with rīz

note" is repeated from the end of the top stave. Here, we should note that each instance of this pattern specifies striking with the hands "right–right–left," that is, mallet strikes by the right hand occur twice consecutively (∨ indicates striking with the left hand). What does this mean?

The training for percussive instruments, including the *santūr*, generally aims at developing the kinetic ability of the nondominant hand to a level as close as possible to that of the dominant hand, while in performance, we observe numerous playing techniques that take advantage of the weakness of the nondominant hand. For instance, in the example just presented, in which the right hand strikes twice consecutively, deploying the left hand's strike on the last note, one might reasonably interpret an intention to assign more significance to the first two notes struck with the right hand than to the final note struck with the left hand.

Another example: Since the *santūr* is played with two mallets (called *mezrāb*), it characteristically often employs *rīz* (*tremolo*; lit. "fine"). There is a strict rule regarding how *rīz* should be used according to note values. Now, our attention should turn to the phrases that often appear in *āvāz,* such as the one in Score 2.4.

According to the rule, *rīz* is employed for notes whose durational values are a dotted eighth note or longer on the notation, so the dotted eighth note in this example is played with *rīz*. At the same time, in free-meter music like *āvāz*, *rīz* must be started with a lightly accented tone, so Score 2.4 sounds much like Score 2.5 (∧ indicates striking with the right hand).

When this phrase is appreciated aurally, the first two tones sound more distinct. And those *are* played by the right hand. Also, in these examples, the tones of the subsequent *rīz* usually blend into the resonance of the initial A note. As a result, what constitutes the core of this phrase are, once again, the first two consecutive tones played by the right hand.

From the two examples, above, it becomes clear that the first two tones are a combination of a short note and a long note, that is, of short and long syllables. Tsuge (1990: 163) states that, among the various meters of classical Persian poetry, the most preferred one uses an iambic (short-long) pattern in its beginning. This pattern is also a unit comprising the *anapaest* (short-short-long) pattern in other meters.

Of course, these patterns are different from each other. But in the elastic rhythm of *āvāz*, what we hear as characteristic is the sequential flow of a short syllable to a long syllable, the rhythmic sensation delivered by a combination of a short syllable immediately followed by a long syllable. In other words, we can understand the iambic pattern as being the most essential. And, as Tsuge points out, this very iambic pattern *is* the "core of the rhythmic texture of the free-metric *āvāz*" (Tsuge 1990: 164). Now, it is time to return to our initial question: "What is the musical experience that underlies activities involving staff notation?"

2.4 *Āvāz* that sounds in the mind

As we develop a somatic understanding of the meter of classical Persian poetry sung with music as demonstrated in the section above, a new way of looking at notation emerges. Whereas we had previously viewed note values solely in a relativistic manner, following the iambic pattern makes it possible to read a cohesiveness of melody and a feeling of the ending by perceiving a short note not as continuing the previous note, but instead forming a set together with the subsequent long note. Accumulated experience in vocal *āvāz* makes this perspective available to us.

As stated in note 1, *āvāz* refers to non-metrical rhythm as well as to a style of songs or vocal music. In Iran, both meanings are often used inseparably. Understanding the word in this way, all the symbols in a transcription are interpreted as representations of, for example, the nuances or feelings of the words being sung, and the range of emphasis for affective expression. Thus, however variable or incomplete in terms of note value a transcription may be, experienced readers can work with it. Interpreted in this frame of mind, the notation for a certain instrument does not necessarily elicit only the sound of that instrument. To give an

Chapter 2

example from my own experience, when I listen to my teacher playing *santūr*, in my mind I hear not only the sound of the *santūr*, but also the vocal *āvāz* as well.

Interestingly, my teacher repeatedly told his students, "Listen to *āvāz* attentively." Initially, my interest was limited to the *santūr*, so I didn't heed this advice. But I gradually came to listen more actively to the performances of vocal *āvāz*, wind instruments such as *ney*, and bowed instruments such as *kamānche*. As if in conjunction with this change in listening style, a disjunction gradually began to appear between the sound being played and the sound I was hearing in my mind.

Perhaps if a music transcription was written only for a specific instrument and was performed "intact," this duality of sounds would not arise. But Iranian notation is read and performed beyond the instrumental frame, even where the notation assumes a specific instrument. This may happen because when reading and writing instrumental music scores, Iranian musicians not only imagine the sound of the particular instrument but also find a vocal *āvāz* there as a universal element. Understanding that beyond the instrumental music the imagined sound of vocal *āvāz* is reverberating, we begin to see that the instrumental notation in Iranian music essentially notates vocal *āvāz* as well, even though it may appear to be a transcription of the tones that are sounding from the instrument. Then, we can consider notation with no bar lines as normal, and interpret note values in a relative way, since *āvāz* is the recitation of classical poetry – that is, one kind of locutionary act – and thus the musical pauses and phrases in it are carried out based on the breath as a fundamental unit.

Following this line of discussion, we can say that all activities involving notation are established by imagining the sound of vocal *āvāz*. This means in essence that even an instrumental performance is executed with a voice in its background. It is exactly there that we can see the position of *āvāz* in Iranian music. For Iranians, *āvāz* is something that flows beneath all music. My teacher's advice, "Listen to *āvāz* attentively" directed us to discover the *āvāz* behind the performance of *santūr*.

Presented with any musical act, Iranians evoke the image of *āvāz*. Various activities, such as transcribing music, interpreting staff notation, or even instrumental performance, exist as efforts to approach as closely as possible to that image. In other words, we can say that this Iranian approach to music pervades even behaviors involving staff notation.

Chapter 3
Improvisation, mental state and memory

3.1 Locating the problem

Traditional Iranian music – especially the form known as *āvāz*, which does not have a definite meter – has generally been described as improvisational. Indeed, Iranian musicians say that their music is "impossible to play in the same way twice" and can "be performed in any number of ways," thereby emphasizing the point that they do not perform what is composed in advance.

In his discussions of improvisation, Bruno Nettl (1974 and 1998, for example) observes that people have, either consciously or unconsciously, evaluated improvisation in contrast to composition. This has resulted in emphasizing the idea that "nothing is prepared for the improvisation until the very moment of the performance," and therefore, "improvisation is impossible to predict." When we reflect on the idea of "predictability," it seems to contain more than a suggestion that improvisation is a device which generates the unforeseen for listeners and performers, and that something new and different should be created there. Further, the musicians' characterization of their music as "impossible to play the same way twice" or "able to be performed in any number of ways" are generally understood to mean that one's own improvisational performance creates something new which differs from previous and other's performances.

However, observing their improvisational performances, it is not uncommon to find the performers making distinctions between objectively identical performances or assessing quite differing performances as essentially the same. My immediate objective in this chapter is to examine such Iranian performers' perspective on improvisation. For this investigation, we must ask: is the product of improvisation truly new (that is, different from previous performance) at all, and if so, in what sense?

It is obvious that even in improvisational performance musicians do not produce music out of nothing. In Iranian music, the modal system called *dastgāh* functions as the foundation (or what Nettl calls the "model") of the improvisation. *Dastgāh* consists of two main components: a collection of traditional melody types (*gūshes*) accumulated in the musicians' being as stock phrases, played as if out of unconscious habit; and the set of rules about the relationship between the *gūshes* in terms of how those stock phrases can be arranged into a whole. However, my purpose here is not to detail the nature of *dastgāh* as a model, but rather to clarify the performers' mental state and memory, that is, to illuminate the ways they confront the model. More precisely, my purpose is to shed light on the state of mind and memory that leads them to perceive objectively identical performances as different and apparently contrasting performances as the same. Let me clarify the thesis of the present study by comparing it with the perspectives of earlier studies.

Generally speaking, research to date has focused primarily on the study of *dastgāh*, the model for improvisation, and then on analyzing examples of actual improvisational performances based on *dastgāh*. Simply speaking, the primary concern has been how musicians treated *gūshes* from *radīf*, which is concrete manifestation of *dastgāh*, in their improvisational performances. As their usual research method in this type of study, scholars have confidently compared the *gūshes* in *radīf* purported to be the sources of the improvisation to the improvisational performance. Some may not have clearly elucidated their methods of analysis, but comparative thinking has been a core premise across studies of Iranian music. In other words, earlier studies sought to consider improvisation (and unpredictability) within the realm of the individual musician's creativity.[1] In this paradigm, *gūshes* in *radīf* were treated as akin to a fixed "text" and improvisation was considered to be a product of the performer's manipulation of that text.

But this perspective does not appear to lead to an essential understanding of improvisation in Iranian music, by which I mean, it cannot explain why performers may claim that objectively identical performances are different or different performances are identical. As I mentioned earlier, researchers invariably experience this perceptional difference when observing improvisational performance, which is a very interesting phenomenon to note when probing the Iranian musicians' view of improvisation. The paradigm at work in the earlier studies, however, overlooks the mechanism with which they judge two performances as the same or different. How so?

In attempting to locate the essence of improvisation in musicians' individual creativity, one must presume that there is both a "separate composer" and a "closed opus" created by him. In this perspective, there is assumed to be no mental state which would identify the objectively identical as different, and the different as identical. Such a phenomenon is overlooked in the paradigm, which incorporates the modern western concepts of "creator" and "opus."

Thus, studies that begin with a modern Western paradigm, incorporating conceptions of "creator" and "opus" as distinct, tend to impose their preconceived idea of creativity upon their observations, rather than reconceiving creativity through a re-examination of improvisation from the perspective of the musicians' mental state and memory. As a result, the question of how it is that various performances are labelled as the same or different has never been examined as a central issue.

This problem does not arise only in the study of Iranian music or in comparisons involving the paradigm of Western modernity, either. As mentioned, Nettl employs terms such as "model" and "points of departure," pointing out that musicians who perform improvisation in the world's various cultures do not produce music *ex nihilo*, but are furnished in advance with a basis for their improvisational performance (Nettl 2001: 96). As a result, previous studies have focused more on those models and points of departure, which differ from one musical culture to another (Nettl 1974: 11–17).

However, studies of improvisation, which centered mainly on an explication of the "model," share a certain paradigm – a view that performers improvise by establishing a balance between "obeying rules" and "doing your own thing" (Nettl 1998: 16). This view looks at the model and points of departure primarily from the aspect of rules or "constraints" alone, and has not explicitly problematized the cultural diversity present in the quality of "arbitrary choice" or the status of freedom which is inextricably linked to the characteristics of constraint.

The goal of this study is to reconsider "freedom," conceived in opposition to constraint in various formulations of improvisation around the world, through examining the case of Iranian music. It aims at adding to the preceding studies of "models" in each musical culture – which discussed only various states of the constraints – a qualitative discussion of "arbitrariness" *per se*, inseparable from the characteristics of the constraints, from the perspective of the mental state and memory of the musicians who deal with the model. Therefore, in this chapter, while touching upon the content of *dastgāh*, an improvisational model, I will describe the mind and memory of the musicians who engage the model, highlighting characteristics of that engagement through comparison with the researcher's mindset. In the process, I hope to clarify, step by step, the sensibility of the musicians' perceptions of "same versus different," and eventually arrive at an understanding of the concept of improvisation in Iranian music.

3.2 What *dastgāh* music signifies

Earlier, I mentioned that the basis for improvisational performance in Iranian music is the modal system called *dastgāh*. Let us first examine what "to be based on *dastgāh*" means for the musicians, before going on to outline it.

If we distinguish compositions and improvisational music in Western art music on the basis of "whether they play what already exists in an unchanged way or not," then we can locate a similar dichotomy in Iranian music, between *mūsīqī-ye radīfī* and *mūsīqī-ye dastgāhī*. Here *radīf* refers to a body of *gūshes* conveyed to students during their music lessons – or more simply, transmitted material. The students must memorize *radīf* verbatim without exception, the result of which is that the handed-down *gūshes* in *radīf* exist as fixed, concrete materials, whether they are transcribed on paper or transmitted verbally from master to disciple.

However, if one played those *gūshes* in a musical presentation precisely as memorized, the performance would be called "*radīf* music." In fact, in some cases, this phrase has negative connotations, derived from the idea that verbatim reproduction of a set of stock phrases is not the aim of learning *radīf*.

The true purpose of learning *radīf* is to provide a foundation for improvisational performance, first comprehending the atmosphere and feeling of each *gūshe* through memorization, and then internalizing the subtle flow of the music through understanding how the *gūshes* are sequentially ordered.

What makes such improvisational performance possible is *dastgāh*. In particular, the phrase "*dastgāh* music" refers to the music produced by following these principles of *dastgāh* – the foundations of the actual musical sound that a disciple understands in the process of learning the *radīf*. Thus, the expression denotes a musical behavior diametrically opposed to the verbatim repetition of a melody passed on from one's teacher. The reason that "*radīf* music" (or performance) holds its somewhat negative connotation in some cases is that it is understood to represent a stage prior to attaining the level of *dastgāh* music.

So, the phrase "*dastgāh* music" is deliberately chosen to refer to personalized music which is performed with an understanding of the modal system intrinsic to the inherited sound material, which goes beyond *radīf* performance.[2]

Then, what is *dastgāh* for the musicians? What image of *dastgāh* does the learner construct as he studies *radīf*? To address this question, we must first examine concrete elements of the *dastgāh* model.

3.3 What is in the *dastgāh* model?

The first direct effect of memorizing the *radīf* is becoming physically familiar with a stock of concrete examples of the *gūshes*. The musical vocabulary or language which emerges automatically during actual improvisational performance is accumulated in the musician's body during this memorization process. For the sake of convenience, I will call this the set of stock phrases. However, it is not only the concrete sound, such as the stock phrases, that is developed through the learning of the *radīf*.

As mentioned in Chapter 1, *radīf* means the "row," and as such it is comprised of many *gūshes* that are connected in sequence temporally. It is worth reviewing the array once again. A *radīf* consists of a series of *gūshes*, each of which has a narrow register in the main part of the piece. The music gradually proceeds from the *gūshes* in the lower register to those in the higher register, and in the end, having reached the highest register of that particular mode, it quickly returns to the original tessitura through a fixed *gūshe* called *forūd* (literally, descent; see Figure 3.1).[3]

Generally, this structure is not referred to in any systematic way by the teacher. But the student gradually realizes the relationship between the *gūshes*, that is, the overall structure of the performance, in the course of internalizing many concrete *gūshes*. In this sense, the first successful break away from *radīf* music toward *dastgāh* music is dependent on the student's ability to recognize the relationships among *gūshes*.

Chapter 3

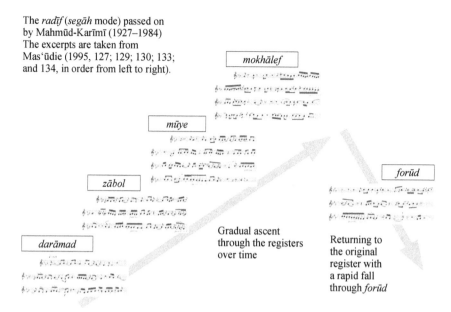

Figure 3.1 Relationship among *gūshes*

As indicated above, we can roughly say that the *dastgāh* model consists of two elements: the stock phrases and the relationship among them – that is, how the stock phrases are arranged and organized as a whole.

Incidentally, my explanation thus far concerns only the *dastgāh*, the model itself. We must think about the mental state of the performer who confronts that model as a separate issue. In particular, musicians have a unique mechanism of remembrance in the employment of stock phrases, which requires researchers to fundamentally shift paradigms to understand. Therefore, in the next section, I discuss the mind and memory of performers who confront the *dastgāh* model, and compare them with the researchers' typical mindset.

3.4 Text-centered vs oral-centered mentality

As mentioned, when told that the *dastgāh* model includes stock phrases, researchers may naturally wonder whether those phrases are played as they are or if they are changed in improvisational performance. However, this question itself is fundamentally contrary to the view of Iranian musicians. To understand the difference between these two perspectives, it might help to think of them as analogous to the difference in mindset between a culture where words operate only via the evanescent voice and a culture in which words are written as text and communicated visually, as Walter Ong suggested in *Orality and Literacy: The Technologizing of the Word* (1982).

For example, by looking at a music score such as the one presented in Figure 3.1, and further, by imagining that it is the original version behind the improvisation, we cannot help asking whether or not these phrases are played as written during improvisational performance. The basis of this orientation lies in the propensity to assume some degree of fixity in a written text, which is perhaps inseparable from the association of the written text with authorship and ownership. In other words, this fixity is linked in the unconscious to one's feeling that "I must play something different from what is shown here since it is improvisation" (I will call this presumption of fixity the "text-centered mentality." To paraphrase, it is the perception that assumes an independent author and that recognizes the work as "closed.")

In contrast, for people *listening* to the music shown in Figure 3.1, these melodies exist only for the duration of their sounding, and they are perceived to exist primarily to embody the relationship between the *gūshes*. Therefore, when the performers improvise, their "verbatim" memory of the melody itself is weak. Nor is their concrete memory, in terms of what and how they played, "verbatim" (I will call this an "orality-centered mentality").

Of course, certain characteristics of Iranian music are also of a fixed nature. The stock phrases are passed on with a certain degree of fixity, for example. But another characteristic is that anyone can use the phrases in improvisational performance. In other words, they are fixed as "shared phrases." In contrast to a text-centered culture in which fixedness is somehow linked to the feeling that "the phrase already belongs to someone, so I must play something else in improvisation," the fixedness of an orality-centered culture carries the perception that the phrases are common property and belong to no one. To put it another way, a text-centered culture adds the sense of individual ownership to its fixity, whereas an orality-based culture incorporates the feeling of sharing.

Chapter 3

Score 3.1 The *radīf* passed on by Abolhasan Sabā (1902–1958) (Sabā 1991: 11)

3.5 The feeling of "being the same"

The fact that performers have both a weak verbatim memory of melodies and a feeling that stock phrases are shared provides an important clue to the problem of identity and difference in Iranian music. Scores 3.1 through 3.4 are examples of *gūshes* which belong to *darāmad* in the *segāh* mode taken from representative *radīfs* passed on by representative musicians.

Looking at these scores as pieces of text, our initial impression is of how divergent the versions of the *darāmad* melody are. However, Iranian musicians are not very conscious of the differences between the four phrases because the seeming variations of the *darāmad* diverge only in a centripetal perspective, in such things as rhythm and melody, but they are all the same in terms of the interrelation between the *gūshes* and the roles of the *gūshes* in the overall performance, as indicated in Figure 3.1. That is, these phrases are all understood as typical examples of certain idiomatic expressions which function as *darāmad*, and they are shared equally by musicians. In that context, all the phrases are perceived as common property which can be shared freely as typical *darāmad* examples and as interchangeable, rather than regarding Scores 3.1–3.4 as different from each other.

Further fueling the feeling that "they are all the same" is that stock phrases do not exist independently in a verbatim manner, as suggested by the score, but rather is like a memory which floats as a "remembrance" (Peabody 1975: 216), stored subconsciously until the performance gives it concrete form. The musicians do not draw on an exactly accurate "text"-like memory when performing (which invites further discussion of the discrepancy between the nuances of the word "stock" and the reality of the musicians' conceptualization). In other words, it is our text-based

Improvisation, mental state and memory

Score 3.2 The *radīf* passed on by Mīzrā Abdollāh (1843?–1918) (Talā'ī 1997: 160)

Score 3.3 The *radīf* passed on by Mūsā Ma'rūfī (1889–1965) (Ma'rūfī 1995: 1)

Score 3.4 The *radīf* passed on by Farāmarz Pāyvar (1933–2009) (Pāyvar 1988: 48)[4]

response to "seeing" the score that makes the melodies in Scores 3.1–3.4 appear to vary in our eyes.

When we observe and analyze (which has strongly visual implications) an improvised performance, we may find that there are *objective* differences among individuals and even between performances by the same musician. However, the two performances – objectively different from the outsiders' perspective – might be seen as identical in the Iranian sense, because 1) the performance exists in the first place as an embodiment of the relationship between *gūshes*; 2) in such performance, the seemingly very different melodies can be categorized as typical idiomatic expressions which play the same roles; and 3) any real differences are diluted retrospectively, as a vague remembrance. Any combination of these factors leaves the musicians who performed the improvisation with the feeling that they performed renditions of the same *dastgāh*. Thus from the Iranian perspective, the two performances may be perceived as identical.

3.6 Feeling of "it is mine and different from others"

Let us now examine the converse: the Iranian musicians' sense of a performance being different from other performances, and that is one's own. In fact, this sense is very closely connected to the understanding that the common phrases do not belong to anyone and thus can be used by anyone. When someone uses such a phrase, it belongs to the performer while it resonates, in the sense that the performer selected it, either consciously or unconsciously, and embodied it as the sound. This, of course, does not mean that it is the performer's music in the sense that he or she created the stock phrases. The "performer's music" here denotes the phrases which are owned by the performer while the music is sounding and which return to the status of common property when the performance is over.[5]

What does this tell us about their sense of difference? In Iranian music, an improvisational performance is understood as original each time, because in each instance the individual performer goes through the process of embodying musical sound according to the modal system, *dastgāh*. In this sense, each performance is different. So, for example, the musician repeats the same rendition and can even say – as often happens – that he has never performed the same way. This "non-numerability" (innumerability) is what I would most emphasize about the character of remembrance among Iranian musicians.

The phrase, "only once," has been heavily used to explain various kinds of improvisation, especially in Middle Eastern music, and was originally used for the "process" of producing music, as discussed. However, if this phrase is applied to an improvisation as product, and, as in popular belief, the musical performance which results is understood to produce unique music, never to be the same in another performance, I must say that it reflects our own misunderstanding deriving from our extremely text-oriented view. Iranian musicians do not perceive improvisation as a countable product, nor do they imagine a performance as fixed or compare the latest performance with previous ones. In other words, the sense of "only once" applied to a process which is not readily apparent from the text-centered perspective is non-countable for improvisational musicians.[6] Rather than the *actual performed* music, as considered from the textual point of view, improvisation is the *procedure* through which music is brought forth each time based on the modal system, *dastgāh*.

We might find individual talent or creativity at first in expressions such as "instantly bringing out actual musical sound," but as I mentioned earlier, this phrase generally refers to mere borrowing from the common property of phrases in the reality of the oral culture. However, "borrowing" here never has negative connotations. To repeat, in a world where the shared phrase does not belong to anyone, the phrase belongs to the performer in the moment it is borrowed. To be more precise, in fact, since the common phrase belongs to no one, there is not even a perception of "borrowing." In that sense, the performer might often say immediately after the performance that he played music according to the sparks of his instinct, but this differs from individual creativity in the modern Western (text-centered) sense. In the first place, in cultures which are strongly dependent on orality, idioms and clichés are not owned by any individual but are shared widely throughout the society. Narrators there repeat virtually the same contents while making subtle distinctions in their expressions. Similarly, their improvisational performance is realized by rephrasing the *gūshes* in various ways, with no assumption of ownership of those phrases. In other words, stock phrases exist in a network of borrowing, appropriating, and paraphrasing by and among the people who use them; such behavior is the reality of improvisation for them, albeit unconsciously.

As we can see, identity and difference for Iranian musicians depend on one's interpretation of the common procedure of bringing music from *dastgāh*. This is not a sense of "either-or" but the more ambivalent feeling of "same but different."

3.7 The text in oral-centered culture

I would now like to consider what it means when Iranian music – which is characterized by an oral-centered perspective – is transcribed into text. As an example, I will present here a transcribed *radīf* which was passed on in a book published by Mūsā-Maʿrūfī (1889–1965) and the criticism it raised.

Normally, *radīf* is transcribed as a sequence of many *gūshes* in temporal order, as depicted in Figure 3.1. In many cases throughout Maʿrūfī's *radīf* book, however, transcriptions of several renditions of a *gūshe* with the same name are included with ordinal numbers such as No. 1–No. 6. As a result, the volume of Maʿrūfī's *radīf* book is much greater than that of any other musician's *radīf* score. For example, the *radīf* in the *shūr* mode which Mirzā Abdollāh passed on, presented in Figure 3.2, has 34 *gūshes*, whereas the *radīf* (*shūr* mode) passed on by Maʿrūfī, indicated in Figure 3.3, contains as many as 70 *gūshes*.

Iranian music, created through mutual borrowing, appropriation, and paraphrasing among musicians, has a strongly redundant and copious nature which Ong identifies as one of the characteristics of oral thoughts and expressions (1982: 39–41). Indeed, the improvisation in Iranian music inevitably becomes redundant and copious, as Maʿrūfī's *radīf* book demonstrates, because even one section of a performance – *darāmad*, for example – is paraphrased by a musician in many ways. In this sense, the transcriptions in Maʿrūfī's *radīf* book maintain this redundant and copious nature of the actual performance of improvisation.

However, this *radīf* book has been criticized. For example, *setār* player Nasrollāh-Zarrinpanjeh (1906–1981) condemned Maʿrūfī's work, calling the 600-page score "fool's gold," not truly comprehensive yet bloated with impure substances (Tsuge 1997: 50). According to Gen'ichi Tsuge, Nasrollāh-Zarrinpanjeh's main objection was that Maʿrūfī did not faithfully pass on his predecessors' *radīf* but added some of his own creations to his benefit.

The criticism that Maʿrūfī added his own creations instead of faithfully passing on the tradition, I think, refers to the fact that Maʿrūfī *transcribed* the redundant and copious nature of improvisation. In other words, the criticism was of Maʿrūfī's implied ownership of the originality, in the sense of a text-centered mentality, that arises from his transcription of redundancy into text.

Improvisation, mental state and memory

دستگاه شور

۲۵	۱۸. خارا	۱	....	۱. درآمد	
۲۶	۱۹. قجر	۲	....	۲. پنجه شعری	
۲۷	۲۰. حزین	۳	....	۳. کرشمه	
۲۸	۲۱. شور پایین دسته: درآمد	۵	....	۴. رهاب	
۲۹	۲۲. رهاب	۶	....	۵. اوج	
۳۰	۲۳. چهارگوشه	۸	....	۶. ملانازی	
۳۳	۲۴. مقدمه گریلی	۹	....	۷. نغمه اول	
۳۵	۲۵. رضوی	۱۲	....	۸. نغمه دوم	
۴۱	۲۶. شهناز	۱۴	....	۹. زیرکش سلمک	
۴۳	۲۷. مقدمه قَرچه	۱۶	....	۱۰. سلمک	
۴۴	۲۸. قَرَچه	۱۷	....	۱۱. گلریز	
۴۶	۲۹. شهناز کُت یا عاشق کُش	۱۹	....	۱۲. مجلس افروز	
۴۷	۳۰. گریلی	۲۰	....	۱۳. عُزال	
۵۲	۳۱. گریلی شستی	۲۱	....	۱۴. صفا	
۵۴	۳۲. رنگ هشتری	۲۲	....	۱۵. بزرگ	
۵۶	۳۳. رنگ شهرآشوب	۲۳	....	۱۶. کوچک	
۷۲	۳۴. رنگ ضرب اصول	۲۴	....	۱۷. دوبیتی	

Figure 3.2 Index of the *radīf* passed on by Mīrzā Abdollāh (Talā'ī 1997)

دستگاه شور :

۵۴ – فرود	۳۶ – ملانازی	۱۸ – سلمک	۱ – مقدمه
۵۵ – مثنوی	۳۷ – پنجه کردی	۱۹ – سلمک قسم دیگر	۲ – درآمد اول
۵۶ – بیات کرد	۳۸ – عزال	۲۰ – ملانازی	۳ – درآمد دوم
۵۷ – بیات کرد قسم دوم	۳۹ – چهار مضراب	۲۱ – ملانازی نوع دیگر	۴ – درآمد سوم
۵۸ – بیات کرد قسم سوم	۴۰ – شروع قسمت شوربالا	۲۲ – مقدمه گلریز	۵ – درآمد چهارم
۵۹ – بیات کرد قسم چهارم	۴۱ – درآمد اول	۲۳ – محمد صادقخانی	۶ – کرشمه
۶۰ – راح روح	۴۲ – درآمد دوم	۲۴ – گلریز	۷ – گوشه رهاب
۶۱ – مجلس افروز	۴۳ – درآمد سوم	۲۵ – صفا	۸ – کرشمه
۶۲ – بیات کرد قسمت پنجم	۴۴ – آواز	۲۶ – چهار مضراب	۹ – درآمد پنجم
۶۳ – چهارمضراب	۴۵ – گوشه گریلی	۲۷ – گوشه ابوعطا	۱۰ – کرشمه
۶۴ – فرود شور	۴۶ – رضوی	۲۸ – مقدمه بزرگ	۱۱ – آواز
۶۵ – گریلی	۴۷ – قجر	۲۹ – مجلس افروز	۱۲ – چهار مضراب
۶۶ – گریلی شستی	۴۸ – شهناز	۳۰ – مقدمه بزرگ	۱۳ – نغمه
۶۷ – گریلی شستی قسم دیگر	۴۹ – قرچه	۳۱ – بزرگ	۱۴ – حزین
۶۸ – هشتری	۵۰ – قرچه نوع دیگر	۳۲ – دوبیتی	۱۵ – زیرکش سلمک
۶۹ – ضرب اصول	۵۱ – قرچه قسم دیگر	۳۳ – خارا	۱۶ – زیرکش سلمک قسم دیگر
۷۰ – شهرآشوب	۵۲ – عقده گشا	۳۴ – قجر	۱۷ – زیرکش سلمک نوع دیگر
	۵۳ – حسینی	۳۵ – حزین	

Figure 3.3 Index of the *radīf* passed on by Mūsā Ma'rūfī (Ma'rūfī 1995)

Chapter 3

As discussed, stock phrases are not owned by anyone but are variously borrowed, appropriated, and paraphrased in the memory of idioms and clichés. The difference in the performances of No. 1–No. 6, as labeled by Maʻrūfī, is therefore merely the result of borrowing, converting, and paraphrasing in the actual improvisational performances, and Iranian musicians would not be conscious of that difference. Whatever his intentions, from an oral-centered perspective, Maʻrūfī's recording those differences – and assigning them numbers – is liable to be interpreted as an attempt to credit the differences to his own originality, although those differences are non-countable and not ownable.

In sum, based on the premise that Iranian music's redundant and copious nature comes from a sense of non-countability, this criticism stresses that the differences which occur in improvisational performance through borrowing, converting, and paraphrasing – which is likely to be interpreted as originality in a text-oriented culture – should never be claimed as Maʻrūfī's own.

3.8 Future studies of improvisation: Text-based culture in relative perspective

It should be clear from the discussion above that we who belong to a text-centered culture, must be cautious in interpreting the words used to describe improvisational performance. Nettl, for example, describes performances based on *dastgāh* as "giving a rendition of something that already exists," and that the musician is "performing a version of something, not improvising upon something" (Nettl 1974: 9).

Nettl uses the word "version" to convey the understanding that the Iranian concept of musical originality is different from what had been assumed in previous studies. However, he does not detail the meaning or background that this word carries, so words such as "create" and "own" which are used in his other writings, risk being interpreted from a text-centered perspective.[7]

The point is, researchers who examine oral-centered cultures and practices should problematize the autonomic nuance that words like "create" and "own," carry, as well as their own culture which assumes this nuance as postulate. Returning to the example of Margaret Caton cited in note 1, she, as a scholar, should have first speculated on her state of mind when using the words "choose" or "choice." That is, she should

58

have relativized her own psychological propensities stemming from text-oriented culture which naturally attributes improvisation to individual creativity and the diversity of autonomous individuals.

Notating sounds and visually recognizing them means to incarcerate the sound as something fixed and to add a sense of individual ownership. In this perception, improvisation must become an act of producing something new and different from what already exists.

When this act is, if only a little (and casually), idealized as generated by something inexplicable, such as an absolute individual creativity with instant inspiration or instinct, examples of actual performances are naturally taken from those of great masters. Here, most problems about improvisation are set aside by assuming that they belong to the musicians' creativity, and as a result, descriptions regarding improvisation fall into magnifying what is unexplainable, for example, by praising the performance of a particular musician as an "act of genius."[8]

Furthermore, if we consider the essence of improvisation as inexplicable, we have few options beyond focusing on what already exists – e.g., *radīf* passed on in the lesson – as something we can explain and reference as fixed material at any time. In other words, assuming that improvisation is inexplicable bolsters the text-centered perspective, reinforcing, for example, the idea that stock phrases are stored verbatim in the musicians' memory. In this paradigm it is difficult to avoid the assumption that improvisation necessarily refers to the act of adding something to already-existing text or making changes – the way we refer to "improvising upon something" (Nettl 1974: 9) – a kind of manipulation which exhibits a fairly visualistic sensibility.[9] Thus, our senses based on committing to paper and visualizing what is written have reduced our sensitivity to the non-textual world in ways that are almost unimaginable.

Only through such reflections can we comprehend the Iranian musicians' narrative about improvisational performance. More specifically, only then can we understand oft-repeated statements such as "I cannot play the same way twice" or "there are countless variations." From the perspective of text-oriented culture, these statements have been accepted literally or dismissed as objects of serious examination. However, by taking their expressions *per se* as unique to an oral-based culture, we can begin to understand their sense of non-countability, and that it is *this* that explains performing the same way while saying it is different, or calling different variations identical. In this sense, Iranian music is truly paraphrasing. In the mind of a musician, there are memories recalled a little differently each time and they are not the only correct texts; as Ong appropriately says, "He remembers these always differently" (Ong 1982: 146). We should consider that a kind of joy in creating new beauty by improvising, as we might imagine, is located after this sense of uncountability.[10]

Chapter 4
Charkh: The circulatory paradigm in performance form and musical structure

4.1 Introduction

Charkh is one of the concepts crucial to understanding Iranian culture. The term principally denotes a wheel, and by extension, firmament or fate which, in Iranian culture, are perceived as circulating. Indeed, the Iranian view of life is often likened to "the wheel of fate" (*charkh-e gardān*), as can be seen in the following passage.

> This world is barren. The firmament endows us with lives and takes them away, in mere capricious play. We, toyed with by the circling wheel of fate, are travelers dreaming overnight in temporary quarters, which is this world. (Okada 1981: 144)

Hence, understanding *charkh* provides significant insight for probing the Iranian people's view of life. While this is quite clear in the study of classical Persian poetry, this concept also sheds light on a variety of fields in Iranology. For example, in Traditional Iranian music, the concept of *charkh* – while not necessarily comprising a view of life – is nevertheless highly suggestive, if only for its implication of "circulation." In this chapter, I seek to establish how *charkh* manifests in the performance form and musical structure of Iranian music, how it appears on multiple levels, and how those levels are interrelated in a single performance.

4.2 *Charkh* in Iranian architecture

Esfahān, an ancient capital of the Safavid dynasty (1502–1722), lies in the center of Iran. Shāh 'Abbās I, who acceded to the throne in 1588, designated this place as the capital in 1597, and erected many buildings – Qeisariye Portal, Ali Qapu Palace, Imam Mosque, and Sheikh Lotf Allah Mosque – around the square which was then called Naqsh-e Jahān. Since those buildings were built facing the square, the square became known as Imam Square as well, and today is a well-known destination for both Iranians and international tourists.

Chapter 4

An article in the newspaper, *Īrān*, dated June 23, 2003, describes Naqsh-e Jahān (or Imam) Square as follows:

> The late Mohammad Karīm Pīrniyā, who had taught us Iranian architecture, used to say this (paraphrasing): Those who know Iranian music would understand well. When you enter [the square] from Qeisariye [Portal], it is just like the *shūr* mode resonating in our ear. At the front vault, the monotonous and calm <u>*darāmad*</u> of the *shūr* mode appears, which becomes <u>*shahnāz*</u> later at Ali Qapu [Palace], <u>*salmak*</u> at Imam Mosque. Subsequently, <u>*zīr afkan*</u> – the zenith of beauty – emerges at Sheikh Lotf Allah Mosque, which reaches <u>*forūd*</u> and returns to <u>*darāmad*</u>. [Similarly,] the square [returns] to Qeisariye [Portal]. In other words, that [square] itself is one fascinating piece of music. (Jihānī 2003: 9; underlining added)[1]

Without knowledge of Iranian music, it would be questionable how much realistic feeling such a metaphor could convey to even Iranians themselves, but it nevertheless conveys the sense that the charm of Iranian music is reflected in the landscape of buildings surrounding the square for 360 degrees – starting with the vault of Qeisariye Portal, passing through Ali Qapu Palace, Imam Mosque, and Sheikh Lotf Allah Mosque, finally returning to Qeisariye Portal.

In order to apply a metaphor like the one above, the speaker must presume that music has a *charkh*-like structure, which begins from a certain point, circles through 360 degrees, and returns to the start. To put it another way, the above description illustrates an Iranian person's recognition that the sequence of *gūshes* underlined in the quote – starting at *darāmad*, passing through *shahnāz*, *salmak*, and *zīr afkan*, returning to *darāmad* through *forūd* – assumes a *charkh*-like character.

So, what exactly is the structure of *charkh* employed in this musical form? In what follows, let us delineate the characteristics of a *charkh*-like musical structure, based on commercial recordings.

4.3 *Charkh* structure in Iranian music

Figure 4.1 details the compositions of performances in the *shūr* mode, as described in liner notes accompanying the commercial recordings available in Iran, the layouts of which are for the most part faithfully

Charkh: The circulatory paradigm in performance form and musical structure

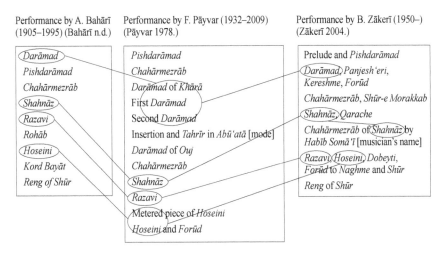

Figure 4.1 Examples of performance in the *shūr* mode by three musicians

replicated from the originals.[2] Here, I have chosen examples of performances by three musicians. As seen, in each performance program, the figure lists from 9 to 16 of the *gūshes*, performed in the *shūr* mode. These are performed in sequence.

In Iranian music, there are a great number of melody types (*gūshe-hā*), both long and short, that are passed on traditionally. These *gūshes* are presented in a systematic way, grouped by mode. Just as modes are generally defined as a "layout of the pitches, including a melodic element, that have a denser relationship with each other" (Mizuno 1992: 33), the name of a *dastgāh* evokes more than merely a scale; rather, it suggests several specific *gūshes*.

Here, what are shown in Figure 4.1 are actually names of the *gūshes* selected by the performers for their recordings from among those belonging to the *shūr* mode. Indeed, while all these performances are in the *shūr* mode, there is diversity in their constructions, perhaps reflecting the idiosyncrasies of each player.

However, when we examine the three performance programs closely (together with the newspaper article about Imam Square, cited earlier in this chapter), we begin to recognize a common flow in them. That is to say, all the performances present *darāmad* around the beginning of the performance, and, after passing through several *gūshes* (*shahnāz, razavi, hoseini*, etc.), finish via the *gūshe forūd*. In particular, the three performances in Figure 4.1 share a common sequence: (*pishdarāmad →*) *darāmad*

63

Chapter 4

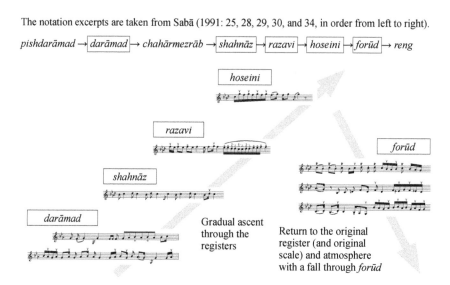

Figure 4.2 The structure of *charkh*

→ (*chahārmezrāb* →) *shahnāz* → *razavi* → *hoseini* → *forūd* (→ *reng*), as indicated by the ovals. As a matter of fact, this sequence represents the *charkh*-like structure of Iranian music.

Roughly speaking, traditional *gūshes* comprising one mode are played in order, as illustrated in Figure 4.2, starting from the *gūshes* in the lower register and progressing to those in the higher register. As the notation excerpts in Figure 4.2 show, a number of *gūshes*, each having its own feeling, gradually unfold in the progression of the ascending tessitura, at times with accompanying *moteghaiyer* notes.[3] Through this, we should be able to hear a gradual heightening of the musical excitement. When the musical voltage reaches its zenith – which occurs with *hoseini* in the highest tessitura of the mode – the music quickly returns to the original tessitura and atmosphere, passing through the fixed *gūshe* called *forūd*.[4] In the same way, the performance of traditional Iranian music in one mode invariably contains within it a flow characterized by changes such as ascending tessitura and a return – that is, the *charkh* – regardless of how much creativity is permitted the musician.

What most makes the above musical structure *charkh*-like is the *gūshe forūd* which appears at the end. *Forūd* (fall or descent) functions to lower the tessitura which had gradually ascended, and serves to return an increasingly altered mood to its original state. Iranian music can have a *charkh* structure only by the existence of *forūd*.

What, then, are *pishdarāmad*, *chahārmezrāb*, and *reng*, which appear in Figure 4.2 but which have so far been left out of the discussion? And what are their relationships to the *charkh*?

4.4 Small *charkh*

The words, *pishdarāmad*, *chahārmezrāb*, and *reng*, are not, strictly speaking, the names of *gūshes*. *Pishdarāmad*, meaning "before *darāmad*," is a calm, prelude-like musical piece. *Chahārmezrāb* means "four plectrums" and is a relatively fast-tempo, metered piece for a solo instrument. *Reng* refers to dance music in a hemiola rhythm incorporating 3/4 meter and 6/8 meter. That is, these words all refer to musical forms but not to specific *gūshes*. However, they do signal the presence of another kind of *charkh*.

Score 4.1 is an excerpt from the notation for *chahārmezrāb* by F. Pāyvar. As stated earlier, *pishdarāmad*, *chahārmezrāb*, and *reng* are the names of specific musical forms, so in the performance, musicians generally do not play particular *gūshes* from *radīf* but instead perform compositions that they had composed in advance for each of those musical forms. Nevertheless, in an independent composition of *chahārmezrāb*, for example, *charkh* also exists on a small scale.

As illustrated in Score 4.1, the music evolves vertiginously from *darāmad* (G) to *shahnāz* (C) and *razavi* (F), including a brief *hoseini* (G one octave higher) portion, and, after a momentary transition, finally returns to the original mood in a movement having a *forūd*-like function in which the return from D *koron* to D natural occurs, as mentioned in note 4. This small-level sort of *charkh* is invariably observed in *pishdarāmad* and *reng* in one scale or another. And this phenomenon (the existence of a small *charkh*) is closely related to the "position" of *pishdarāmad*, *chahārmezrāb*, and *reng* in the overall flow of the performance.

Thus, both *pishdarāmad* at the beginning and *chahārmezrāb*, which comes after *darāmad*, can contain a small *charkh* with *darāmad* as a starting point precisely because the music has not yet gone through a full-fledged change (i.e., the sound is still *darāmad*-based). Likewise, *reng* can have a small *charkh* in it just because it occurs after the music has returned completely from its changes through *forūd* (that is, because the music is already back to the *darāmad*-based state).

65

Chapter 4

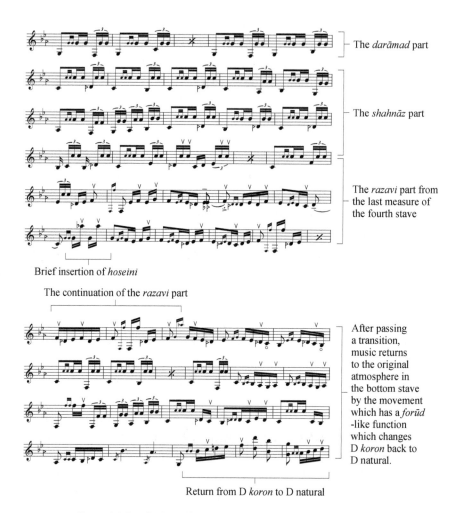

Score 4.1 Small *charkh* in *Chahārmezrāb* (Pāyvar 2019: 13–14)

In other words, it is extremely unlikely that pieces of music which have a small *charkh* starting with *darāmad* appear in the middle of the entire performance – for example, after *razavi*. I demonstrate this point in Figure 4.3.[5]

4.5 *Charkh* as "play"

Figure 4.1, as noted earlier, demonstrates the flow of the *charkh* (shown in the ovals): (*pishdarāmad* →) *darāmad* → (*chahārmezrāb* →) *shahnāz* → *razavi* → *hoseini* → *forūd* (→ *reng*). Examining the figure more closely,

66

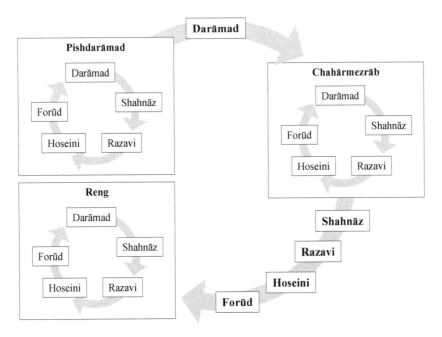

Figure 4.3 Multi-layered *charkh*

however, we find several descriptions that do not correspond to this flow. I am referring specifically to the *forūd* listed on the second line of the performance example by Zākerī or the absence of *forūd* at the end of Bahārī's performance (see Figure 4.1-a). How should we interpret these two cases?

Conveniently, Pāyvar's example offers an apt explanation of Zākerī's case. The former includes a description on the sixth line which says "insertion." This indicates that the musician arbitrarily as in an act of play inserts something different from the overall flow of *charkh*. Such an insertion may be a single rhythmic phrase or a temporary "modulation" (to be discussed in Chapter 12) to another mode (in this case, *Abū'atā* mode). However, even if the insertion is temporary, it must have the appropriate form for the music to return to the original *charkh*. Thus, the *forūd* seen on the second line of Zākerī's performance functions to return to the original *charkh* from the playful insertion. (Incidentally, the *kereshme* immediately before the *forūd* is a rhythmically fixed phrase, and is a typical insertion.)

After the insertion in Pāyvar's performance, a *forūd* is played without fail in order to return to the larger flow of *charkh*. But this return is so

Chapter 4

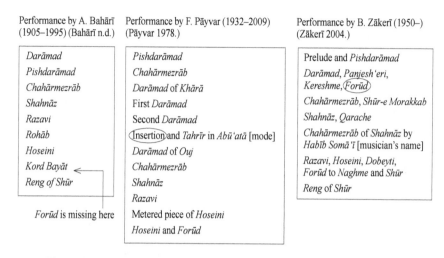

Figure 4.1-a Examples of performance in the *shūr* mode by three musicians

natural that the *forūd* is omitted from the description. The missing *forūd* in the description of Bahārī's performance stems from the same reason. These examples are evidence that the flow of *charkh* functions as a tacit premise in the performance of traditional Iranian music.

4.6 *Charkh* inscribed on the musician's body

The flow of the *gūshes* which comprise the *charkh* is not passive, such that the *charkh* is formed as a consequence of the arrangement of *gūshes*. To give an example, the *radīf* passed on by Abolhasan-Sabā (1902–1958), referenced in Figure 4.2, contains some *gūshes* which anticipate the next *gūshe* even before it starts (see Chapter 5, note 7). This reveals that a single *gūshe* entails the desire to form a *charkh*; musicians improvise by feeling that desire, resident in a single *gūshe*, as their own.

Musicians memorize these *gūshes* through intense training. But the work of internalizing *gūshes* is not limited to receiving them acoustically and reproducing them. As stated in Chapter 3, during my fieldwork in the 1990s, the masters scarcely mentioned the structure of *charkh* or the relationship between *gūshes* in concrete terms. They certainly are not explained theoretically using figures or provided to the students as a piece of knowledge. Instead, the students learn this structure (or relationship) on their own by sensing, experiencing and somatically feeling it through the practice of repeatedly playing a number of *gūshes* – by accumulating them, as it were, in their bodies. This way, the relationship between the *gūshes* is developed as the students' own physical desire, in which the *gūshe* melody is not listened to as an object but is felt as a subject that contains a yearning for the next sound or *gūshe*.

The phrase "memorize *gūshes*" – a phenomenal description – is apt to lead us to imagine sound as *an external object* that should be memorized. But, in fact, memorization occurs through one's physical body. Thus, it may not be an exaggeration to say that *charkh* is felt not so much in the sound itself, but rather in our physical experience of playing the sounds, embodied in the way that our physical or motor sense of playing a phrase – our perception of hand position on an instrument – anticipates the phrase to come. Indeed, the relationship between *gūshes* is itself embedded in the physical body performing each *gūshe*, and the improvisational performance unfolds as it follows that desire.

In other words, the *charkh* is very important on the concrete level of things such as how improvisational performance should be conducted over time (that is, what should be performed next). Precisely because each *gūshe* operates in relation to *charkh*, it contains dynamic force and functions to drive the improvisational performance forward. Such drive exists not only in the *charkh* but also at the microscopic level within a single *gūshe*.

Let us look broadly at the basic structure of a single *gūshe*. It contains the following: [prelude – *darāmad*[6]] → [poetry – *sh'er*] → [ornamental melismatic passage deriving from vocal technique – *tahrīr*] → [ending phrase – *forūd*]. This indicates that, besides the element which provides the basis of its name, a *gūshe* also includes other functions such as *forūd*.

Score 4.2 presents *darāmad* in the *segāh* mode, excerpted from the *radīf* passed on by Abdollāh-Davāmī (1899–1980). In it, we can clearly observe that the music which accompanies the sung poetry (*sh'er*) from the third stave, and which increases in excitement through *tahrīr* after the 16th rest in the fifth stave, returns via the use of *forūd*.

What is of importance here is that for musicians who improvise, this structure is not merely static. For them, *darāmad* – a relatively calm introduction – is also the part leading to the poetry section called *sh'er*. And the drive toward *tahrīr* is set off with the completion of the recitation of *sh'er*. That is, the musicians, having finished singing the *sh'er* part, are imbued with the impulse to create excitement in the next section by developing the music virtuosically with the use of *tahrīr*. After that, the

Chapter 4

Score 4.2 *Darāmad* in the *segāh* mode from the *radīf* by *Davāmī* (Pāyvar 1996: 115)

excitement is invariably directed at conclusion through the ending phrase *forūd*. Of course, this structure is not always maintained, depending on the *gūshe*. But even if it is condensed or compressed, the flow of the music is imprinted in each phrase within a *gūshe*, or even further, in the physical body of the performer who plays those phrases. The prospect of heading for the *forūd* and its resolution is embodied in the physicality of the musician performing the exciting *tahrīr*. In this way, the performer's consciousness of "what to play next" – an important topic in the study of improvisational performance – is led by the structure of the *gūshe*, containing within it a flow of changes and resolving, even on a small level within a single *gūshe*, as well as in the progression of the *gūshes* (that is, *charkh*).

From the cases above, we understand that the *gūshe* is a compound entity that exists in relation to other *gūshe*, not as a single body but as a functional part, embedded in a sequence within a mode. When we look at *radīf* from this perspective, the danger of judging a *radīf* according to

70

the name or the number of the *gūshes* becomes obvious. There are many cases that, as with *forūd*, the name of the *gūshe* does not appear on the list because its existence is axiomatic. However, even if it is not named, the minimal elements for forming a mode are invariably incorporated in the sequence of the *gūshes* as *charkh*. Thus, understanding and extracting these elements is a significant challenge for the students of improvisational performance.

4.7 Musical listening and perception based on the *charkh* sensibility

The *charkh*-like structure of Iranian music as explicated thus far constructs a world in which small *charkh* and large *charkh* intertwine on multiple levels, as if in an arabesque pattern. In that world, there is a type of musical listening and perception which is unique to the *charkh* view.

For example, in passages of a performance which may sound exciting if heard independently, one can, from the *charkh* perspective, perceive a subdued feeling, preparing for the further excitement that is yet to come. We might also recognize that the *forūd*, which may seem to be simply descending if heard in isolation, is actually performing its function of "return" to the original state from the ever-changing development, when heard in context.

This *charkh*-based view provides a significant clue for understanding improvisational performance, which is of great value in the study of Iranian music. As stated earlier, previous studies pointed out that Iranian musicians do not create music from a void, but are prepared with the foundations for playing improvisation. As we have seen, Bruno Nettl called such foundations of the performance "models" or "points of departure" (Nettl 2001: 96). Indeed, Iranian musicians go through years of memorizing and understanding hundreds of *gūshes* before reaching the state of being able to perform improvisationally.

According to Nettl, what had been identified as "building blocks" (1974: 13) were a variety of *gūshes* and their central tones, *forūd*, and so on. Yet, how they relate to one another and how they are perceived as a whole has not been fully discussed. Models have been thought to be concrete things (such as *gūshe* itself), whereas the relationship among the *gūshes* does not seem to have been clearly verbalized as an important issue, as is evidenced by the fact that this has not been expressed by a common term, despite it being another pillar of the improvisational model.

In this context, the term "the *charkh* frame of mind" (the idea of "the *charkh* mind") goes one step beyond what previous studies pointed at and accommodates the perception of musicians in terms of how stock phrases accumulated in their memory are placed not randomly but in order as a whole and how they organize their entire improvisational performance, using those memorized phrases. In the world of traditional Iranian music, learning music does not signify merely memorizing sets of *gūshes* as repertoire but denotes the acquisition of a *charkh* frame of mind through such practice. Hence, by focusing on the word *charkh*, we can see how Iranians appreciate and create music out of a sense of *charkh* and, through a structural listening, feel its beauty – the beauty of the way in which the sequence of *gūshes* proceeds and the way they are connected.

Chapter 5
Analysis of *gūshes*

5.1 Introduction

In the chapters thus far, I have mainly demonstrated ways in which *gūshes* – shared melody types – are used, and repeatedly pointed out that they are paraphrased in practice. We can observe copious examples of such characteristics of *gūshes,* not only in improvisational performance but also in *radīfs* – an aggregate of traditional *gūshes* – presented to students in music lessons.

As stated earlier, there are multiple *radīfs* transmitted by the inheritors of each respective tradition. Of those prevailing in contemporary Iran, the *radīf* transmitted by Mirzā Abdollāh (1843?–1918) is considered to be the most important. The *radīfs* which are either passed on or published in the capital, Tehran today can be traced back to the court music of the Qajar Dynasty (1796–1925), which is considered to be Mirzā Abdollāh's *radīf*. His was not an independent creation, but he is credited with having organized it based on the material he had learned from his father, 'Alīakbar Farāhānī. Farāhānī's art was passed on to Abdollāh's brother, Āqā Hoseinqolī (?–1915), as well. The musicians who studied with the brothers, and the disciples of those disciples, would transmit the *radīf* under the name of Mirzā Abdollāh as the figure who had especially contributed to the systematization of the materials. By the same token, as the disciples became mature musicians through practicing the tradition of their lineage and were recognized as such in society, they in turn promulgated their own musicality by publicizing their versions of *radīfs* under their own names. In other words, they generated their own *radīfs* from those of their forerunners. Consequently, we have today several *radīfs*, each of which indicates its performers' school or pedigree.

In this chapter, I will analyze some of these *radīfs* to illustrate through various examples how musicians create their music by using shared *gūshes* and paraphrasing them. At the same time, I will demonstrate that, without fail, every musician establishes the overall flow of *charkh* through such a process of music-making.[1] For the analysis, I have selected six *radīfs*:

73

Chapter 5

1. *Radīf* passed on by Mirzā Abdollāh (Talā'ī 1997) (transcription for *tār* and *setār* by Dāryūsh Talā'ī)
2. *Radīf* passed on by Abolhasan Sabā (1902–1958) (Sabā 1991) (transcription for *santūr*)
3. *Radīf* passed on by Mūsā Ma'rūfī (1889–1965) (Ma'rūfī 1995) (transcription for *tār*)
4. *Radīf* passed on by Mahmūd Karīmī (1927–1984) (Mas'ūdie 1995) (transcription for vocal by Mohammad Taqī Mas'ūdie)
5. *Radīf* passed on by Abdollah Davāmī (1899–1980) (Pāyvar 1996) (transcription for vocal by Farāmarz Pāyvar)
6. *Radīf* passed on by Farāmarz Pāyvar (1933–2009) (Pāyvar 1988) (transcription for *santūr*)

These *radīfs* are published in Tehran today and are widely used for the study of Persian music. I have chosen the *segāh* mode for the analysis (for reference, see Figure 3.1). As we have seen, a *radīf* consists of a number of small, traditional melody types or short musical pieces called *gūshes* that are arranged sequentially; the number of *gūshes* varies greatly between musicians. Thus, as the criterion for selection of *gūshes* in this chapter, I focus on *gūshes* included in the Mirzā Abdollāh *radīf*, and exclude any that appear only in a single *radīf*; the results of this are presented in Table 5.1. In the next sections, I will analyze these *gūshes* in order.

It is worth repeating that the *gūshes* shown in Table 5.1 generate *charkh* – temporal flow – when they are performed successively. However, since as many as nine examples will be presented per *gūshe*, vertically dissecting the horizontal temporal flow of *charkh* for the purpose of detailed analysis, the reader may lose their place within the overall flow of *charkh*. Therefore, in Table 5.1, I arranged the names of *gūshes* horizontally to show the flow of *charkh* and listed the names of the six *radīfs* vertically, with corresponding scores under each *gūshe* name, so that the reader can comprehend the analyses per *gūshe* from the perspective of *charkh*. The table should be useful as a bird's-eye reference as one proceeds through the following analysis.

Table 5.1 The *gūshes* and corresponding scores analyzed in this chapter, as taken from the six *radīfs*[2]

	Darāmad	*Naghme*	*Kereshme*	*Zang-e shotor*	*Zābol*	*Baste negār*	*Mūye*
Mirzā Abdollāh	Scores 5.1 and 5.8	Scores 5.10 and 5.12	Score 5.14	Score 5.17	Score 5.19	Score 5.25	Score 5.31
Sabā	Score 5.4				Score 5.20		Score 5.32
Pāyvar	Score 5.6				Score 5.21		
Karīmī	Scores 5.3 and 5.5				Score 5.23		Score 5.29
Ma'rūfī	Scores 5.7 and 5.9	Scores 5.11 and 5.13	Score 5.15	Score 5.18	Score 5.22	Score 5.26	Score 5.28
Davāmī	Score 5.2				Score 5.24		Score 5.30

	Shekaste mūye	*Mokhālef*	*Hājī hasanī*	*Baste negār*	*Maghlūb*	*Kereshme*	*Zang-e shotor*
Mirzā Abdollāh		Score 5.37	Score 5.49	Score 5.48	Score 5.54		Score 5.46
Sabā		Score 5.38			Score 5.53		Score 5.44
Pāyvar		Score 5.39					
Karīmī	Score 5.35	Score 5.41			Score 5.51		
Ma'rūfī		Score 5.40	Score 5.50	Scores 5.27 and 5.47	Score 5.52	Score 5.43 (bottom)	
Davāmī	Score 5.36	Score 5.42			Score 5.55		Score 5.45[3]

	Hazin	*Forūd*	*Hoddī o pahlavī*	*Reng-e delgoshā*
Mirzā Abdollāh	Score 5.56	Score 5.60		Scores 5.69-a through 5.69-f
Sabā		Score 5.61	Scores 5.65 and 5.67	
Pāyvar		Score 5.62		Not included**
Karīmī		Score 5.58	Scores 5.66 and 5.68	
Ma'rūfī	Score 5.57	Score 5.59		Not included**
Davāmī		Score 5.63		

** Pāyvar and Ma'rūfī each have *Reng-e delgoshā*, but they are not included in this book.

5.2 *Darāmad*

In analyzing the musical characteristics of *gūshes*, we must first pay attention to the sounds called *shāhed* and *ist*. *Shāhed* is a tone that appears frequently throughout a *gūshe*, thereby emphasizing itself. The word *shāhed* primarily means "evidence" or "proof," and as these definitions suggest, the repeated appearance of the tone, in an emphatic manner, serves as an authenticating mark to characterize its *gūshe*. Meanwhile, the sound with which a phrase in a *gūshe* or an entire *gūshe* ends is called *ist* (the root of the verb *īstādan*, meaning "to stop"). The *shāhed* and *ist* often share the same note; for example, the *gūshe* called *darāmad* employs a single tone that functions as both *shāhed* and *ist*.

Chapter 5

Score 5.1 *Radīf* passed on by Mirzā Abdollāh (A *koron*) (Talā'ī 1997: 160)

Score 5.2 *Radīf* passed on by Abdollāh Davāmī (B *koron*) (Pāyvar 1996: 115)

Score 5.3 *Radīf* passed on by Mahmūd Karīmī (E *koron*) (Mas'ūdie 1995: 127)

Darāmad is a non-metered *gūshe* performed at the beginning of each mode; the word means "prelude" or "introduction" (and it may be simply called *āvāz,* depending on the mode). This *gūshe* expresses the most orthodox characteristics of the mode being performed. Thus, when given only the name of the mode, *segāh*, without a specific *gūshe* name, what is evoked is the character of *darāmad*. The mode is defined as, for example, "the *segāh* of A *koron*" or "the *segāh* of B *koron,*" and so forth, according to the note functioning as *shāhed* and *ist*.

As we have seen, the *radīf* transmitted by Mirzā Abdollāh shown in Score 5.1, for instance, is in the *segāh* mode constructed with A *koron* as its *shāhed*, while Davāmī's *radīf* in Score 5.2 is in the *segāh* mode with

76

B *koron*; likewise, the *radīf* by Karīmī in Score 5.3 is in the *segāh* mode with E *koron*.

As we have already seen in Nobuo Mizuno's definition of modes – a "layout of the pitches, including a melodic element, that have a denser relationship with each other" (Mizuno 1992: 33) – what is important in Iranian music is not absolute pitch but the relative relationship among notes within a mode. At the same time, a mode cannot simply be constructed on any pitch. For example, musicians conventionally use three kinds of the *segāh* mode shown above. This may create a slight difficulty in our examination of the structure of *charkh* and the relationship between *gūshes*, as well as in comparing the ways in which shared phrases comprising those relationships are paraphrased. Nevertheless, I would like to quote the variations of the mode just as they are, respecting the fact that each has been established as a *segāh* mode that is most suited to the particular registers and attributes of vocals or instruments. Thus, in each example below, I will indicate the *shāhed* of the specific *gūshe* in parentheses.

In each of the first staves of the three *radīfs* shown in Scores 5.1–5.3, we see a gradual descending movement to *shāhed* from the pitch a third degree above it, inserting some fine ornaments. This melodic movement is often observed in actual improvisational performances identified as the *darāmad* of the *segāh* mode, indicating that musicians share a certain movement of tones as the characteristic of *darāmad*. However, we should not identify the melodic movement in these examples as the shared sound movement. To repeat Peabody's explanation from Chapter 3, the norm of *darāmad per se* exists only as a "remembrance" floating in musicians' memory, which musicians bring into concrete sounds every time they play improvisationally. Each example above should be understood as a sample result of a musician "recalling" the movement of shared sound in a concrete manner. Thus, it is more appropriate to view the variation revealed in these three scores as an inevitable difference caused by each performer's "remembrance" of the *darāmad* as a real sound, or to attribute the difference to restrictions or conditions of the "hardware" (i.e., the respective musical instrument or the performer's physical body) rather than to the idiosyncratic creativity of the musicians, as previous studies proposed.

As the study of *radīf* often demands, as an abstract activity, it may be possible to analyze the melodies in these three examples and extract

Chapter 5

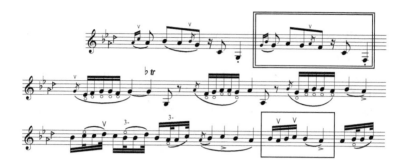

Score 5.4 *Radīf* passed on by Abolhasan Sabā (A *koron*) (Sabā 1991: 11)

Score 5.5 "Another kind of *darāmad*" from *radīf* passed on by Mahmūd Karīmī (E *koron*) (Mas'ūdie 1995: 127)

the typical character of *darāmad*. However, it is impossible to present that character solely as a concrete sound or a score, because what is presented in that way would already involve someone's interpretation once he/she turned it into audible sound or a transcription. Hence, the normative characteristics of this mode can at best only be described as "a gradual downward movement to *shāhed* from the pitch a third degree above it while inserting fine ornamental notes." In Chapter 3, I stated that the scores presented were shared phrases. In fact, however, what is shared is not the sound itself but the image I describe above, from which such concrete sounds or musical scores are generated. Thus, the students of Iranian music do not recognize *radīf* – the materials passed down to them – as a basic model, that is, as the object they should process or manipulate directly for improvisational performance. Instead, they perceive it merely as a typical representation. And, while there are many such typical representations, there is also a *radīf* that appears in a slightly varied way, as seen in Score 5.4.

78

Analysis of *gūshes*

Score 5.6 *Radīf* passed on by Farāmarz Pāyvar (A *koron*) (Pāyvar 1988: 48)

The melodic movement of Sabā's *radīf* in the example above does not descend to *shāhed* from the pitch the third degree above. Yet, since the movement from the pitch a third above is never the basic model but merely a typical manifestation, this melodic activity cannot be viewed as a variation of the archetype, but should instead be treated as another sample, like the other three recognized in the same way. Karīmī's *radīf* in Score 5.5 supports this claim: it displays a *gūshe* named "another kind *darāmad*" which follows the ordinary *darāmad* we saw earlier, and like Sabā's *radīf* in Score 5.4, this *gūshe* also exhibits a melodic movement that temporarily stops at the pitch a third degree below *shāhed* (see the area indicated by the double box).

Put simply, the musical characteristics of these melodic movements that can be objectively identified are hard to describe, other than as "a desire to move toward *shāhed*." Even Sabā's *radīf* in Score 5.4, which "manifests differently," moves toward *shāhed* from the second stave forward, and Pāyvar's *radīf* in Score 5.6 starts almost from the note of *shāhed* itself, gradually descending to settle down on the *shāhed* one octave below.

Thus, it becomes clear that the long descending and ascending melodic contours conspicuous in Ma'rūfī's *radīf* from Score 5.7 are actually progressions toward *shāhed*. By the same token, we can see that the stepwise ascension of motives in the second stave of Sabā's *radīf* in Score 5.4 and in the middle of Pāyvar's *radīf* in Score 5.6, as well as the descending line seen in Davāmī's *radīf* in Score 5.2, are also passing sections which head toward their respective *shāhed*.

79

Chapter 5

Score 5.7 *Radīf* passed on by Mūsā Ma'rūfī (E *koron*) (Ma'rūfī 1995: 1 of *segāh* mode)

Score 5.8 *Radīf* passed on by Mirzā Abdollāh (A *koron*) (Talā'ī 1997: 160)

Score 5.9 *Radīf* passed on by Mūsā Ma'rūfī (E *koron*) (Ma'rūfī 1995: 1 of *segāh*)

The characteristic we should note here is that the movement toward *shāhed* is more or less realized by employing fixed phrases. In Scores 5.4, 5.6, and 5.7, the structure of notes in the boxed-in areas are typical ending phrases, and we see an iambus (short-long) pattern in which the melody moves to *shāhed* from the pitch a third degree below it at the end of the *gūshe* (see the doubled boxes in Scores 5.8 and 5.9), which is widely used as the ending phrase of the *darāmad* of *segāh* mode. Because of such practice, the listener can tell that it is the *darāmad* of *segāh* by listening to just the first two tones of Pāyvar's *radīf* in Score 5.6.

At this point, it is worth probing the significance of these phrases within the *charkh* structure. Clearly, the shared phrases presented above do not exhibit such strong characteristics in themselves. That is to say, the characteristic which determines *darāmad* is not necessarily conveyed by its specific melodic features, but rather by a more abstract level of norm, like "an atmosphere or feeling of having a directional tendency toward *shāhed*." In addition, we can observe that its pitch range tends to consist of a frame encompassing only about three degrees above and below the *shāhed* note.

However, we should recognize here the important fact that this *gūshe* is viewed as the backbone of the *segāh* mode overall. This indicates that the *gūshe* serves as a foundation upon which ensuing *gūshes* display a multitude of transformations, such as ascending pitch ranges. We have already seen that the sequence of *gūshes* within a mode have an overall flow in which they exhibit changes, with the rise of tessitura followed by a descending melodic phrase called *forūd,* finally returning to the original pitch range and its atmosphere. When viewed in terms of the temporal flow of *charkh*, the melodic activity of *darāmad* which appears subdued at this moment will be recalled as hugely significant in the later part of the performance.

5.3 *Naghme, Kereshme,* and *Zang-e shotor*

5.3.1 *Naghme*

We are now at the point where a variety of new musical elements begin to unfold, with *darāmad* as their origin. First to appear is *naghme,* which means "melody;" here, though, the melody not only exhibits an inclination to move toward a certain note as we saw in *darāmad,* but also displays a more concrete feature.

The melodic figures boxed-in in Scores 5.10 and 5.11 are core units of *naghme* which appear repeatedly throughout this *gūshe* with some variation in pitch.

These figures eventually return to the *shāhed* of *darāmad*, but before settling completely, they execute a decorative passage called *tahrīr* which imitates melismatic vocal technique (Scores 5.12 and 5.13). The insertion of *tahrīr* at this position is intentional. For the musician who has internalized the structure of a *gūshe*: prelude/*darāmad* → poetry/*sh'er* → ornamental melismatic passage deriving from vocal technique/*tahrīr* → ending phrase/*forūd*, as discussed in Chapter 4, the physicality of playing

Chapter 5

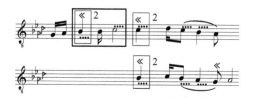

Score 5.10 *Radīf* passed on by Mirzā Abdollāh (A *koron*) (Talā'ī 1997: 161)

Score 5.11 *Radīf* passed on by Mūsā Ma'rūfī (E *koron*) (Ma'rūfī 1995: 1 of *segāh*)

Score 5.12 *Radīf* passed on by Mirzā Abdollāh (A *koron*) (Talā'ī 1997: 160)

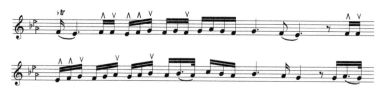

Score 5.13 *Radīf* passed on by Mūsā Ma'rūfī (E *koron*) (Ma'rūfī 1995: 2 of *segāh*)

tahrīr already foretells that the music will soon settle down after *tahrīr*. In this light, it is natural for the musician to play *tahrīr* or similar melodic figures before the music resolves in *shāhed* or *ist*.

I mentioned that in analyzing this *gūshe*, we will first find *naghme* having its own unique melody. While *darāmad* is distinguished by its typical movement toward a certain tone, *naghme* is principally recognized by its particular melody: it is a type of *gūshe* that has a concrete musical characteristic that is perceived as its basic formula in addition to a directional inclination.

5.3.2 *Kereshme*

The *gūshe* called *kereshme* (glad eye, flattering), which follows *naghme*, exhibits a distinct musical character incorporating hemiola, in which the compound duple meter (6/8) and the triple meter (3/4) alternate (Scores 5.14 and 5.15). This reflects the meter of the poetry which is most often presented in this *gūshe*.

In this *gūshe*, the rhythm of the poetry and that of the music dovetail perfectly. Let me quote an excerpt from a poem by the fourteenth century poet Hāfez, which is frequently sung in the *kereshme* section.

بیا و کشتی ما در شط شراب انداز

خروش و ولوله در جان شیخ و شاب انداز

Biyā o keshtī-ye mā dar shat-e sharāb andāz

Khorūsh o velveleh dar jān-e sheikh shāb andāz

"Come and let us cast our boat into the river of wine;

Let us cast a shout and clamor into the soul of the sheikh and the young man." (Zonis 1973: 128)

The meter of this poem is called *mojtass-e makhbūn*, which has the following pattern: short-long-short-long + short-short-long-long. It is created by altering the meter called *mojtass* (long-long-short-long + long-short-long-long) – itself a combination of *mostaf'alon* (long-long-short-long) and *fā'elāton* (long-short-long-long) – with a type of variation called *makhbūn* which changes the first long syllable of each of the two meters into a short one. The same rhythm of this meter is observed in this *gūshe*.

This *gūshe* can be used regardless of mode because it is primarily discernible by its rhythm. For example, the *homāyun* mode shown in Sabā's *radīf* (Score 5.16) presents a *gūshe* by the same name, in which the above poem is sung accompanied by music with identical rhythm.

Chapter 5

Score 5.14 *Radīf* passed on by Mirzā Abdollāh (A *koron*) (Talā'ī 1997: 163)[4]

Score 5.15 *Radīf* passed on by Mūsā Ma'rūfī (E *koron*) (Ma'rūfī 1995: 3 of *segāh*)

Score 5.16 *Kereshme* in the *homāyun* mode from the *radīf* passed on by Abolhasan Sabā (Sabā 1990: 7)

In short, a musician can play this *gūshe* anywhere, irrespective of mode, or, as I will discuss, of register. In this way, *kereshme* also differs completely from *darāmad* in the sense that a specific and distinct rhythmic pattern is recognized as its basic formula and is shared among musicians.

Analysis of gūshes

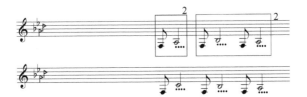

Score 5.17 *Radīf* passed on by Mirzā Abdollāh (A *koron*) (Talā'ī 1997: 167)

Score 5.18 *Radīf* passed on by Mūsā Ma'rūfī (E *koron*) (Ma'rūfī 1995: 5 of *segāh*)

5.3.3 *Zang-e shotor*

What follows *kereshme* is the *gūshe* called *zang-e shotor*. *Zang-e shotor* means the bell of a camel, and the *gūshe* is thought to imitate the sound of a bell as the camel strides. Thus, it carries a rhythm that evokes the image of strolling.

The repeated figures of beamed 16th notes in Ma'rūfī's *radīf* (Score 5.18) are inserted to extend the half notes of the basic rhythmic pattern from the *radīf* of Mirzā Abdollāh (Score 5.17) in a decorative fashion, but Ma'rūfī's *radīf* still displays the rhythm and melody that are unique to *zang-e shotor*.

Thus, the respective characteristics of *naghme*, *kereshme*, and *zang-e shotor* can be identified as the concrete formulae of each *gūshe*, and in this sense, these *gūshes* are differentiated from *darāmad*.

Having said that, however, the examples demonstrate that these *gūshes* also comprise the pitch range of *darāmad* as their center, and eventually return to *shāhed* of *darāmad* while exhibiting distinct rhythms and melodies. In other words, the relationship between *darāmad* and the ensuing *gūshes* is such that *darāmad* presents a keynote atmosphere and sonority whose characteristics cannot be extracted as a prototype, whereas the subsequent *gūshes* display more concrete features within the

Chapter 5

Score 5.19 *Radīf* passed on by Mirzā Abdollāh (C) (Talā'ī 1997: 169)

Score 5.20 *Radīf* passed on by Abolhasan Sabā (C) (Sabā 1991: 14)

Score 5.21 *Radīf* passed on by Farāmarz Pāyvar (C) (Pāyvar 1988: 49–50)

mood and tones of *darāmad*. After this point, however, a change occurs with the ascension of the tessitura.

5.4 *Zābol*

Zābol is the name of a city in Sīstān and Balūchestān Province in eastern Iran. In music, it refers to the *gūshe* that has its *shāhed* on the third degree above that in *darāmad* (Scores 5.19 through 5.24).

The beginning of this *gūshe* presents a fixed melody (in the double rectangles), heading toward *shāhed* of *zābol*. This phrase rarely changes

Analysis of *gūshes*

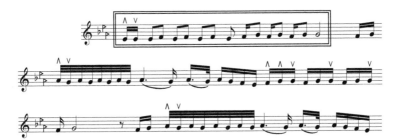

Score 5.22 *Radīf* passed on by Mūsā Ma'rūfī (G) (Ma'rūfī 1995: 6–7 of *segāh*)

Score 5.23 *Radīf* passed on by Mahmūd Karīmī (G) (Mas'ūdie 1995: 129)

Score 5.24 *Radīf* passed on by Abdollāh Davāmī (D) (Pāyvar 1996: 115)

in any *radīf*. As previously noted, variations in the transcriptions should be considered as the inevitable results of individual musicians *recollecting* the image of those fixed phrases held in "remembrance" as real, concrete sounds, or perhaps caused by restrictions or provisions (conditions, features) in the "hardware," such as a particular musical instrument or the condition of a performer's physical body. In that respect, the fixed melody in each example illustrates the way it is shared as a phrase belonging to no one – existing in the mesh of a common domain that is educed and restated every time a musician plays it.

Chapter 5

Furthermore, it is hard to describe the characteristics of the ensuing sections of this *gūshe* other than by saying that the melodic activities are executed with *shāhed* as their core note. That is, any of the six examples in *zābol* shown here cannot be identified as such by a concrete feature, as in the case of *darāmad*. Thus, we cannot assume the existence of a prototype; all renditions manifest representative characteristics and it is impossible to say that one is closer to the prototype than another. The idiosyncrasy of musicians has almost no involvement with the operation of shared phrases, which can even be described as paraphrasing each other as interchangeable expressions.

Having seen the characteristics of this *gūshe*, we begin to understand that *zābol* and *darāmad* share a common attribute in the sense that neither can be extracted as a concrete entity. This indicates that *zābol* and *darāmad* function in a similar manner in the structure of *charkh*. In other words, *zābol*, like *darāmad*, acts as a foundation for subsequent *gūshes* by setting a new tessitura. This is well-illustrated by the fact that the *gūshes* which appear subsequent to *zābol* begin with a typical introductory phrase to *zābol*, while each *gūshe* displays its specific rhythm and melody.

5.5 *Baste negār*

Likewise, we can see the introductory phrase to *zābol* placed at the beginning of this *gūshe* (see the first stave of Scores 5.25 and 5.26), followed by a rhythmical melodic figure specific to this *gūshe* (shown in doubled boxes), displayed with the *shāhed* of *zābol* as its center.

Like *kereshme*, this *gūshe* with clear characteristics – especially in its rhythm – may occur in other registers, as in Score 5.27.

Since this *gūshe*'s unique rhythmic pattern is its essential characteristic and is shared as such, musicians can perform this *gūshe* regardless of the order of the *gūshes* and their place in the rising tessitura. This characteristic is also qualitatively different from *zābol* in terms of whether the *gūshe* influences the *charkh*'s structure or not.

When we further examine *baste negār* performed in the pitch range of *zābol*, we find an interesting feature in the structure of *charkh*. As previously seen, the structure of a *gūshe* consists of the following parts: prelude/*darāmad* → poetry/*sh'er* → ornamental melismatic passage deriving from vocal technique/*tahrīr* → ending phrase/*forūd*. What is peculiar here is that the ending phrase, *forūd*, of *baste negār* in the

Analysis of *gūshes*

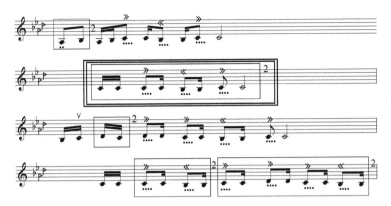

Score 5.25 *Radīf* passed on by Mirzā Abdollāh (C) (Talā'ī 1997: 170)

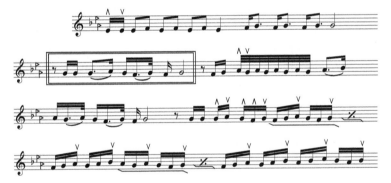

Score 5.26 *Radīf* passed on by Mūsā Ma'rūfī (G) (Ma'rūfī 1995: 8 of *segāh*)

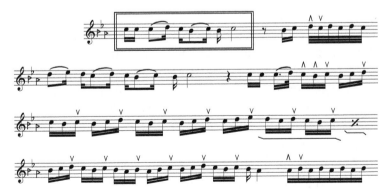

Score 5.27 *Baste negār* in another pitch range (C), from the *radīf* passed on by Mūsā Ma'rūfī (Ma'rūfī 1995: 18 of *segāh*)

Chapter 5

tessitura of *zābol* does not end on the *shāhed* of *zābol* but settles instead on the *shāhed* of *darāmad*.

I have stated that the pitch level shifted from *darāmad* to *zābol* in the temporal scheme of *charkh*. However, the example above illustrates that the shift of stage in *charkh* is not accomplished all at once with the introduction of a new *gūshe*, but that the music instead proceeds gradually, having characteristics of both the preceding and the new *gūshes*. That is to say, the *gūshe* called *zābol* (and *baste negār* under the influence of *zābol*) is not completely independent from *darāmad*, although it exhibits its uniqueness with its own *shāhed* and musical figure, which are distinct from those of *darāmad*. Recall that *darāmad* is a representative *gūshe* of the *segāh* mode and expresses the most orthodox characteristics of the mode. *Zābol* in this mode is recognized essentially by its pitch range which contrasts with the tessitura presented by *darāmad*. Under this relationship between the two *gūshes*, *darāmad* functions as the *gūshe* that *zābol* should periodically reference. In this way, *charkh* is not a sum of clearly delineated, independent *gūshes* that are visually recognizable in transcriptions, or as a table of contents, as will be discussed in chapter 6. Rather, it should be understood as one continuous temporal flow in which *gūshes* proceed in mutual reference.

5.6 *Mūye*

In the *gūshe mūye* ("lamentation"), the pitch range of the melodic activity is raised further (see Scores 5.28 through 5.32). Like the *gūshes* thus far whose function is to introduce a pitch range frame, *mūye*'s musical characteristic cannot be identified as a concrete entity, such as a basic formula. Perhaps the only way to describe it would be that it constantly emphasizes the note a minor third above the *shāhed* of *zābol* and the (*koron*) note a neutral second above the *shāhed*, descending to end appropriately on the *shāhed* of *zābol*.

These phrases are all similar to one another and practically interchangeable, which hampers the idiosyncrasy of the performers. Any difference generated in performance is at most the result of paraphrasing. "Sharing the phrases" is, in fact, a non-idiosyncratic activity, and yet, it is not necessarily viewed negatively. Thus, the musicians improvise by *recollecting* phrases they may have heard before or by using melodies

Analysis of gūshes

Score 5.28 *Radīf* passed on by Mūsā Ma'rūfī (G–B flat) (Ma'rūfī 1995: 9 of *segāh*)

Score 5.29 *Radīf* passed on by Mahmūd Karīmī (G–B flat) (Mas'ūdie 1995: 130)

Score 5.30 *Radīf* passed on by Abdollāh Davāmī (D–F) (Pāyvar 1996: 116)

that are stored fragmentarily in their memory *without alteration*, that is, by referencing *dastgāh* as a process.

So far, I have discussed the significance of each *gūshe* from the perspective of the overall temporal scheme of *charkh*. Now let us ex-

Chapter 5

Score 5.31 *Radīf* passed on by Mirzā Abdollāh (C–E flat) (Talā'ī 1997: 171)

Score 5.32 *Radīf* passed on by Abolhasan Sabā (C–E flat) (Sabā 1991: 16)

plore another implication which is observed in *gūshe mūye* beyond the *charkh* view.

In this *gūshe*, the major part is constructed within a fairly narrow interval, from *shāhed* of *zābol* to the note a minor third above, and the melody observed here is not so distinct. So, ostensibly this *gūshe* appears to have few elements to bring about changes. In fact, however, I should note that the descending melodic activity in the frame of the minor third interval passing through two 3/4-tone intervals (the minor third above → 3/4-tone down to *koron* of the second degree above *shāhed* → 3/4-tone down to *shāhed* of *zābol*) carries certain implications in Iranian music.

Score 5.33 shows *darāmad* in the *shūr* mode from the *radīf* of Mirzā Abdollāh. Here, the note G is presented as a melodic center which functions both as *shāhed* and *ist* in this mode, as in the *darāmad* of the *segāh* mode. What is noteworthy is the melodic activity which

92

Analysis of *gūshes*

Score 5.33 *Darāmad* in *shūr* from the *radīf* passed on by Mirzā Abdollāh
(Talā'ī 2015: 3 in score section)

moves from the note a minor third above to *shāhed*, by passing through microtones, which is also observed in *mūye*.

I have presented an example in the *shūr* mode here, but the frame with two neutral tones within the interval of the minor third is fairly common in the structure of other modes. For example, it occurs in four derivative modes of *shūr* (*bayāt-e tork, abū'atā, dashtī,* and *afshārī*) which share the same comprising notes and also in the *navā* mode. Significantly, the modes in the *shūr* group are found most frequently in the folk music of provincial areas, and are considered the representative mode that builds the backbone of Iranian music, even for the art music influenced by such folk music. Thus, it is understandable that this descending movement of melody with two neutral tones within the interval of the minor third in *mūye* within the *segāh* mode can evoke other modes in the listener, and by extension, elicit the image of other typical Iranian music.

To conjure that image, however, it should be demonstrated that the image evoked by *segāh* differs from that of typical Iranian music. Now then, let us probe the general characteristics of the sound activity in Iranian music by closely examining the way the melody descends, employing the two neutral tones within the interval of the minor third, which I described as evoking typical Iranian music.

The most notable feature of the intervals in Iranian music is the use of microtones, such as *koron* (lowering a quarter tone) or *sori* (raising a quarter tone). These tones in the modes contribute to generating the unique atmosphere of Iranian music. Nevertheless, the effect of such microtones is most fully realized when they are used in passages that bring their characteristics into play, rather than simply because they are part of the scale. This can be seen in the *gūshe āvāz* in *afshārī* mode taken from the *radīf* by Sabā.

Chapter 5

Score 5.34 *Āvāz* in the *afshārī* mode taken from *radīf* by Sabā (Sabā 1992: 18)

Here, the note C is repeated emphatically as the *shāhed* of the *afshārī* mode, and as such, presented as a stable sound, which is followed by the advent of D *koron* (the second degree above) a couple of times as auxiliary notes, eventually returning to C. This is a typical melodic activity of *afshārī* in which we can feel the tone of *shāhed* increasing in stability by repetitious return from a microtone. In other words, microtones are treated here as a sound that contrasts with and brings out the stability of *shāhed*. While I agree that one cannot generalize the characteristics of microtones as "unstable," it is worth paying attention to this capacity of microtones in contrast to other "ordinary" tones. Perhaps one could say that those microtones embrace unstable elements in the sense that they head toward slack or release, and the feeling of instability is resolved by the descending melodic movement toward regular tones. Let us look at the examples of *mūye* from this perspective.

The descending movement containing microtones in *mūye* presented above can also be viewed as demonstrating this feature of microtones. That is, in this *gūshe*, we can also observe a directional inclination of microtones – almost a "physiological drive" – moving from instability to stability as seen in the example of *afshārī*. As mentioned earlier that the descending movement passing through two neutral tones in the minor third interval frame appears widely in the structure of other modes as well; there are numerous examples throughout Iranian music that demonstrate such characteristics of microtones. Thus, Iranian music is performed with the perception that microtones possess a feeling of instability that is to be resolved later, or a "tension resembling that of the leading tone," to use the terminology of Western music.

However, when we look at each example of *darāmad* in the *segāh* mode, the note functioning as both *shāhed* and *ist* – that is, the *gūshe*'s melodic center itself – *is* a microtone. Thus, we should not regard this tone as an instability to be resolved, but rather view it as revealing the unique stability specific to the *segāh* mode. When considering the role

Analysis of *gūshes*

Score 5.35 *Radīf* passed on by Maḥmūd Karīmī (A *koron*) (Mas'ūdie 1995: 131)

Score 5.36 *Radīf* passed on by Abdollāh Davāmī (E *koron*) (Pāyvar 1996: 116–17)

of *mūye* within this distinct sound of *segāh*, we begin to understand that the narrow interval frame of the minor third plays an important role in triggering the evocation of the wider world beyond. *Gūshe* is not only characterized by its relation to *charkh* – the temporal scheme – within a mode, but also by having mutual linkage beyond the boundary of mode in various ways. The execution of "*charkh* as play," about which I wrote in Chapter 4, is also possible through this interactive relationship.

5.7 *Shekaste mūye*

"*Shekaste*" means "broken," and *shekaste mūye* is a *gūshe* which breaks with the feeling maintained in the preceding *gūshes* and renews the mood in some way. In the examples here, this *gūshe* alters the original feeling of *mūye* by extensively stressing the *koron* in *mūye* as *shāhed* (Scores 5.35 and 5.36).[5]

The characteristic of this *gūshe* is also hard to explain except by saying that it repeatedly emphasizes the *koron* in *mūye*, other than in the figures at the beginning indicated by rectangles. Rather, the purpose here is to present the unique atmosphere itself, which is brought about by prolonging the microtone (*koron*) without resolving it. Therefore, in the improvisational performance of this *gūshe*, a musician is required to highlight its distinct mood by extending *koron* as a matter of high priority. Such a performance cannot be denigrated as a mannerism or lacking viridity. In this light, the *gūshe* also illustrates precisely how the sharing of phrases works.

5.8 *Mokhālef*

As the word *mokhālef* – meaning "opposing" or "antagonistic" – indicates, this *gūshe* carries strong characteristics that counteract the feeling of the mode to which it belongs, more so even than *shekaste*. Its idiosyncrasy is created not only by the further ascension of *shāhed* and *ist*, but also by incorporating notes that do not appear in the *gūshes* up to this point.

As shown in Scores 5.37 through 5.42, the *shāhed* in this *gūshe* is located at the fourth degree above that in *zābol*.

Furthermore, due to the two altered tones indicated in notes 6, 8, and 9, this *gūshe* no longer supplies the feeling of *darāmad*. The reason that this *gūshe* is also called *ouj* (summit) at times is not only because it is positioned in the highest register of the music, but also because the upsurge of mood with a step-by-step ascension of tessitura by playing a series of *gūshes* now quickly reaches its climax with the strong, distinct character of *mokhālef*. Incidentally, this *gūshe* is occasionally performed alone, independent of the *segāh* mode. This may serve as evidence that the character of *mokhālef* is recognized as being distinct from the attributes of the *segāh* mode.

As seen above, *mokhālef* is defined by its explicit idiosyncrasy. However, this does not imply that the *gūshe* also contains a fixed musical phrase that can be recognized as clearly as that in *kereshme*, as a basic formula specific to that *gūshe*. On the contrary, there are only a few elements identifiable as the typical movement, such as the melodic direction to *shāhed* or a temporary stop on the *koron* tone a third degree below *shāhed* as *ist-e movaqqat* (temporary *ist*. see the phrases in doubled boxes in the scores below). Nevertheless, because the notes that comprise *mokhālef* differ significantly from those in the preceding *gūshes*, we can easily recognize this *gūshe*, even only by its directional inclination to *shāhed*. Furthermore, the melody heads toward *shāhed* by borrowing

Analysis of *gūshes*

Score 5.37 *Radīf* passed on by Mirzā Abdollāh (F)[6] (Talā'ī 1997: 173)

Score 5.38 *Radīf* passed on by Abolhasan Sabā (F)[7] (Sabā 1991: 18)

Score 5.39 *Radīf* passed on by Farāmarz Pāyvar (F) (Pāyvar 1988: 51–52)

97

Chapter 5

Score 5.40 *Radīf* passed on by Mūsā Ma'rūfī (C)[8] (Ma'rūfī 1995: 16 of *segāh*)

Score 5.41 *Radīf* passed on by Mahmūd Karīmī (C) (Mas'ūdie 1995: 133)

Score 5.42 *Radīf* passed on by Abdollāh Davāmī (G)[9] (Pāyvar 1996: 117)

Analysis of *gūshes*

Score 5.43 *Kereshme* in *darāmad* (top) and *kereshme* in *mokhālef* (bottom), from *radīf* passed on by Mūsā Ma'rūfī (Ma'rūfī 1995: 3, 21 of *segāh*)

phrases, that is, by paraphrasing. We can see this clearly in the six scores of *radīf* (5.37–5.42), which display similarities in their phrasing.

As such (while *mokhālef* has such characteristics), *mokhālef* also functions to establish the tessitura of the ensuing *gūshes*, as we saw in *darāmad* and *zābol*. Some *gūshes* that appeared prior to *mokhālef* – particularly the ones distinguished by their rhythmic characteristics – reappear in the tessitura of *mokhālef*. For example, in Sabā's *radīf* (Score 5.38), *kereshme* – first performed in the pitch range of *darāmad* – reappears in the fourth stave. In contrast, in Ma'rūfī's *radīf* (Score 5.43), this portion is presented separately as an independent *gūshe*.

Also, *zang-e shotor*, which was first played in *darāmad*, has another melody that is completely different, but which also evokes a camel's bell. This is performed in the tessitura of *mokhālef*, as shown in Scores 5.44 and 5.45. Incidentally, in the *radīf* of Mirzā Abdollāh in Score 5.46,

Chapter 5

Score 5.44 *Radīf* passed on by Abolhasan Sabā (F) (Sabā 1991: 19)

Score 5.45 *Radīf* passed on by Abdollāh Davāmī (G) (Pāyvar 1996: 118)

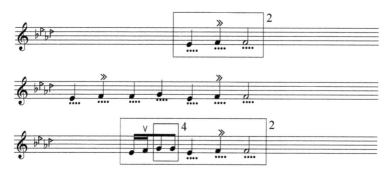

Score 5.46 *Radīf* passed on by Mirzā Abdollāh (F) (Talā'ī 1997: 182)

the same melody as *zang-e shotor* in *mokhālef* is played under the name of *naghme*.

Baste negār, which was performed in the echelon of *zābol*, also reprises its unique rhythmic phrase in the tessitura of *mokhālef* (see the phrases in double rectangles in Scores 5.47 and 5.48. In Score 5.48, the melody up to the end of the third stave is the introduction to *mokhālef*).

As is clear from these examples, some *gūshes*, such as *kereshme*, *zang-e shotor*, and *baste negār*, have their own distinct rhythmic pattern or melody, which is recognized as a basic formula and shared as such. That is why these *gūshes* can be placed without regard to the cycle of *charkh* and are performed in the pitch range of *gūshes* like *mokhālef*, *darāmad*, or *zābol*, which have no identifiable, concrete, basic formula but instead

Analysis of gūshes

Score 5.47 *Radīf* passed on by Mūsā Ma'rūfī (C) (Ma'rūfī 1995: 18 of *segāh*)

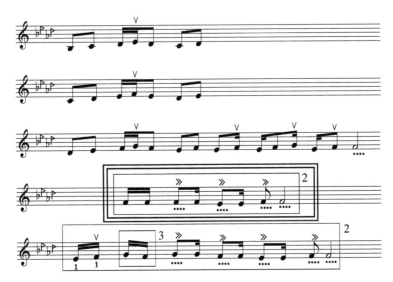

Score 5.48 *Radīf* passed on by Mirzā Abdollāh (F) (Talā'ī 1997: 178)

play the role of a keystone in the flow of *charkh*. This dichotomy in the roles of *gūshe* forms the orthodox relationship between the *gūshes* with an identifiable basic formula and those without one.

5.9 *Hājī hasanī*

The melodic movement that frequently appears as the signature of *hājī hasanī* is shown in the phrases marked by double lines in Scores 5.49 and 5.50. Above, I mentioned the orthodox relationship between the *gūshes* with identifiable basic forms and the ones which do not have a fixed formula. This implies that, for example, if *hājī hasanī* did not exhibit the movement indicated in the double rectangles, it would become difficult to tell *hājī hasanī* apart from *mokhālef*. This is the relationship between the two types of *gūshe* that I described with the term "the orthodox relationship."

Chapter 5

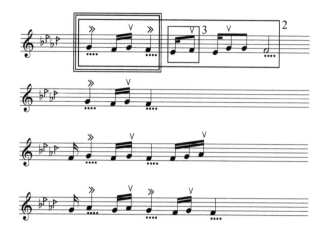

Score 5.49 *Radīf* passed on by Mirzā Abdollāh (F) (Talā'ī 1997: 176)

Score 5.50 *Radīf* passed on by Mūsā Ma'rūfī (C) (Ma'rūfī 1995: 18 of *segāh*)

5.10 *Maghlūb*

Generally, this *gūshe* is placed immediately after *mokhālef*. The *mote-ghaiyel* (altered note), which was lowered to a flat note in *mokhālef*, is restored to a *koron*, maintaining the register an octave higher in some *radīfs*, and there appears the melody which ascends to *shāhed* from a neutral third below – like those in the ending phrase of *darāmad* (see the phrase in the doubled boxes in Scores 5.51 through 5.55).

While set an octave higher, this melodic motion conveys the feeling that we are suddenly pulled back to the atmosphere of *darāmad* from *mokhālef*, thus making a strong impression on the listener's ear, especially at this point of the *charkh* flow.

Such an impression created by the *maghlūb* melody is indissolubly connected with its position in the performance order – subsequent to *mokhālef* – in the overall scheme of *charkh*. This indicates that in an

Analysis of *gūshes*

Score 5.51 *Radīf* passed on by Maḥmūd Karīmī (E *koron*) (Mas'ūdie 1995: 134)

Score 5.52 *Radīf* passed on by Mūsā Ma'rūfī (E *koron*) (Ma'rūfī 1995: 19 of *segāh*)

Score 5.53 *Radīf* passed on by Abolhasan Sabā (A *koron*) (Sabā 1991: 19)

improvisational performance of this *gūshe*, the musicians are expected first and foremost to reproduce the atmosphere. The musicians meet this expectation, not by exerting their originality but by applying phrases that are shared as *maghlūb*. We can clearly see the ways in which they apply shared phrases in Scores 5.51–5.55, which exhibit no significant variation from one to the other.

Chapter 5

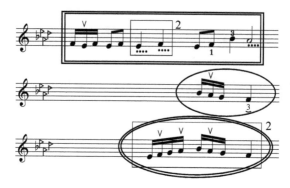

Score 5.54 *Radīf* passed on by Mirzā Abdollāh (A *koron*) (Talā'ī 1997: 181)

Score 5.55 *Radīf* passed on by Abdollāh Davāmī (B *koron*) (Pāyvar 1996: 118)

Furthermore, the melodic activity of *maghlūb* is stereotyped over the entire *gūshe*, as well as in the introductory section. Following the introduction in the doubled boxes, we can observe clichéd phrases everywhere, including a figure that temporarily stops at the note a third degree below *shāhed* (in the oval), and the repetition of a melodic motive with a stepwise ascent and descent (in the double oval). This all illustrates how the performers play improvisation by applying shared phrases with little or no introduction of personal idiosyncrasy.

5.11 *Hazin* through *forūd*

The *maghlūb* seen above returns temporarily to the pitches of *darāmad*, but the *mokhālef* undercurrent persists, if viewed in terms of the overall flow of *charkh*. There, a melodic formula with a distinct rhythm might be inserted within the *mokhālef* pitch frame, as we saw in *hājī-hasanī*. For instance, in the two *radīfs* shown in Scores 5.56 and 5.57, the motive called *hazin* (lit., "grievous") – a figure characterized by repeating the same note several times while instantly slowing the tempo – is inserted at this position in the *charkh* scheme.

Analysis of *gūshes*

Score 5.56 *Radīf* passed on by Mirzā Abdollāh (F) (Talā'ī 1997: 184)

Score 5.57 *Radīf* passed on by Mūsā Ma'rūfī (C) (Ma'rūfī 1995: 22 of *segāh*)

Here, *hazin* is seen with a repeated undulating melodic motion in the vicinity of *shāhed* (the same note as that in *mokhālef*), which descends to a temporary stop on the *koron* tone at the neutral third degree below *shāhed*. In other words, because it is inserted, this kind of phrase is performed in a way that accommodates the character of the insertion point, including the component pitches of the *gūshe* into which it is placed.

In addition, because such a *gūshe* is a phrase to be inserted, performing it is not obligatory. As evidence of this, only two out of the six *radīfs* presented in this chapter contain *hazin*. In other words, *gūshes* that can be inserted independent of the flow of *charkh* are dispensable. In contrast, the *gūshes* comprising the *charkh* cycle, listed in Figure 3.1 – including *darāmad*, *zābol*, *mūye*, and *mokhālef* – cannot be omitted. Classifying the *gūshes* into two types – one with concrete, identifiable formulae and the other without – might be seen to suggest the latter is a "lesser" type, but

105

Chapter 5

Score 5.58 *Forūd* presented in the latter half of *gūshe* "*mokhālef be maghlūb*" excerpted from the *radīf* by Mahmūd Karīmī. (The melody descends from C to E *koron*. In that process, B *koron* returns to B flat. See the circled note.) (Mas'ūdie 1995: 134)

Score 5.59 *Forūd* presented in *gūshes* "*hazin*" through "*hozān*" excerpted from the *radīf* by Mūsā Ma'rūfī. (The melody descends from C to E *koron*. In that process, B *koron* returns to B flat. See the circled notes.)[10] (Ma'rūfī 1995: 23 of *segāh*)

that is certainly not the case. The most important *gūshes* are of the latter type, in which we cannot identify a basic formula but which constitute a flow of the *charkh* with a characteristic keynote atmosphere.

The melodic activity that was executed within the framework of *mokhālef* now loses that characteristic, little-by-little, and begins to exhibit an inclination to descend. In this process, the two *moteghaiyel* tones that were altered in *mokhālef* gradually return to the comprising notes of *darāmad*; thus, the music prepares to return to the foundational sound of the *segāh* mode: *darāmad* (see Scores 5.58 through 5.63). These melodic activities – the descent of the echelon and the return to

106

Analysis of *gūshes*

Score 5.60 *Forūd* presented in the latter half of *gūshe* "*hazin*" excerpted from the *radīf* by Mirzā Abdollāh. (The melody descends from F to A *koron*. In that process, E *koron* returns to E flat. See the circled note.)[11] (Talā'ī 1997: 184)

Score 5.61 *Forūd* presented in the latter half of *gūshe* "*masnavī-ye mokhālef*" excerpted from the *radīf* by Abolhasan Sabā. (The melody descends from F to A *koron*. In that process, E *koron* returns to E flat. See the circled note.) (Sabā 1991: 20)

the comprising notes of *darāmad* – are in many cases also executed by employing clichéd formulae.

In the four *radīfs* presented in Scores 5.58 through 5.61, we can clearly see the typical pattern in which the *moteghaiyer* note that was altered in *mokhālef* returns to the original pitch as the melody gradually descends in the wake of the phrase in the double rectangle. The melodic movements in Scores 5.62 by Pāyvar and 5.63 by Davāmī are somewhat different, and yet, as in the case of *darāmad*, they are not irregular. They simply show another way of expressing the image of the melody returning to the *darāmad* as it descends. This activity also should be understood as part of paraphrasing – the sound of which one can recognize as somewhat familiar – rather than as an execution of the idiosyncrasy of the performer.

The melodic motion described above is called *forūd* (lit., "fall"). While the *gūshes* until then unfold various aspects of the *segāh* mode

107

Chapter 5

Score 5.62 *Forūd* presented in the latter half of *gūshe "maghlūb"* excerpted from the *radīf* by Farāmarz Pāyvar. (The melody descends from F to A *koron*. In that process, E *koron* returns to E flat. See the circled note.) (Pāyvar 1988: 56)

Score 5.63 *Forūd* presented in the latter half of *gūshe "masnavī-ye mokhālef"* excerpted from the *radīf* by Abdollāh Davāmī. (The melody descends from G to B *koron*. In that process, F *sori* returns to F natural. See the circled note.)[12] (Pāyvar 1996: 119)

Score 5.64 Another kind of *mūye* excerpted from the *radīf* by Mirzā Abdollāh (Talā'ī 1997: 186)

as they raise the register step-by-step, the *forūd* functions to bring the music – which had attained the climax of transformation at the highest echelon – back to the original atmosphere. In such a scheme of changes and convergence programmed in each mode, *forūd* is an indispensable constituent of a mode and no mode is complete without it.

We should also note that *forūd*, which plays an indispensable role, is nominally part of other *gūshes*, like *hazin*. That is to say, the *forūd* is so axiomatic to a circuit of the cycle – *charkh* – that it does not necessarily require notation.

From the perspective of Iranian musicians, this axiomatic feeling toward *forūd* is such that they are always conscious of *forūd* in the tiniest unit of music at any moment of the performance, regardless of when, where, and what they play. With this perspective, one can recognize *forūd* even in two notes, like the ones shown in the next example.

Score 5.64 presents a different kind of *mūye*, positioned after *hazin*. Even in this extremely simple figure made up of four notes, one can observe the function of *mūye* (*shekaste mūye*) in the first two notes, and of *forūd* in the last two notes. Furthermore, whether one can perceive *forūd* and its feeling of closure specific to the *segāh* mode via only these two notes or not could be a measure of receptivity toward *charkh* embedded in Iranian music.

5.12 *Hoddī o pahlavī*

Positioned after *forūd*, *hoddī o pahlavī* begins in the register of *darāmad*, and exhibits relatively similar melodic activity across different *radīfs*, with the short-long-long metrical pattern of poetry called *fa'ūlon* as its underlying rhythm (Scores 5.65 and 5.66). The introductory section of this *gūshe* ends with a short *tahrīr* (boxed-in phrases).

In the latter half, by contrast, the pitches of *mokhālef* (re)appear, displaying the rhythm of *fa'ūlon* in a more definite fashion (Scores 5.67 and 5.68). But, shortly after that, the music moves to conclude quickly by inserting *forūd* (boxed) and ends with another *tahrīr*.

By itself, this *gūshe* exhibits a wide melodic activity in which elements of the preceding *gūshes* reappear here and there. This breadth of activity is generated by revisiting the overall flow of *charkh*. Therefore, when playing this *gūshe*, what the musicians bear in mind is the bird's-eye

Chapter 5

Score 5.65 *Radīf* passed on by Abolhasan Sabā (A *koron*) (Sabā 1991: 21)

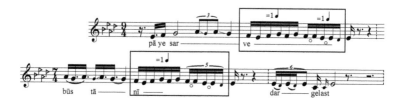

Score 5.66 *Radīf* passed on by Mahmūd Karīmī (E *koron*) (Mas'ūdie 1995: 135)

Score 5.67 *Radīf* passed on by Abolhasan Sabā (The melody descends from F to A *koron*. In *forūd*, E *koron* returns to E flat.) (Sabā 1991: 21)

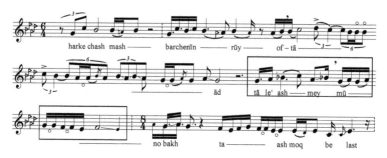

Score 5.68 *Radīf* passed on by Mahmūd Karīmī. (The melody descends from C to E *koron*. In *forūd*, B *koron* returns to B flat.) (Mas'ūdie 1995: 135)

view of the flow of *charkh*, in addition to the rhythm of *fa'ūlon* (short-long-long) that loosely defines this *gūshe*.

As is clear from the discussion so far, *gūshes* can be broadly classified into two types according to their nature. One type bears its own keynote role as a comprising member of *charkh*. The other includes *gūshes* characterized by their unique rhythms or melodies.

Analysis of *gūshes*

The former – the *gūshes* which serve as framework in the construction of *charkh* – include *darāmad*, *zābol*, *mūye*, and *mokhālef* (*forūd*), as illustrated in Figure 3.1. These *gūshes* exhibit their respective frames of pitch range, centered on the *shāhed* in each, as they ascend from the lower to the higher echelons of the *segāh* mode. Since the characteristics of mode in Iranian music gradually manifest themselves in the presentation of each *gūshe* successively in the overall scheme of rising tessitura, each *gūshe*, together with its order in performance, is considered as an essential component of a mode.

In the latter – the *gūshes* with unique rhythms or melodies – display fixed rhythms or melodies in the pitch range established by their preceding *gūshe*. The *gūshes* that have relatively fixed rhythms include *kereshme*, *zang-e shotor*, *baste negār*, and *hazin*; the *gūshes* that have more or less fixed melodies include *naghme* and *hājī-hasanī*. As we have seen, these *gūshes* would be absorbed into the former type if their characteristic rhythms or melodies were absent. In other words, their identity is established by specific rhythms or melodies. This enables these *gūshes* to be inserted and played in any pitch range or setting without drastically altering their characteristics.[13]

Except for Chapter 2, I have thus far focused on the former type of *gūshe* because I believe that gaining perspective on the interrelationships in *charkh*, that is, the nexus among *darāmad*, *zābol*, *mūye*, *mokhālef*, and *forūd*, provides the key to understanding how musicians view *dastgāh* as a model, and by extension, improvisational performance. Unlike the "freestanding" *gūshes* that can exist independently of other *gūshes*, these are the ones which drive the music forward and manifest beauty in the way *gūshes* are connected, which musicians vividly feel but which may be difficult to perceive from the outside. As evidence of this, in the last *gūshe* of the *segāh* mode, *reng-e delgoshā*, all the elements of the major *gūshes* played thus far reappear in the same order, forming the epitome of the *segāh* mode as a whole.

5.13 *Reng-e delgoshā* ("fun and exhilarating *reng*")

Reng means a dance piece. In *radīf* it plays the role of concluding a mode. Thus, this *gūshe* is a finale crowning the close of the *segāh* mode. *Reng* is usually in 6/8 meter often containing a hemiola rhythm with the insertion

Chapter 5

Score 5.69-a Beginning of *reng* in the *radīf* passed on by Mirzā Abdollāh (A *koron*) (Talā'ī 1997: 192)

Score 5.69-b The part of *darāmad* (A *koron*) (Talā'ī 1997: 192)

Score 5.69-c The part of *zābol* (C) (ibid.)

of 3/4 meter. The examples presented here are excerpts from a *reng* in 2/4 meter.

The motive shown in Score 5.69-a appears regularly throughout the *gūshe*, providing the uninterrupted foundational tone of the *segāh* mode. This kind of two- or four-measure phrase functioning to set the underlying tone is called *pāye* (lit., "foundation" or "basis"). The structure of this *gūshe* distills the essence of the *segāh* mode with a brief recapitulation of the features of all the major *gūshes* played thus far, while employing *pāye* as their foundation (Scores 5.69-b through 5.69-f).[14]

Although examples are not presented here, *reng* in the *radīfs* transmitted by Ma'rūfī and Pāyvar exhibit the same structure. Like this, the nonverbalized constraint is deeply embedded in the improvisational performance of Iranian music, however much the performers maintain that their artistic freedom is guaranteed in improvisation.

Analysis of *gūshes*

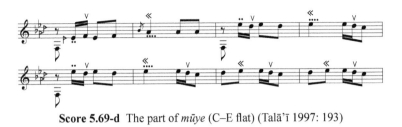

Score 5.69-d The part of *mūye* (C–E flat) (Talā'ī 1997: 193)

Score 5.69-e The part of *mokhālef* (F) (ibid.)

Score 5.69-f The part of *forūd* (movement down from F to A *koron*) (Talā'ī 1997: 193–4)

Bruno Nettl used the term "density" to express the degree of constraint and fixity in the improvisational performance of various musical cultures, by which he makes comparison among them (Nettl 1974: 13). While the question arises of whether it is possible to gauge the degree of constraint in phenomena which have different qualities – for example, the fixity that can be identified as a concrete sound and the constraint in relationships such as *charkh* – in the same arena, Nettl regards the density of constraint in Iranian music as relatively high. Indeed, Iranian music does have high density if viewed in terms of the structural constraints observed in *charkh* and the fixity of sounds in the sharing of phrases, which we have discussed in this chapter.

The problem, however, is that the performers do not perceive this "constraint" negatively. Quite the contrary, they find joy in re-creating the flow of *charkh* through paraphrasing. Thus, the objective of this chapter was to shed light on the nature of paraphrasing – the ways in which musicians apply those shared phrases – more specifically, using a wealth of examples from the lineages of six musicians.

Chapter 6
Change in the context for learning improvisation: The influence of writing on Iranian music

6.1 Introduction

I have mentioned that, in Iran, music was traditionally passed on orally. With the introduction of Western music, however, the use of staff notation has fully taken root, and textbooks and *radīfs* notated on staves are used in various ways for instruction in traditional music. Perhaps this can be viewed as a problem of modernization in music. Like the introduction of Western music in Japan during the Meiji period (1868–1912), the modernization of music in Iran brought Western music perspectives and pedagogical methodologies into the realm of traditional music in many forms. For example, staff notation has been introduced in the teaching of traditional music, which was originally transmitted orally, and the concept of étude, which aims at mastering technique, has been brought into music instruction, where the goal had previously been solely the transmission of *gūshes*.

This chapter examines the issues of such musical modernization through a focus on changing views of education and knowledge inherent to instruction in traditional music. Stated differently, it will look at Iranian music – which I have so far examined from various aspects of oral culture – from the perspective of the influence of text-based culture, that is, the influence of the mindset of writing. As I will discuss, instruction in traditional Iranian music had been conducted in an apprentice system similar to that of classical Japanese dance, in which the learners must first imitate the *form* alone which the master demonstrates instead of being taught the ABCs of the dance step-by-step. That is, transmission of the art was executed situationally (or contextually), emphasizing an awareness rarely gained outside of the apprentice system, wherein the learner can closely observe the daily life of his teacher.

However, textbooks such as *Dastūr-e Tār* (1921), by ʿAlīnaqī Vazīrī (1887–1979), which appeared with the introduction of staff notation, significantly changed traditional music pedagogy. For example, many

Chapter 6

innovations were made including recording microtonal pitches in staff notation, introducing the concept of étude, arranging music in a Western style, and modifying instrument holding positions to facilitate playing. These changes introduced a modern educational mode of knowledge transmission, providing more specific, direct, and systematic instruction, in contrast to the traditional apprentice system in which each student would raise questions and seek answers in the course of concentrating on imitating the teacher.

This chapter will discuss how attitudes toward teaching and learning – that is, views of knowledge and education – in the apprenticeship have been changed by a methodology involving staff notation and études, together with the modern educational perspective inherent in that methodology and, furthermore, by the mindset of writing. It will also look at the changes those factors have brought to music. I will begin with a review of the perspectives on knowledge and education which had previously governed the teaching of traditional Iranian music.

6.2 Situationally acquired knowledge

According to Ong (1982: 49), knowledge in an oral culture has always been situational, in a form "close to the human lifeworld" (ibid.: 42). In the past in Iran, the master and disciple lived in a close relationship. *Tār* and *setār* player Hosein Alīzādeh recalls his training period as follows:

> In the past, the relationship between a master and his disciple was not limited to being together only during lessons; even outside class, they were together all the time, as if they were friends. (interview, July 18, 2002)

In fact, it was impossible to learn from the master in a mode other than "observing and stealing" while living together. In those circumstances, teaching was never solely the provision of detailed instructions. Nevertheless, this does not imply an absence of concrete instruction. It means that even if there was concrete instruction, there were also abundant opportunities outside direct instruction that would convey the essential meaning of the teaching to the student.

In Chapter 1, I described how a student's perspective toward the fixity of *radīf* changes depending on stage of mastery, in order to explicate the extent to which the *radīf* learned as a fixed text determines the improvisation (see Section 1.3). There, it became clear that the *gūshe* passed on from the master remains in a fixed text as long as the learner trains exclusively with the same master. However, through exposure to other musicians' performances in other contexts, the learner begins to experience the *charkh* which realizes the text. Thus, the sensibility towards *charkh* that enables improvisational performance is acquired not only by learning *gūshes* in front of one's master, but by the experience *outside* the place of learning.

Studying the *radīf* taught by a teacher not as a mere text but with the intention of gaining a feeling for *charkh* while finding a positive meaning in the learning for future improvisational performance, is prompted by focusing on an entire circle of musicians who practice improvisation. Learning *gūshes per se* in front of the master is a necessary process, but does not suffice to enable the performance of improvisation. As Alīzādeh points out, disciples who live with their master learn the meaning and significance of the *gūshes* passed on by closely observing the behavior of their master as a musician *outside* the setting of music instruction.

In her discussion of the educational values of apprenticeship, Kumiko Ikuta points out that the difference between apprenticeship and school education, or further, the root of what generates the organizational difference, lies in the differences between their respective views of knowledge and education (Ikuta 2001). Modern education is built on the perspective that one can extract knowledge – including its appropriateness (or significance) and application – and teach that knowledge independently, whereas in apprenticeship, although a "form" is passed on from a teacher, how it should be used (in improvisation, for example) or what it means to use the form in improvisation is never taught, and it is understood that the students should learn this by *voluntarily* observing and absorbing the master's practice or the customs of the society to which the master belongs. This process of learning is not a "thing" which can be "extracted" from the rest and taught as a piece of knowledge. Among other scholars, Margaret Caton, quoted in Chapter 3 (2002: 141), states that "the art of improvisation was usually not taught separately." This statement derives from the different perspectives on knowledge and education between apprenticeship and the school system. In other words, the scholars' question, "whether or not to be able to teach" *per se* represents the text-based culture of modern education.

Prior studies tended to describe the learning processes – which cannot be taught as an object or extracted as an independent piece of knowledge – using phrases such as "learning *naturally*." However, this "naturalness" is not a vague or passive attitude which only awaits the presentation of knowledge. Rather, it refers to a learner actively turning their antennae toward the world outside the apprenticeship to seek the meaning of what was taught – in other words, a conscious act which Ikuta describes as "infiltration to the world." Therefore, this "naturalness" only refers to the students' internal perceptual world, whereas for us researchers, it is instead an "intentional" and "voluntary" act that should be vigorously studied.

The learner's goal is mastery of the "types" rather than a superficial "form." The *radīf* which students are provided and individual examples of improvisation are, after all, merely "forms," whereas "type" refers to that which actualizes such forms (or appearance) – namely, the *charkh*-based perspective. The view of knowledge and education that enables one to learn the types, in short, perceives the *radīf* – passed on from the teacher as a "form" – as meaningful only in relation to its application (improvised performance), and does not focus on how to use the form in isolation. This is a "situational" perspective on knowledge which is "close to the human lifeworld," that is, "not a realistic but a relational knowledge" (Ikuta 2001: 244) in the world of traditional Iranian music.

6.3 Change brought by the concept of the étude

6.3.1 Abstract knowledge

Soon after Iranian music began to be written in staff notation, a number of textbooks, such as the *Dastūr-e Tār* appeared. Knowledge became abstracted, detached from the context in which a disciple lived in a close relationship with a master; the transmission of that knowledge *per se* thereby became possible. This abstract knowledge, however, refers to the knowledge of playing techniques on each instrument. Gen'ichi Tsuge recalls his experience of learning *radīf* as follows:

> Each student came to lessons with the melodic instrument which was his/her strength. A female Iranian student and I brought *setār* whereas one of the male Iranian students brought a *tār*; two others had violins while another two – a male and a female student – received a lesson with *santūr*. (Tsuge 1989: 279)

This statement reveals the fact that, in Iran, studying music traditionally did not mean learning the techniques of playing specific instruments. As discussed in previous chapters, learning Iranian music does not refer to expanding a repertory, such as mechanically memorizing many *gūshes*. The purpose of learning *radīf* is to enable improvisational performance by first comprehending the atmosphere and feel of each *gūshe* through memorization, and then internalizing the subtle flow of the music (that is, gaining the sensibility of the *charkh*) through understanding how the *gūshes* are sequentially ordered. In the traditional context, the study of *radīf* took place in such a way that students of various instruments gathered for comprehensive lessons with a master beyond the differences between the instruments, and thus the students could feel that the aim of the lesson was not mastering each instrument but acquiring the *charkh* feeling.

But with the appearance of textbooks such as the *Dastūr-e Santūr*, abstracted knowledge has brought the traditional practice of music teaching to a new pedagogic stage with a modern educational sense, that is, specific instruction on playing techniques. The new style of teaching informs the students of the specific practice to be done and the expected results of that effort. In this way, it emphasizes the transmission of direct and specific knowledge – instrumental performance techniques – rather than the "situational" ways of learning in which students *sense* the *charkh* feeling. In this, we can observe that the transmission of musical tradition which had been aimed at acquiring the *charkh* feeling, was qualitatively changed by beginning instruction with the instruments' playing techniques. This change has significantly influenced the sound of Iranian music as well. In what follows, we will examine more specifically how the concept of étude, which aims at the mastery of performance techniques, has influenced the sound of Iranian music.

6.3.2 Sound as reflection of the voice

As we have seen, learning music in Iran traditionally involved a process of a teacher passing on *gūshes* to a disciple. Improving instrumental technique was not the primary intention. Instead, the focus was on the feeling of *āvāz* (vocal), no matter the instrument, as discussed in Chapter 2. In other words, what the student needed to learn initially were the sounds and phrases which evoke *āvāz*.

Chapter 6

Score 6.1 Etude for *Takie* imitating *Tahrīr* (Pāyvar 1961: 43)

These *āvāz*-like sounds can be found in many of the examples presented in this book. The Score 6.1 is one example.

The technique of repeating a small embellishment in Score 6.1 is called *takie*. *Takie* means "to lean against," and when one hears the sound produced by this technique, its intention is obvious. It imitates a melismatic vocal technique called *tahrīr* which alternates natural voice and falsetto voice rapidly and repeatedly.

Musicians acquire *takie* as a universal Iranian musical idiom, not as a technique intrinsic to a particular instrument. As a result, musicians maintain the feeling of "producing a voice" as if it were their own, even though they may be instrumentalists. For example, when the *tahrīr* is executed in a higher register as the mood becomes heightened in the latter half of a performance, the singer must perform it with an especially strong sense of excitement and urgency. Such urgent and intense feelings are equally expressed in the *takie* performance of an instrumentalist who plays as if they were singing. The playing of *takie* evokes the feeling of raising one's voice although the musician merely moves their hands. Thus, the musical language of *takie*, which is common to Iranian music, does not exist statically to evoke the sound of the voice. It *is* the physicality of vocalization for the players which is underpinned by feelings of urgency, eurhythmy, and breathing which vocalization brings, and it makes the player feel as if they are singing through their hands.

6.3.3 Employment of the sound determined by the instrument

When, however, the instrument-centered view that was introduced by the concept of étude comes into play, a desire emerges for the quality of sound intrinsic to each instrument, in addition to the sound evoking *āvāz*. Here, I will examine this phenomenon through a performance of the *santūr*.

Change in the context for learning improvisation

Score 6.2 Transcription of Mirzā Abdollāh's *radīf* by Kiyāni (Kiyāni 1990: 3)

Score 6.3 Excerpt from "Khazān" composed by Meshkātian (Javāherī 1997: 7)

As discussed in Chapter 2, training in percussive instruments, including the *santūr*, uses various practices for strengthening the non-dominant hand.[1] Because the higher register on the *santūr* is located to the player's left and the lower register is on the right, it becomes technically important that the left hand can play as freely as the right hand to achieve proficiency in the mid-to-high registers. Nevertheless, when observing contemporary *santūr* musicians' use of the left hand, we find considerable differences in the degree of skill and usage of the left hand depending on the performer and the piece.

Score 6.2 provides one of Mirzā Abdollāh's *radīf* (shown in Score 5.33), performed and transcribed by *santūr* player Majid Kiyāni (1941–). Kiyāni is known for playing *radīf* faithfully, and his performance differs little from what was transcribed for the *tār* and *setār* shown in Score 5.33. As such, his playing style rarely incorporates techniques unique to the *santūr* (i.e., it does not make full use of the left hand).

In contrast, however, *santūr* players such as Parvīz Meshkātian,[2] Ardavān Kāmkār (discussed in Chapter 11), and others, apart from their conventional *radīf* playing, actively incorporate techniques unique to the *santūr* in their newly composed works for instrumental music. For example, as is clear from the Score 6.3, the music employs virtuosic

Chapter 6

repeated strikes with the left hand (shown with ∨ on the score).[3] Naturally, extensive training of the left hand is required to play such a piece. Of course, the differences between Meshkātian and Kiyāni begins from the fact that one plays traditional *radīf* and the other a composed piece. But, whatever does "training the left hand" mean in *santūr* playing?

6.3.4 The meaning of left-hand training

I had the opportunity to observe Kiyāni's lessons in 1998. What impressed me most about the experience was that there was almost no instruction provided regarding how to play the instrument or details about performance techniques. For example, when students asked for instruction on how to hold the mallets (*mezrāb*), Kiyāni always replied with an affirmative answer, saying "you are doing fine." Considering that at the time, various musicians had already published textbooks such as the *Dastūr-e Santūr* and were attempting to establish a systematic pedagogy for teaching playing techniques from the introductory level, Kiyāni's lessons appear to have been a conscious refusal of the new style of teaching. Under his tutelage, training the left hand was scarcely imaginable, and other students didn't feel the need for that training either while they were studying with Kiyāni. What is this telling us?

Here, we need to think about the respective roles of the right (dominant) hand and left (non-dominant) hand in the playing of *santūr* and how each hand is related to the other. The aforementioned *takie* provides a clue toward answering this question.

As indicated in Score 6.1, in the performance of *takie* – which imitates *tahrīr*, the vocal technique that rapidly and repeatedly alternates the natural and falsetto voice – the natural voice part, which plays the dominant melody, is performed with the right hand, and the embellishing falsetto tone is played with the left hand. Although training in percussive instruments, including *santūr*, incorporates various exercises to raise the ability of the non-dominant hand to near that of the dominant one, in the performance of *takie*, we can see that the weakness of the non-dominant hand is effectively used in contrast to the competence of the dominant hand. This type of composition is not limited to *takie*; we can identify many techniques in the performance of *santūr* that assign the relaxed part of a phrase to the left hand. In other words, in the effort to produce a sound based on the voice, the weakness of the left hand is used. From this perspective, it is clear why Kiyāni did not specifically train the left hand.

It appears that the idea of training the left hand was a distant concern for Kiyāni because the quality of vocal sound is, by and large, the foundation of his style. For him, questions of technique, such as what one should do in order to quickly strike the strings with the left hand (or to produce a firm sound with the left hand) or what the hand position should be, and the training required to realize it are unnecessary for the primary goal of achieving the quality of voice. When the goal is the production of a voice-like sound, the left hand can remain weak. The weakness of the left hand is effectively utilized in imitating nuances of all kinds of voice.

However, for those who seek the musical language unique to the *santūr*, the left hand – which is in charge of the higher register of the scale – naturally becomes the target of training. The supremacy of the instrument demands that the weakness of the left hand must be overcome "for the performance of the *santūr*." From this perspective, use of the left hand becomes much more intense for musicians such as Ardavān Kāmkār. Of course, the sound that results from such training is entirely different from that derived from the voice.

The well-known *tār* player Mohammadrezā Lotfi (1947–2014) reportedly complained that adopting Western music études into the practice of Iranian instrumental music destroys Iranian music, presumably referring to the danger that the voice, which is intrinsic to the sound of Iranian music, may disappear or become diluted.

6.3.5 Intertwining the voice and the instrument

Having examined this phenomenon, it becomes clear that Iranian music has both sounds reflecting the physical sense of vocal production and sounds that are deeply constrained by the physicality of the instrument, and that these two elements have increasingly intertwined and dynamically penetrated each other, particularly after the appearance of textbooks.

Obviously, all musical instruments share these entwined physical senses. But their engagement is especially vivid on the *santūr* because – as a hammered dulcimer – the more instrumental the passage, the more it awakens a physical sense of striking. That is, because the *santūr* cannot sustain sounds with a single strike, and must therefore fill the temporal space with repeated strikes, the act of striking is apt to surface in the

Chapter 6

consciousness of the players. Therefore, players can realistically feel the parallels and coexistence of the qualities of sound emphasizing the physicality of striking and sound as a reflection of vocal production. Although both are produced by the same action of striking, the feeling induced by the former type of *santūr* playing strongly contrasts to that resulting from the latter which evokes the physical sense of "singing" or "vocalizing."

This contrast between the two playing styles may be somewhat diminished in the performance of instruments which can, in contrast, sustain tones, such as the *ney* or *kamānche*. For an instrument which can produce sustained sounds, its playing, *per se*, is close to the physical sense of vocalization, resulting in the evocation of the act of singing. In this sense, the contrastive relationship in Iranian music between sound as a reflection of the voice and sound controlled by the physicality of the instrument may be observed as more prominent in the performance of instruments that use mallets for striking or that are plucked. This should be taken into consideration as a reason that playing the *santūr* – among all Iranian instruments – has become notably virtuosic.

Thus far, we have looked at the influence of the appearance of textbooks, including the concept of étude. Now, let us turn to the influence the notation of *radīf* onto staves has had on traditional Iranian music.

6.4 Change brought by staff notation for *radīf*

6.4.1 Loss of the *charkh* feeling

When *radīf* themselves began to be notated and published, the names of the *gūshes* were listed in the table of contents. This highlights the fact that each individual *gūshe* – traditionally recognized as parts of a continuous temporal flow (*charkh*) – had begun to be understood as something clearly delimited and that could be extracted.

Figure 6.1 shows the liner notes included with the cassette tape of the *radīf* for vocal, passed on by Abdollāh Davāmī (1899–1980). As shown, it lists the names of the *gūshes* in each mode (thus, the breaks between each *gūshe* are visually clear).

However, if we listen to the recording of the performance by Davāmī, we find that he proceeds to sing from one *gūshe* to the next, without particular concern about the name of each *gūshe*, since he often forgets

Change in the context for learning improvisation

ب	الف
• آوازِ افشاری	• دستگاهِ شور
درآمد اوّل	(همراهِ تار محمدرضا لطفی)
جامه‌دران	درآمد اوّل
عراق	درآمد دوّم
قرایی	کرشمه
• آوازِ کرد بیات	درآمد رهاوی
درآمد اوّل	سلمک
درآمد دوّم	قرچه
حزین	رضوی
• آوازِ بیات ترک	عزال و حسینی
(همراهِ تار محمدرضا لطفی)	زیرکشِ سلمک
درآمد اوّل	(با تار اجرا شده است)
جامه‌دران	• آوازِ دشتی
دوگاه	درآمد اوّل
شهابی	دشتستانی
روح‌الارواح	حاجیانی
قطار	غم‌انگیز
مثنوی	اوج
• آوازِ ابوعطا	گیلکی
(همراهِ تار محمدرضا لطفی)	
درآمد	
رامکلی	

Figure 6.1 Liner notes of the *radīf* passed on by Abdollāh Davāmī (Davāmī 1997)

to announce the name of the *gūshe* before singing it, instead enumerating them at the end. I think this illustrates that Davāmī grasped the *radīf* in the continuous temporal flow of *charkh* rather than as an accumulation of *gūshes*, each of which is a clearly delimited melody type.

For the generation who first experience *radīf* in notation, though, *radīf* may initially be recognized *visually* as an accumulation of *gūshes*, readily delimited and extracted (or broken down). Of course, this should not be a problem if the traditional process of learning – proceeding from copying the "form" to understanding the "type" – is maintained. But as discussed above, this learning process does not exist as a concrete form of pedagogy. By contrast, the names of the *gūshes* in a list are exposed to the eyes of all students in concrete forms, such as a table of contents of the *radīf* or liner notes of recorded materials. So, depending on the student – if there is not enough "infiltration into the world" – there is the possibility that the learner's understanding of the *radīf* will not evoke the feeling of *charkh* structure. When we consider that improvisational performance is enabled not by manipulating the concrete "forms" but by understanding "types," it is likely that the loss of the feeling of *charkh*

Chapter 6

Score 6.4 Transcription example by Jean During (1995: 90)

Score 6.5 Transcription example by Dāryūsh Talā'ī (1997: 12)

will significantly influence the execution of improvisation, *per se*. I will return to this later.

6.4.2 Analytical views on music

Today, when it has become commonplace to transcribe *radīf* in staff notation, analytical *radīf* scores have emerged. Scores 6.4 and 6.5 are transcriptions of *radīf* passed on by Mirzā Abdollāh. These transcriptions demonstrate that Jean During's (1947–) score notates the music along its temporal course, whereas Dāryūsh Talā'ī's[4] transcription notates the structure of the phrases analytically.

126

Here, we must question whether Talā'ī was truly *listening* to the *radīf* analytically from the start. I suspect that he probably acquired analytical views through transcribing the music, rather than by *listening* to the *radīf* analytically from the outset. In which case, the notation reveals his interpretation of the *radīf* that he transcribes. Furthermore, the scores, once notated analytically, will greatly influence the next generation who look at them.

6.4.3 The need to be unique

The sense of "owning phrases" brought about by writing (that is, transcribing in staff notation) restricts the borrowing and appropriation of other performances, which were previously a commonplace in improvisation using the "common property" of exemplary phrases. That restriction derives from a performer's sense that improvisation ought to be something *original*.

As a result, contemporary performers, who are restricted (or who were driven to restricting themselves) in their use of the common property of exemplary phrases, suffer from self-questioning whether they are truly creative, and struggle to find ways in which they can be creative. Stated differently, contemporary Iranian musicians are required to be more creative than their predecessors, because what were once ephemeral sounds that disappeared almost instantly now persist as text or sound recordings, and because of the general view that "the opus is closed." The traditional Iranian concept of "originality," which might be described using words such as "version," "remembrance," or "paraphrase," as discussed earlier, is thus gradually changing through the assimilation of text-based culture by Iranians themselves.

6.4.4 The weakened significance of *radīfdān*

Before the *radīf* were transcribed onto staves, there were *radīf* experts, called *radīfdān* (literally, a person who knows *radīf*). These experts had to play *radīf* repeatedly to maintain their memory of them, and so their attitude was conservative by necessity. Today, however, performers can more freely allow themselves to engage in new artistic activities by notating *radīf* as text. For example, they can compose music – even using *radīf* and manipulating them as textual material.

Chapter 6

Since the remaining *radīfdān* are now elderly and *radīf* are, at the same time, notated, the role of *radīfdān* is declining, and there is even a tendency for some who value creativity to ridicule them.

6.4.5 Disappearance of the process of learning "types"

Thus far in this chapter, I have discussed various impacts of the textual mindset on Iranian musical activity: the lesson system and the concept of étude lead students to unconsciously prioritize concrete knowledge (namely, the learning of playing techniques and *gūshes* as repertory) above relational knowledge (the *charkh* sensibility), while the notation of *radīf* makes them experience music – which is naturally a continuous temporal flow – visually, as something that can be broken down, resulting in the collapse of the *charkh* perspective.

Perhaps the greatest affect such a textual mindset might have on traditional Iranian music is that the practice of creating one's own *radīf*, as discussed at the end of Chapter 1, will change in quality or remain misunderstood. Let us review Nettl's statement quoted in note 7, Chapter 3.

> The fact that the *radifhā* of various teachers differ somewhat is due in part to the fact that each musician, once he has learned his master's *radif*, may set out to create his own version, making changes and innovations, and also in part because many musicians studied, successively or simultaneously, with two or more teachers and created their own *radifhā* by combining their teachers' versions. (Nettl 1972: 19; underlining added)

Here, the phrase "combining their teachers' versions" suggests two possibilities of interpretation. One, as noted earlier, is that because Nettl's views are based on the perspectives of text-based culture, he may conceive the generation of a "type" as being the combination of "forms." Another possibility is that younger musicians may refer to the combinations of forms they create as their "types," or even imagine that they are truly creating types. In this way, the mindset of written culture incorporates an aspect that may jeopardize the generation of one's own type, *radīf*.

PART II

Chapter 7
How can individuality be described and explained?

7.1 Before admiring great musical masters

How can individual character be a subject of music study? Some might wonder why this question should be revisited and problematized, especially at this time, because our musical discourse is replete with themes such as "the splendor of the work" or "the talent and genius of those who produced a formidable opus." In short, individual character is already a topic of research and analysis. For example, although we have seen some changes lately, writings on Western music history are replete with a cavalcade of "great musicians" and "masterpieces," and the prevailing descriptive style was to admire the unique characteristics of those musicians and their works. As a result, we who have inherited this perspective see nothing odd about being steered to "the individuality and the creativity of the genius" and admiring those characteristics. This attitude toward music is also observed in ethnomusicology.

Let me cite an excerpt in which a scholar refers to a specific musician in discussing improvisational performance in Iranian music.

> The music of Banān is a good example of improvisation. He would first choose a poem, basing the choice on his mood and his assessment of the audience's mood and desires. He would also choose the *dastgāh* to go with that poem. (Caton 2002: 141)

This statement reveals a common tendency in the way that scholars describe something for analysis by first citing a specific musician; it assumes musicians' idiosyncrasy or talent as axiomatic, and elaborates its discussion as a means of confirming it. Let us continue to look at Caton's description.

> The art of improvisation was usually not taught separately. Instead, in the process of aural transmission of the *gūshe-hā* the musician internalized a pool of melodic figures as well as the underlying

> structures that he was intuitively able to draw on during performance. In listening to master musicians, the student was able to comprehend the possibilities and limits of improvisation. In developing a rapport with his audience, he also learned to match his choices to his own mood and the mood of his audience, according to the inspiration of the moment. (ibid.)

This description seemingly explains in a scholastic manner what the musician does during the performance. However, it in fact ends up only mystifying it, because one cannot in the end explain anything with expressions like "intuitively" or "the inspiration of the moment" without further elucidation of those terms.

This pitfall lurks in the approach to writing that begins by citing the names of master musicians. There, a musical practice (in this case, improvisational performance) as the subject of the study is unconsciously idealized as something executed inexplicably through the sheer creativity of individuals fed by intuition or the inspiration of the moment. And, in fact, this naive idealization of individual uniqueness originates in the fact that the materials to be analyzed are taken from the performance of master musicians in the first place.

In this approach, most of the problems that should be described and analyzed are attributed to the idiosyncrasy and creativity of individual musicians, and the explanation ends up emphasizing a virtually inexplicable realm, admiring specific musicians, for example, with descriptions like "acts of genius." Thus, the details of musical practice that should be explicated are reduced to "individual character" which is itself scarcely defined. In this way, the discussion falls into the tautology that "master musicians are great."

What, then, should we do to avoid such a circular discussion? I propose that the scholar should put aside the musician's unique quality or talent *per se*, rather than extoling it as something ineffably magnificent, and attempt to describe as closely as possible the ways the musician makes choices in the details of music-making. Which elements are considered, and what judgment is at work? These questions should also be linked to the type of description that clarifies which aspects of music the musicians and others find valuable. Such perspectives should be connected to an attitude that does not view individual character solely as a finished product, but probes and describes how that unique character emerged.

Scholars of Middle Eastern music have approached the issue of how music is created from various directions but can be roughly divided into two types. One is to elucidate the music-generating system called *maqām* or *dastgāh*. There are many aspects of the modal system that remain unexplained, and it is a huge challenge for scholars to systematize and describe them. The other turns its gaze toward the specific musicians who operate the modal system, which is also indispensable for the study of *maqām* or *dastgāh*. However, this latter group of studies sometimes devolves into a "cult" of the individual musicians, as outlined above.

Thus, perhaps what we need now is to describe phenomena that lie in-between these two camps of traditional studies – those researching fundamental principles and those praising outstanding individuals – thereby connecting the two. Essentially, research provides new insights by illuminating a subject or process that had previously been opaque. Ultimately, the "unique character" may not be explicable, but we should eschew that sweeping judgment since many factors – such as differences in learning environment – are, in fact, describable and might explain how individuality is created. By attempting to detail those factors, we can perhaps identify contributing factors which are not reducible to either the general principle of *dastgāh* or an outstanding individual character. With that in mind, this chapter will explore factors that generate individual characteristics in Iranian music without viewing the process of that generation as opaque.

7.2 Difference according to the *radīf* to be learned

When thinking about the creation of individual characteristics, we should first consider the different environments in which students learn traditional music – that is, differences of the *radīf* to be learned – as the primary factor.

Radīf is a group of melody types (*gūshe*s) transmitted by traditional Iranian musicians. Once admitted to the study of traditional Iranian music, students learn the music initially by memorizing each *gūshe* in *radīf* together with its order of performance. However, the number of *gūshe*s and the details of them in the *radīf* vary depending on the teacher or the lineage of the school, as indicated in Scores 7.1 and 7.2.

The *gūshe*s in these examples are both called *darāmad* in the *segāh* mode. I will describe below how these *gūshe*s differ from each other

Chapter 7

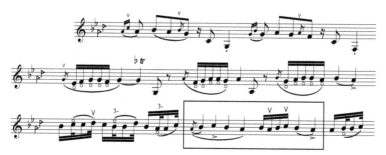

Score 7.1 *Darāmad* passed on by Abolhasan Sabā (Sabā 1991: 11)

Score 7.2 *Darāmad* passed on by Mirzā Abdollāh (Talā'ī 1997: 160)

despite having the same *gūshe* name. Prior to that, though, let me point out that there are a host of *radīfs*, each of which exhibits the art of an individual school or pedigree, and that students normally learn more than one *radīf*. The purpose of learning *radīf* is not the mere mechanical memorization of the *gūshes* or the accurate reproduction of them. Rather, its true purpose is comprehending the atmosphere and feeling of each *gūshe* through memorization, and then familiarizing oneself with the overall scheme of the music by internalizing the subtle flow of the music through understanding how the *gūshes* are ordered sequentially, thus making improvisational performance possible.

The modal system that enables improvisational performance in Iranian music is called *dastgāh*. Students do not aim at reproducing the *gūshes* that they learned from their teacher, but study the *radīf* in order to gain understanding of *dastgāh*, which provides the base of concrete sounds – in other words, to build up one's own image of *dastgāh*.

The image of *dastgāh* which each musician establishes does not rely on one source of *radīf*. Even though the learning environment may vary, the image of *dastgāh* becomes to some degree a shared subjectivity through learning multiple *radīf*s. Nevertheless, it is probable that the musician's image of *dastgāh* is greatly influenced by the *radīf*s that he or she learns, in the particular order in which they are learned. Let us return to the examples.

Scores 7.1 and 7.2 show the *gūshe* called *darāmad* in the *segāh* mode with the note A *koron* as their *shāhed*. In both examples, the music concludes on A *koron*. However, if you listen to those *gūshes*, their impressions are quite different. For example, in Score 7.2, the melody ends on A *koron* (i.e., it arrives at A *koron*) as early as the fourth note of the first stave, followed by multiple phrases ending on A *koron* in various ways to emphasize the feeling of closure on that note, while in Score 7.1, the melody starts with A *koron*, but that is merely the beginning of the melody going down and away from the *shāhed*, and we instead feel a sense of closure on the notes F, C, and the lower F at the end of the first stave, which seemingly have no relationship with the *shāhed* of A *koron* there.

Such differences may seem trivial once we comprehend the characteristics of the *segāh* mode. In fact, this pause on F is also the typical movement of the *segāh* mode, which increases the desire to go to the A *koron*, and indeed, in Score 7.1, the melody on the second stave gradually rises toward A *koron*. But it is predictable that the movement which temporarily ends on F will leave a strong impression on students who don't yet have a full understanding of the *segāh* mode.

This is because the feeling of ending that is unique to each *dastgāh* must be the target of the student's acute attention when learning that particular *dastgāh*. To master a *dastgāh* means to develop one's capacity to empathize completely with the feeling of ending or phrases that are unique to that *dastgāh*. Otherwise, it would be impossible to perform improvisation with a sense (or the illusion) of deriving music from the performer's own wellsprings.

Of course, once students accumulate musical experience, they will understand that the feeling of complete ending in the *segāh* mode is revealed in the area indicated by the box in the third stave. But for beginners with less experience in *radīf*, the "unique" melodic motion in Score 7.1 may shake their image of the *segāh* mode. Furthermore, the musicians' image of the *segāh* mode may vary depending on whether they have learned this as their first *radīf* or not. We should consider this factor when exploring the generation of individuality.

7.3 Social and private "habit"

Another factor to consider in exploring how individual character is formed is the various "habitual customs" in playing that emerge from the unconscious in improvisational performance.

When we examine the geographical areas and musical genres in which a number of case studies of improvisational performance were conducted, as Bruno Nettl notes – the issue of "playing habit" seems to be discussed relatively often in the field of jazz, both by scholars and in general discourse. In those narratives, "habit" is at times valued positively as a vivid expression of individual character in the improvisational performance, and sometimes negatively, as humdrum, by those who seek novelty in improvisation.

Compared to jazz, the question of habit in Iranian music – or more accurately, the issue of physicality – was not clearly addressed as an independent issue, either positively or negatively. However, examining habits provides various clues for understanding the generation of individual character.

Let us begin by classifying habit into two categories – the private and the social. The private habit is literally a completely individual style – that is, inexplicable – and thus, will not be discussed here; nor will the "ultimate unique character" mentioned earlier.

The social habit, however, clearly expresses the character of the musical genre (traditional Iranian music, in this case) in which the habit occurs, and it includes, for example, musical idioms unique to pan-Iranian music that exist beyond the specificity of particular hardware, such as particular musical instruments. Thus, we can think of learning *radīf* as the act of imprinting such idioms as second nature and accumulating them as habits of motion. Naturally, this social commonality subsumes some variation depending on the *radīf* one has learned, as discussed in the previous section. But here, I would like to consider those disparities as differences between social groupings rather than among individuals.

7.3.1 The language of each musical instrument

If the "social habit" is divided into smaller groups, the social character of some groups can be defined by various factors stemming from the specificities of their musical instruments – that is, certain physical functions and playing techniques called for by each instrument according

How can individuality be described and explained?

Score 7.3 *Radīf* for *āvāz* passed on by Mahmūd Karīmī (Mas'ūdie 1995: 13)

Score 7.4 *Radīf* arranged for *santūr* by Arfa'e Atrā'ī (Atrā'ī 1990: 1)

to its respective structure. In other words, one variable of social habits is the different musical instruments that are mastered. Indeed, certain tones or sounds are determined not only by the pitches and duration of the music itself, but also by the physicality and playing technique of the instrument. This point is illustrated in Scores 7.3 and 7.4, which show a *radīf* for vocal music and its *santūr* version, respectively.

In Iranian music, the phraseology characteristic of vocal music, *āvāz*, has been traditionally regarded as a universal language that all musicians should master. In Score 7.4, we can observe that while the music attempts

Chapter 7

to simulate the idiom of *āvāz*, instrument-specific techniques appear here and there.

To give an example, portamento which appears everywhere in the *āvāz* in Score 7.3 (indicated by squares) is impossible to play on the *santūr* in the strict sense. Instead, in Score 7.4, the portamento is replaced by a tremolo introduced by a grace note an octave lower, which occurs only in the first note of a phrase, and phrases are frequently shifted to other registers (indicated by arrows), taking advantage of the layout of the strings which makes a quick change of register easy. Thus, Score 7.4 is replete with idioms that are unique to the *santūr* and that are distinct from the *āvāz* phraseology.

I have given only one example above, but it should suffice to demonstrate that each instrument has its own distinct musical language which constitutes a part of the creation of individual character. Another, and more notable, example of the generation of individuality is the intersection of multiple musical languages.

7.3.2 Intersection of multiple musical languages

Intercrossing of languages between various musical instruments

The "intersection of multiple musical languages" refers to mixing musical idioms by different musical instruments. In the following section, I will explore this phenomenon in the case of tuning the *santūr* and its musical language influenced by the music of the *tār* and the *setār*.

Score 7.5 depicts the tuning of the *santūr* in which each of the low, middle, and high registers that stretch over three octaves is tuned from the lower to higher notes in the order of E through F, respectively. Recently, however, the lowest note E (in the square) is often lowered even further by the third degree to C.

In the middle and high registers, it is indispensable to have two kinds of E – E flat and E *koron* (in the various triangles) – to accommodate music that distinguishes those notes. However, the lowest E, which stands alone, had no such role and was not used frequently.

However, lowering the lowest E note by only the third degree to C in recent tuning systems produced a new sound and musical idiom of *santūr*, as seen in Score 7.6.

How can individuality be described and explained?

Score 7.5 Tuning system of *santūr* (Pāyvar 1961: 46)

Score 7.6 Excerpt from "Rāz o Niyāz" by Pashang Kāmkār (Kāmkār 1996: 29)

Here, the music successfully adds the effect of harmony or drone by playing the lowest note tuned to C simultaneously with other notes in the low register such as F and G. The chordal effect obtained with the new tuning, in fact, mimics the sound of open strings that are frequently played on the *tār* and *setār*, as is noticeable by the fact that an independent melody appears in a contrastive fashion in the middle tessitura (in the rectangle). Hence, this tuning system not only produced a deep, low-pitched, sustaining sound that was not available in the traditional tuning, but also new prospects for the *santūr* as an accompanying instrument, as well as a melodic instrument.

Influence of musical idioms from Western music

In examining the encounter of multiple musical languages, we should also consider the influx of musical idioms from outside Iranian music.

139

Chapter 7

Score 7.7 Excerpt of "Khātere" by Ardavān Kāmkār (Kāmkār 2016: 70–71)

Let us look at a performance example of *santūr* by Ardavān Kāmkār in Score 7.7.

The example exhibits Western tonal music, an impression reinforced by the accompaniment of arpeggios. Also, there is no use of microtones in creating the tonal music.

Furthermore, I would point out that from the physical perspective, as exemplified in the transcript of score 7.7, many pieces which incorporate Western musical idioms require difficult and unique playing techniques, rarely seen in traditional *radīf* performance, in which the left hand plays the melody and the right hand accompanies it (because on the *santūr* the strings in the lower register are located to the right side of the performer and those in the higher register are to the left side). Such physical dexterity has become recognized as an indispensable skill, functioning as a new "physical habit" for Western music-oriented performers.

Triggered by the question of how to explain the individual character, we have explored above – although narrowly – two factors that generate individuality: differences in which *radīf* one learned and physical habit. In particular, physical habit is a fascinating angle from which to speculate on sociality and its interplay in Iranian music at many levels. We can see this in the way that the techniques unique to each instrument and the social nature of Iranian music's universal language (imitating the voice) that lies beyond the individual characteristics of the instruments are vigorously intertwined. This point is evident if we take a look at some introductory textbooks for various Iranian musical instruments (see Sections 6.3.2 through 6.3.5).

Our discussion did not include private habits, but there may in fact be many explainable cases in which such habits are generated from a complex intertwining of the various factors discussed above. Furthermore, although a particular individual's style may not be explicable, the way it circulates and its impact in society can be described and analyzed.

In any case, in the research of individual uniqueness in music, it is perhaps not by, for example, generalizing the problem of habit into the broad category of black boxes under the name of individuality, but by breaking down the phenomenon into the various elements from which individual characteristics emerge – and by speculating on their interrelationship – that we will achieve insights for the future study of individuality.

Chapter 8
Verbal rhythm and musical rhythm

8.1 Introduction

Iranian music has a variety of genres. According to the *New Grove Dictionary of Music and Musicians*, Iranian music may roughly speaking be divided into two categories, "art music" and "folk music" (Farhat et al. 1980: 292–309). "Folk music" refers to religious recitation, narrative and didactic song, lyric song, popular entertainment, and dance music, whereas "art music" refers to the music based on the modal system called *dastgāh*, which was organized mainly at the royal court during the Qajar dynasty, and in which the Persian mystic poems of Rumi, Hāfez, and others are usually sung. In this chapter, our focus is on the latter, music based on *dastgāh*, to examine the relationship between verbal and musical rhythm.

In the field of Iranian traditional music studies, much has been written about the relationship between verbal and musical rhythm (Zonis 1973; Tsuge 1970; Miller 1999). In Iranian traditional music, the *zarbi* (literally, rhythmic), meaning parts with a fixed rhythm, and *bi-zarbi* or *āvāz*, meaning parts with no fixed rhythm, typically alternate in succession. However, compared to the music of neighboring countries, Iranian music is characterized by having less measure in rhythm. Previous studies have therefore mainly focused on the *bi-zarbi* or *āvāz* parts, which cannot be divided into measures in a Western sense, to ascertain how the Persian poetic meter is incorporated in those sections (see, for example, Tsuge 1970). Additionally, *bi-zarbi* or *āvāz* is basically improvised in a free rhythm and performed based on poetic meter, whereas *zarbi* is typically pre-composed music in which the musical rhythm has already been established. *Bi-zarbi* and *āvāz* have thus been considered to be an appropriate focus for observing the poetic meter.

In this chapter, however, I will examine how the original poetic meter changes when the poetry is sung in *zarbi* by way of exploring the dynamic relationship and balance between verbal rhythm and musical rhythm.

Chapter 8

8.2 Various relationships between verbal and musical rhythm

In Iranian music, there are a large number of melody types (*gūshes*), both long and short, that have been passed down by tradition. These *gūshes* (literally 'corner, section, piece') do not exist haphazardly, but rather are organized in a systematic fashion grouped by musical mode called *dastgāh*. Musical modes are generally defined as a "layout of the pitches, including a melodic element, that have a denser relationship with each other" (Mizuno 1992: 33). The name of a *dastgāh* evokes more than merely a scale for audiences in Iran; rather, it suggests several specific *gūshes*.

In the next section, I will illustrate various relationships between verbal and musical rhythm for several *gūshes*. First, the *gūshe* called *kereshme* will be introduced to demonstrate a perfect correspondence between musical rhythm and the poetic meter. We will then turn to two *gūshes*, the *Sāqīnāme* and *Chahārpāre*, and examine cases of each where the poetry is sung in *zarbi* to illustrate more complex relationships between verbal and musical rhythm.

8.3 *Kereshme*: Perfect correspondence between musical rhythm and poetic meter

Let us begin with the *gūshe* called *kereshme*. This *gūshe* has an hemiola rhythm in which six-eight time and three-four time appears alternately, and can be considered to show a perfect correspondence between musical rhythm and poetic meter, because most poetry sung in this *gūshe* has the same rhythm, as in the following poem by *Hāfez*, mentioned in section 5.3.2.

> *biyā o keshtī-ye mā dar shat-e sharāb andāz*
> *khorūsh o velveleh dar jān-e sheikh o shāb andāz*

بیا و کشتی ما در شط شراب انداز
خروش و ولوله در جان شیخ و شاب انداز

Come and let us cast our boat into the river of wine;

Let us cast a shout and clamor into the soul of the sheikh and the young man. (Zonis 1973: 128)

Verbal rhythm and musical rhythm

Score 8.1 *Kereshme* in *homāyun* mode, from the *radīf* passed down by Abolhasan Sabā (1902–1958) (Sabā 1990: 7)

The meter of this poem consists of a series of "short-long-short-long + short-short-long-long" sequences called *mojtass-e makhbūn*. *Mojtass* originally consists of two different types of feet, *mostaf'elon* "long-long-short-long" and *fā'elāton* "long-short-long-long." *Makhbūn* refers to the transformation that changes each first long syllable into a short syllable.

As Score 8.1 makes clear, this *gūshe* has the same rhythm as the *mojtass-e makhbūn*. As others have pointed out (Tsuge 1970: 220; Miller 1999: 249; Zonis 1973: 128), this is a typical example of perfect correspondence between musical rhythm and poetic meter. Whenever this *gūshe* is performed, its character does not change, regardless of musical mode, scale and register.

8.4 *Sāqīnāme*

The next example comes from the *Sāqīnāme*, the well-known verse by *Hāfez*. Let us see how the original meter changes when the poem is sung in *zarbi*. Its original meter is as follows:

> *Biyā sāqī ān mey ke hāl āvarad*
> *Kerāmat fazāyad kamāl āvarad*
> *Be man de ke bas bi del oftādeam*
> *Vaz in har do bi hāsel oftādeam*

بیا ساقی، آن می که حال آورد

کرامت فزاید، کمال آورد

به من ده که بس بی‌دل افتاده‌ام

وز این هر دو بی‌حاصل افتاده‌ام

145

Chapter 8

Table 8.1 The original meter of *Sāqīnāme* by *Hāfez* (based on Miller 1999: 246)

short syllable	long syllable	long syllable
1. *bi*	2. *yā*	3. *sā*
4. *qī*	5. *ān*	6. *mey*
7. *ke*	8. *hāl*	9. *ā*
10. *va*	11. *rad*	

Table 8.2 *Sāqīnāme* in *zarbi*

super short syllable (appoggiatura)	super long syllable (half note)	long syllable (quarter note)	long syllable (quarter note)
1. *bi*	2. *yā*	3. *sā*	4. *qī*
	5. *ān*	6. *mey*	7. *ke*
	8. *hāl*	9. *ā*	10. *va*
	11. *rad*		

Score 8.2 *Sāqīnāme* in *māhūr* mode, from the *radīf* passed down by Mahmūd Karīmī (1927–1984) (Mas'ūdie 1995: 177)

Come, cupbearer, that wine which brings ecstasy,

Increases grace, brings perfection,

Give me for sufficiently disheartened have I fallen (become).

And of these both (grace and perfection) have I been deprived.
(Miller 1999: 219)

As indicated in Table 8.1, this poetry is usually sung in *motaqāreb* meter, consisting of repetitions of *fa'ūlon*, i.e. the "short-long-long" foot.

When this poetry is sung in *zarbi*, whose rhythmic structure is "half note + quarter note + quarter note," its original meter changes.

As Table 8.2 shows, the original meter of poetry appears to change in *zarbi*. The [4. *qī*], [7. *ke*], and [10. *va*], which are originally short syllables, are all treated as long syllables (quarter notes) of the same length as [3. *sā*], [6. *mey*], and [9. *ā*], except for [1. *bi*], which is treated as a super short syllable. Nevertheless, if we examine them in more detail, it turns out that each occurrence of [4. *qī*], [7. *ke*], and [10. *va*] is accompanied by [5. *ān*], [8. *hāl*], and [11. *rad*], i.e. super long syllables. In this sense, if we consider them in relation to the sound immediately after them, and not to the one preceding, I would claim that [4. *qī*], [7. *ke*], and [10. *va*] sound shorter and in that sense function as short syllables. Furthermore, in those super long syllables (half notes) which are repeated four times in total ([2. *yā*], [5. *ān*], [8. *hāl*], and [11. *rad*]), a vocal technique peculiar to Iranian music called *tahrīr* is usually employed, by which the length of the syllables is prolonged and emotionally emphasized.

In other words, if we confine our observations to the actual "short-long" rhythmic pattern of the poetry, certainly its meter can be disregarded in *zarbi*. However, from the perspective of where the emphasis is placed, not just that of "short-long" sequences, it turns out that the emphasis continues to be on the long syllables by means of the vocal technique of *tahrīr*. In this sense, a similar contrast to that between short and long syllables is preserved, even if differently realized.

8.5 *Chahārpāre*

Let us once again examine how the original meter changes when poetry is sung in *zarbi* using a *gūshe* called *chahārpāre*.

Chahārpāre is one of the *gūshes* which belongs to *abū'atā* mode, and features a "short-short-long-short-long" rhythm in *bi-zarbi* or *āvāz* rhythm. As indicated in Chapter 2.3, below is a typical poem usually sung in this *gūshe*, by *Hātef Esfahānī*, together with its meter:

> *che shaved be chehre-ye zard-e man nazarī barāye khodā konī*
> *ke agar konī hame dard-e man be yekī nazāre davā konī*

> چه شود به چهرهٔ زرد من نظری برای خدا کنی
> که اگر کنی همه درد من به یکی نظاره دوا کنی

> What would happen if, for heaven's sake, you give one look at my pallid face;
> For if you do, all my pain with one glance you cure. (Miller 1999:189)

147

Chapter 8

Table 8.3 Metrical structure in the original meter of *Chahārpāre* by *Hātef Esfahānī*

short	short	long	short	long
che	sha	vad	be	cheh
re	ye	zar	d-e	man
na	za	rī	ba	rā
ye	kho	dā	ko	nī

Score 8.3 *Chahārbāgh (Chahārpāre)* in *abū'atā* mode, from the *radīf* passed down by Mahmūd Karīmī (1927–1984) (Mas'ūdie 1995: 44)

As indicated in Table 8.3, this poem is composed in the *kāmel* meter, which consists of repetitions of *motafā'elon*, i.e. a "short-short-long-short-long" foot. In the following section, let us consider four *zarbi* pieces and observe how this meter changes when poetry is sung in *zarbi*.

8.5.1 *Chahārpāre* sung in *tasnīf-e dogāh*

Here, I would like to examine how the meter of *chahārpāre* changes when poetry is sung in the *zarbi* called *tasnīf-e dogāh*. *Tasnīf-e* ("composed song") *dogāh* ("second place") is one of the *gūshes* which belongs to *bayāt-e tork* mode. In the following piece, which has three-four time, the meter is structured as described in Table 8.4 and Score 8.4.

In this case, we can say that the poetry meter is retained in *zarbi* as is.

8.5.2 *Chahārpāre* sung in "*mehrabānī* in five-eight time" and "*mehrabānī* in two-four time"

Another *gūshe* which belongs to *bayāt-e tork* mode is *mehrabānī*. In "*mehrabānī* in five-eight time," the meter is structured as follows:

As we see in Table 8.5, the first half of the meter is similar to *tasnīf-e dogāh*. However, in the second half of the meter, short syllables and long syllables are treated equally (see the shaded cells in Table 8.5).

148

Verbal rhythm and musical rhythm

Table 8.4 Metrical structure in *tasnīf-e dogāh*

1st beat	2nd beat	3rd beat
short/short	long	⟶
short	long	⟶
che /sha	vad	
be	cheh	
re/ye	zar	
d-e	man	

Score 8.4 *Tasnīf-e dogāh* in *bayāt-e tork* mode (Tsuge 1999: 34)

Table 8.5 Metrical structure in "*Mehrabānī* in five-eight time"

1st beat	2nd beat	3rd beat	4th beat	5th beat
short/short	long	⟶	short	long
che /sha	vad		be	cheh
re/ye	zar		d-e	man

Score 8.5 "*Mehrabānī* in five-eight time" in *bayāt-e tork* mode (Pāyvar 1982: 35)

Furthermore, in "*mehrabānī* in two-four time" (indicated below), after the first "short-short" part, the following "long-short-long" segments are all treated equally. (See the shaded cells in Table 8.6. To maintain unity with "*mehrabānī* in five-eight time" in Table 8.5, the eighth note is calculated as one beat in Table 8.6.)

On this basis, one might once again conclude that the original meter changes in *zarbi*. However, when considered from the perspective of where the emphasis is placed and where we find a similar contrast to "short" vs "long," an interesting point becomes clear: where the *shāhed*

149

Chapter 8

Table 8.6 Metrical structure in "*Mehrabānī* in two-four time"

1st beat	2nd beat	3rd beat	4th beat
short/short	long	short	long
che/sha	vad	be	cheh
re/ye	zar	d-e	man

Score 8.6 "*Mehrabānī* in two-four time" in *bayāt-e tork* mode (Pāyvar 1982: 36)

(core note) is located. *Mehrabānī* is usually sung in *bayāt-e tork* mode, in which the *shāhed* is always located in the last long syllable (in Scores 8.5 through 8.7, note B♭). Furthermore, all the melodies in these examples end with the *shāhed*.

Table 8.5.1 The location of the *shāhed* in "*Mehrabānī* in five-eight time"

1st beat	2nd beat	3rd beat	4th beat	5th beat
short/short	long		short	long (*shāhed*)
che/sha	vad		be	cheh
re/ye	zar		d-e	man

Table 8.6.1 The location of the *shāhed* in "*Mehrabānī* in two-four time"

1st beat	2nd beat	3rd beat	4th beat
short/short	long	short	long (*shāhed*)
che/sha	vad	be	cheh
re/ye	zar	d-e	man

Thus, syllables that were treated equally in terms of length are not equal in terms of the stability of *shāhed* and *ist*, that is, the feeling of the end of the phrase or sentence. Consequently, we can again see that the last long syllable is perceived as *heavy* or *prominent* compared to the other notes.

8.5.3 *Chahārpāre* sung in "*mehrabānī* in six-eight time"

As a final example, let us examine *"mehrabānī* in six-eight time." This case appears relatively complicated, having 12 beats (six beats repeated twice) and beginning with an anacrusis. The allotment of the meter to the beat is as follows:

Verbal rhythm and musical rhythm

Table 8.7 Metrical structure in *"Mehrabānī* in six-eight time"

1	2	3	4	5	6	1	2	3	4	5 (*shāhed*)	6
(rest)	(rest)	short	short	long	→			short	long	→	(rest)
(rest)	(rest)	short	short	long	→			short	long	→	(rest)
(rest)	(rest)	che	sha	vad				be	cheh		(rest)
(rest)	(rest)	re	ye	zar				d-e	man		(rest)

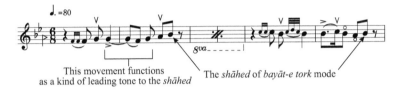

This movement functions as a kind of leading tone to the *shāhed*

The *shāhed* of *bayāt-e tork* mode

Score 8.7 *"Mehrabānī* in six-eight time" in *bayāt-e tork* mode (Pāyvar 1982: 36)

As Table 8.7 indicates, there are two types of metrical allotment; however, both maintain the original meter in *zarbi*. As previously mentioned, this is not simply because long syllables are allotted to long notes, but also because the *shāhed* of *bayāt-e tork* is located in the final long syllable. Thus, the final long syllable is perceived as longer than its actual duration. In other words, the hearer feels more heaviness in this final note. Furthermore, in this case we can observe that there is one note stretched a third lower than the *shāhed*, before the music reaches the *shāhed*, as if to build anticipation for it (see Score 8.7). This note thus functions as a kind of leading tone, and leads to the *shāhed*.

Stated differently, through this type of movement, the audience perceives greater heaviness when the melody reaches the *shāhed*. Moreover, and especially in this case, since the rest is located immediately after the *shāhed*, the *shāhed* sounds longer than its duration due to the lingering tone. All these factors contribute to the result that one feels the long syllable as *heavy*, not only because of the length of the tone but also because of the various musical elements described here.

8.6 Conclusion

It is generally said in musicological studies that the meter of poetry tends to change when sung in the *zarbi* parts, whereas it appears to remain relatively the same in the *bi-zarbi* or *āvāz* parts. To be sure, if we understand rhythmic patterns in the literal sense of short and long syllables, certainly the meter can be often disregarded in *zarbi*, where

151

musical rhythm takes precedence over poetic meter. However, from the examples discussed above, we may conclude that the long syllable is still perceived as heavy or prominent compared to other notes, either by means of the *"tahrīr* technique," which attracts the audience's attention, or from the perspective of where the *shāhed* or *ist* is placed.

In this sense, it is insufficient to describe meter solely with terms such as "long" and "short." We must rather recognize poetic meter as something complex which comprises wide-ranging elements, and not just arrangements of "long" and "short" syllables. For this purpose, it may be best to return to the original definition of syllabic weight and develop alternative terms starting with "heavy" and "light" in order to understand the interaction of meter and musical rhythm as a whole.

Chapter 9
Trial and error on hammered dulcimers: Iranian and Indian *santūr*

9.1 Introduction

The diverse range of stringed instruments found in India and Iran are typically divided into three categories according to how they are played: plucked (including the *sitar, sarod, tamboura, tār, setār,* and *'ūd*), bowed (including *sarangi, dilruba, kamānche,* and *gheichak*), and hammered. This chapter focuses on the *santūr*, a hammered dulcimer with strings stretched over a trapezoidal sound box struck with mallets held in each hand. As a performer, I specialize in the Iranian *santūr*, but when considering the place of the hammered dulcimer in a given musical genre, there are many intriguing similarities between the *santūr*'s place in traditional Iranian music and in the classical Hindustani music of northern India. In this chapter, I will explore the *santūr*'s disadvantages as a hammered dulcimer and examine the trial-and-error efforts of *santūr* players to overcome these disadvantages.

Photo 9.1 An Iranian *santūr*

153

9.2 The place of the *santūr*

The Iranian *santūr* has had many eminent players, including Farāmarz Pāyvar (1933–2009), Parvīz Meshkātian (1955–2009), and Ardavān Kāmkār, along with countless students and enthusiasts. Within these circles, the *santūr* is an important instrument. Outside the *santūr* scene, however, negative views of the instrument are not uncommon.

There are many reasons for this. One is the inconvenience of tuning. A standard *santūr* has 72 strings, and they must be tuned to match the *dastgāh* to be played in. The instrument's simple tuning pins make accurate tuning in the strict sense impossible, and it must be regularly retuned due to the effects of temperature and humidity on the strings.

In Iranian music, the ability to skillfully imitate the feeling of the *āvāz* (voice) is a crucial part of musical expression, even for instrumentalists. However, the *santūr*'s construction precludes techniques like portamento or vibrato, and a struck note's timbre cannot be varied over time. This puts the *santūr* at a disadvantage when imitating the voice. During an interview I conducted with *tār* and *setār* player Mahiyār Moshfeq in February 2018, when the topic of improvising in a group of different instruments came up,[1] he stated that it is "very difficult for the *santūr* to participate fully in the session" due to the limitations imposed by its construction,[2] and that it is "also difficult to match the range of the singer," which differs from session to session.

These limitations of the *santūr*'s construction are not unique to Iran, though. The instrument now used in northern India is originally from the Kashmir region, and in *Journey with a Hundred Strings*, Shiv Kumar Sharma (1938–2022) describes the various ways he modified the Kashmiri *santūr*'s construction and playing technique to adapt it to Hindustani music. His comments about that trial and error process are particularly intriguing in light of the disadvantages of the Iranian *santūr* described above. The next section draws on Sharma's book to explore his efforts in detail.

9.3 From Kashmir to Hindustani music

In Kashmir, the *santūr* was played as accompaniment to the Sufi songs of devotion known as *sufiana kalam*, "over half of which are in Persian, with most of the rest in Kashmiri, and a few in Urdu" (Powers 1980: 818).

Shiv Kumar Sharma, who is credited with introducing the *santūr* to Hindustani music and remained a preeminent player of the instrument throughout his life, was born in Jammu and Kashmir. His father began educating him in vocal music and tabla at a young age. When Sharma was fourteen years old, his father encountered the *santūr* during a temporary assignment to a radio station in Srinagar, and was so moved by the experience that he had his son begin learning to play the instrument (Sharma 2002: 13). In the years that followed, Sharma remodeled the *santūr* in various ways to adapt it to Hindustani music (ibid.: 56).

First, he held the *santūr* on his lap as he played it, instead of using the traditional wooden stand. This helped dampen unwanted resonances during particularly fast passages. He also reduced the number of strings per course from four to three, which further reduced unwanted resonances and made the *santūr* faster to tune.

Sharma also changed the arrangement of the strings. A standard *santūr* has two columns with bridges placed alternately in the left and right column. Each bridge supports a course of three to four strings strung horizontally across the instrument and tuned to the same note. Since the player can theoretically strike either to the left or right of any given bridge, there are four "planes" of strings that could be struck: left of the left bridge column, right of the left bridge column, left of the right bridge column, and right of the right bridge column. Normally, however, players used only the two central planes, right of the left bridge column and left of the right bridge column.

According to Pacholczyk's description of the original string arrangement on the Kashmiri *santūr*, if all the strings were steel, then the two central planes were tuned in unison to a heptatonic scale (from g to g^2 with 15 bridges per column). If the strings were of steel and brass, the brass strings were strung on the bridges in the right column and tuned an octave below the steel strings. Only a few musicians used the plane to the left of the left column, and this was tuned exactly one octave above the plane to the right of the left column (Pacholczyk 1996: 35). In the Iranian *santūr*, on the other hand, which is strung with both steel and brass strings, the three planes mentioned above are tuned in three registers, each in a different octave: a vertical heptatonic scale (from e^1 to f^2 with 9 bridges per column) repeated one octave lower on the right (low register) and one octave higher on the left (high register).[3]

Chapter 9

Photo 9.2 Kashmiri *santūr* (collection of the National Academy of Music, Delhi)

Photo 9.3 Shiv Kumar Sharma (right) and the author at Sharma's home in Mumbai, August 2016

Photo 9.4 Kashmiri *santūr* (right) on a wooden stand (collection of the National Academy of Music, Delhi)

Photo 9.5 Placing the *santūr* on the player's lap. Player: Takahiro Arai, a pupil of Shiv Kumar Sharma (photograph provided by Arai)

Photo 9.6 Kashmiri *santūr* with four strings per course (photographed in the Museum of Performing Arts at the National Academy of Music, Delhi)

Photo 9.7 A contemporary *santūr* played in Hindustani music with three strings per course

Trial and error on hammered dulcimers

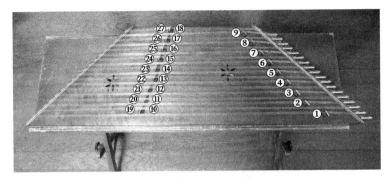

Photo 9.8 An Iranian *santūr* from above

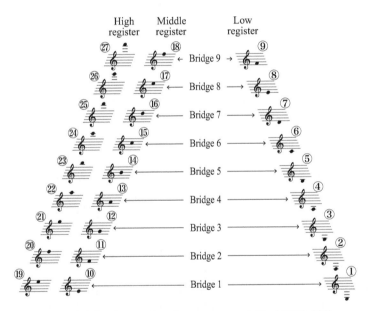

Figure 9.1 Iranian *santūr* string arrangement (Tani 2016: 101)

To adapt the Kashmiri *santūr* to Hindustani music, Sharma first removed the brass strings, returning to an arrangement with steel strings only, which forms the two central planes. Then, instead of tuning the left and right of the steel strings in unison, he tuned the left plane to altered notes, creating a chromatic scale (Sharma 2002: 56). This enabled the instrument to accommodate multiple modes, eliminating the structural limitation of seven notes per octave that made it difficult for *santūr* players to accommodate modes or altered notes other than those the instrument had been tuned to, as noted by Moshfeq above.

Chapter 9

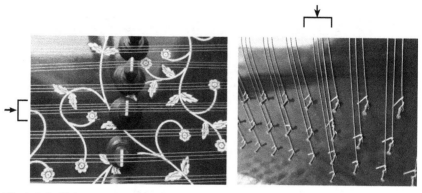

Photo 9.9 *Chikari* course on a *santūr* played in Hindustani music (Note that, unlike the other courses, it has four strings instead of three.)

Players of the Iranian *santūr* sometimes compensated for "missing" notes by borrowing (playing) a note from another register (plane), but Sharma's redesign was more radical. It located all the notes necessary for the current mode on the right-facing plane and altered notes in the same register on the left-facing plane, making the instrument capable of accommodating different modes at any time.

Even more distinctive was Sharma's addition of *chikari* strings. Many string instruments used in classical Indian music have, as well as the main strings played by the performer, open strings called *chikari*. *Chikari* are used for drones and rhythmic accents and reinforces the atmosphere of the mode. Although the strings in each course of the *santūr* are usually tuned in unison, Sharma tuned the strings on one particular bridge to several different notes – for example, *sa, sa, ga,* and pa^4 – to create a *chikari* course (ibid.). This allows harmony to be produced in a single stroke, reinforcing the basic atmosphere of the raga being performed. The Iranian *santūr* has nothing like the *chikari* course.

9.4 The challenge of imitating the voice

The most difficult challenge Sharma faced, and the most crucial to resolve, was that of imitating voice. As noted, the player of the *santūr* strikes only open strings, which are never manipulated with the other hand to alter their pitch. This makes it impossible to use the portamento-like technique in classical Indian music called *meend*, in which notes are prolonged and connected to others to create unbroken musical phrases. When *meend* is not used and the notes are "cut," the *alaap* (an introductory phrase performed in free rhythm to introduce a *raga*'s basic atmosphere) is "incomplete" (Sharma 2002: 52). Sharma had to overcome this problem somehow to win recognition for the Kashmiri *santūr* in Hindustani music.

The solution Sharma hit upon was a playing technique called *ghaseet* (rubbing). Sharma never documented this technique in detail, either in writing or on video, but I will attempt an explanation based on the testimony of *santūr* players Takahiro Arai and Setsuo Miyashita.

The mallets used for the *santūr* in India are distinctly heavier than those used for the Iranian instrument. Additionally, while the striking surface of an Iranian *santūr* mallet is usually covered with felt or similar material, the Indian mallet's striking surface is bare wood.[5] As a result, if the mallet is allowed to fall onto the string with its full weight, it will rebound as it strikes. *Santūr* players in India use this feature to produce a series of these rebounds, like a one-handed drumroll, to lengthen the note.[6] Particularly intriguing on the *santūr* mallet in India is the many grooves carved into its striking face from left to right, matching the orientation of the strings. These grooves let the player create a series of minuscule rebounds to sustain the sound simply by "rubbing" the mallet back and forth across the string. This is the technique Sharma called *ghaseet*.

On the Iranian *santūr*, the only technique for prolonging notes is tremolo, which is played by repeatedly striking the same string with the left and right mallet alternately.[7] *Ghaseet* allows *santūr* players in India to extend a note simply by moving the mallet back and forth (much practice is required, of course). By moving the mallet far enough to reach the next string, the player can even add the portamento-like nuance of *meend*. Here, too, we see why the string arrangement Sharma adopted was necessary: when all the notes for the main mode are on the right plane (in a single vertical column), the player can produce the basic scale of the *raga* in a smooth, *alaap*-like manner by using *ghaseet*.[8]

9.5 A different solution in Iran: Reinforcing the instrumental character

In Iran, we find few individual creative adaptations to enable portamento-like nuance that are as radical as Sharma's. Instead, we see the imitation of a vocal technique called *tahrīr*, in which the singer alternates rapidly between natural and falsetto voice, which is considered necessary not just for the *santūr* but for all instruments.

Chapter 9

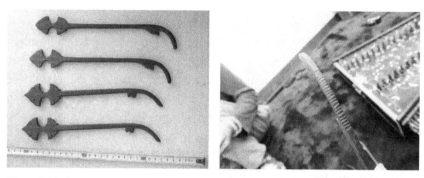

Photo 9.10 *Santūr* mallets in India (left), showing grooves in the striking face (right)

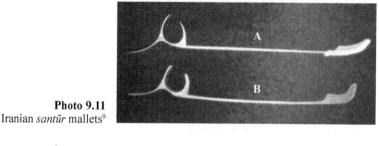

Photo 9.11
Iranian *santūr* mallets[9]

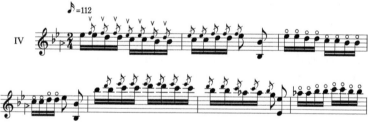

Score 9.1 Etude for *Takie* imitating *Tahrīr* (Pāyvar 1961: 43)

Score 9.1, which was previously discussed as Score 6.1, is a passage from an étude in a *santūr* tutor. Tutors for other instruments invariably include similar études. In other words, as a way of approaching the sound of the human voice, instrumentally imitating *tahrīr* is not an example of a creative adaptation unique to the *santūr*. In its finer details, of course, there are techniques in *Iranin santūr* playing for expressing the subtle nuances of the voice, but nothing we might call truly groundbreaking. This is related to the fact that while the challenge of imitating the voice remains crucial to performance, the instrumental character of the Iranian

Trial and error on hammered dulcimers

Photo 9.12 Lesson with Ardavān Kāmkār, a master of contemporary Iranian *santūr*, who is known for his virtuosic techniques

santūr has developed dramatically under the influence of "fast playing" and "virtuosic technique," as will be described in Chapter 11.

This contrasts with the instrumental character of the *santūr* in India, which evidently has a rhythmic side to it. For example, in Hindustani music, the *santūr* and the *tabla* are in clear and constant "conversation," but there is very little such interaction between the Iranian *santūr* and Iranian percussion instrument the *tonbak*. This is further evidence that the Iranian *santūr* has been developing for the past two or three decades under the mutually reinforcing influences of virtuosic technique and an orientation toward solo performance.

Additionally, while in this chapter I discussed the Kashmiri *santūr* solely in terms of Sharma's adaptations, one reason his creative adaptations took root in India was surely because the number of people seeking to introduce the *santūr* to Hindustani music was small, including only a handful of individuals, such as Bhajan Sopori (1948–), who played chiefly in and around Delhi. In Iran, however, the size of the *santūr*-playing population makes the adoption of major changes to the established string arrangements and playing methods much less likely.

Ultimately, in Iran, the disadvantages faced by a hammered dulcimer seeking to imitate the voice were converted into the advantage of virtuosic technique, greatly increasing the number of players. In India, however, notwithstanding Sharma's considerable recognition and accomplishments, the number of *santūr* players remains small as a proportion of the music making population. These two countries share similar philosophies of imitating the voice, but experience contrasting results.

161

Chapter 10
Perceiving and understanding through the fingers: Toward a comparative study of instrumental somatic sensibilities

10.1 Introduction

This chapter attempts an account of the different somatic sensibilities among musicians of various specializations – including *āvāz* (vocal), *tonbak*, *tār* (and *setār*), *santūr*, *ney*, *kamānche*, and *'ūd* – while they experience the "common ground" of traditional Iranian music.

When we say that a musician specializes in a certain kind of music, what exactly do we mean? Even within the same musical genre, expertise varies greatly from person to person. Even when we try to imagine music in the abstract, we do not necessarily conceive of it as sound alone, in isolation. Those who dabble in piano might unconsciously treat music in terms of the piano's construction and the physical limitations (and advantages) of the player's body; those who are more familiar with singing might create music within the limits of their register but unthinkingly enjoy positive aspects like "vocal grain." As a result, even when people appear to be dealing with sound alone, each individual's output bears the deep imprint of different concrete, somatic experiences, derived from the instrument they play.

In the context of Iranian music, the *santūr* is similar to the piano in that, compared to other instruments, the act of producing a note is relatively easy – the player simply strikes a pre-tuned string with a mallet. This gives it an affordance that could be called virtuosic, in which players seek to fill the music through the sheer number of notes. Most other instruments, however, including the *tār* and *setār*, are played using one hand to determine (or vary) pitch and the other to produce the sound (and control its volume). Simply producing a note requires a certain degree of effort, but because that effort is inseparable from vibrato, dynamics, and timbre control, the musician is inclined toward making each note sing with musicality, rather than producing a greater number of notes. For

Chapter 10

instruments like the *ney* and *kamānche*, which can prolong notes, that trend is even more pronounced.

Musicians are, of course, aware that an instrument's physicality, the affordances it offers the musician, strongly influences the character of the sound created. When composers orchestrate an ensemble work, physicality is doubtless among the individual instrumental characteristics they consider, even if unconsciously. For researchers, instrumental physicality is richly suggestive of how performers grasp and understand Iranian music. In this chapter, I draw on fieldwork conducted in Iran from January to February 2014 to contemplate differences in somatic experience as they relate to musical cognition and understanding, by comparing the physicality of the *setār* and *'ūd* to that of the *santūr*.

10.2 Differences in musical experience that cause hierarchy among instruments

Importantly, even within the shared context of Iranian music, a player's experience differs greatly depending on the instrument they specialize in. What is more, these different experiences even create a hierarchy of instruments. Consider the following statements which I heard from a vocalist during fieldwork in Iran. He asked me, as someone who had devoted most of his musical efforts to learning the *santūr*:

> Why did you choose the *santūr*? You should have chosen a different instrument. (February 2009)

He said to *santūr* player Kourosh Matin (1974–):

> You ought to burn that *santūr*. (Interview with Matin, January 2014)

The fact that the speaker was a vocalist is essential background to these comments. The *āvāz* stands above all else at the center of Iranian music, and while other instruments may shine through specialized techniques and artistry, ultimately a player's status as a musician rests on how skillfully they can imitate the atmosphere of the *āvāz*. And, although all Iranian instruments face this challenge, the *santūr*, as we have seen, is at an extreme disadvantage. The instrument's construction precludes techniques like portamento or vibrato on individual notes. Nor can a note's timbre be altered after it is struck. All professional musicians (and amateur enthusiasts) are cognizant of this to some degree, and when instruments are ranked in terms of their ability to produce the "sound and feel" typical of Iranian music – after the *āvāz*, of course – the list is generally headed by the *tār* and *setār* (and even *ney* and *kamānche*, in my opinion). Thus, even expressions of admiration for a virtuosic *santūr* player are nevertheless linked to an insistence that the instrument struggles to express the "sound and feel" typical of Iranian music.

Musicians understand this "typical sound and feel" differently, so an objective definition cannot be provided. I will therefore attempt to explain the background against which these statements arise, based on the different somatic sensibilities of those who play each type of instrument.

10.3 *Santūr* physicality and *setār/tār* physicality

Let us consider the different physicalities involved in playing a simple melody on different instruments – for example, the ascending scale G-A-B-C-D-E-F. A *santūr* player would usually play the scale at points (3) to (8) and then (11) in Figure 10.1 below. Thus, in terms of physicality, the most salient issue would be the need to overcome the separation between E and F. Put another way, the instrument's construction presents the player with a technical challenge in trying to effect a smooth transition from E to F.

For a *setār* player, however, the most salient aspect of somatic sensibility is the fact that – after the G, which can be played on an open string, with no left-hand action necessary – the two subsequences A-B-C and D-E-F are both played using the index, middle, and ring finger to fret the same relative positions (pitch relationships), but on different strings. As depicted in Figure 10.2, A-B-C is played on the lower, second string, and D-E-F on the higher, first string. As a result, the *setār* player is cognizant that the figure to be played is composed of two conjunct, identical tetrachords (four-note series spanning a perfect fourth): G-A-B-C and C-D-E-F.

This kind of musical cognition is a natural consequence for players of instruments like the *setār*, *tār*, and *kamānche*, but not for a *santūr* player. *Santūr* players do not need to fret or otherwise determine the pitch of, for example, D, D flat, or D koron, from moment to moment; in that respect, playing the *santūr* is somewhat like playing the *setār* with open strings –

Chapter 10

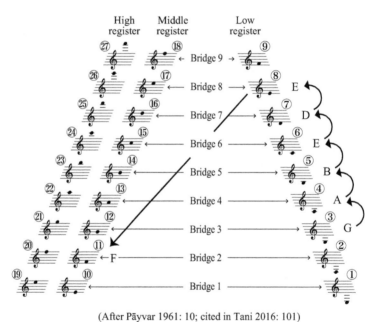

(After Pāyvar 1961: 10; cited in Tani 2016: 101)

Figure 10.1 String arrangement on a *santūr*

with the strumming and plucking hand alone, and not using the fretting hand at all.

Probing the different physicality of players of different instruments leads to the conclusion that music is not known only as sound. Indeed, we suggest that the twelve modes of Iranian music (referred to by terms like *dastgāh* and *āvāz*) are sensed both aurally and through the fingers.

Perceiving and understanding through the fingers

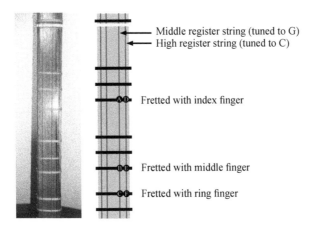

Figure 10.2 Fretting positions on a *setār*

10.4 Tetrachord cognition and hand/finger position

Generally speaking, the tetrachord is more important than the octave for understanding modal systems like *dastgāh*. A tetrachord is a four-note series spanning a perfect fourth, and modal systems are often better understood and analyzed in these terms to understand the movement of the melody, rather than in terms of the octave. A mode can be viewed as two tetrachords, either conjunct (sharing one note in the middle) or disjunct (separated, generally by a major second), which usually permits a better understanding of how the notes move.

According to Dāryūsh Talā'ī (1953–), the twelve modes of Iranian music comprise the four tetrachords shown in Figure 10.3, in various combinations. By numerical necessity, a given tetrachord will be a component in multiple modes, which creates opportunities for modulation. In Iranian music as played today, an improvised performance comprises more than one *dastgāh* – indeed, listeners will evaluate it in part on the beauty of its modulations from one *dastgāh* to another. Understanding *dastgāh* and *āvāz* in terms of their component tetrachords is thus essential for understanding the practices of Iranian music.

Figure 10.3 shows the interior note structure (and fingering, on the string instrument) of each tetrachord in terms of cents, with the full tetrachord understood as a 500-cent perfect fourth.[1] In a February 2014 exchange, *setār* player Bābak Modarresi (1974–) demonstrated these internal structures for each tetrachord, converting Talā'ī's theory so that

167

Chapter 10

	zāyed (an "extra" fret not named for a finger)		Middle finger (vostā)	Ring finger (benser)	Little finger (khenser)	
Open strings	140		240		120	C
	140	140		220		S
	200	80		220		D (N)
	200		180		120	M
	Index finger (sabbābe)			Ring finger		(Talā'ī 1993:23)

Figure 10.3 Four tetrachords by Talā'ī

50 cents (one quarter tone) was considered 1.[2] Modarresi's explanation of the tetrachords are as follows:

1. *Shūr* (S): 4:3:3 (e.g., C — D — E koron — F)
   C — whole-tone interval — D — 3/4 -tone interval — E *koron* — 3/4 -tone interval — F.

2. *Māhūr* (M): 4:4:2 (e.g., C — D — E — F)
   C — whole-tone interval — D — whole-tone interval — E — semi-tone interval — F.

3. *Chahārgāh* (C): 3:5:2 (e.g., C — D koron — E — F)
   C — 3/4 -tone interval — D koron — 5/4-tone interval — E — semi-tone interval — F.

4. *Dashtī* (D):[3] 4:2:4 (e.g., C — D — E flat — F)
   C — whole-tone interval — D — semi-tone interval — E flat — whole-tone interval — F.

The main point here is how musicians recognize each of the four tetrachords, and to note the wide differences in cognition among different musicians even on something as important as the tetrachords. As audible notes, of course, the tetrachords are distinguished aurally, but I want to illuminate how differences within the same perfect fourth are distinguished physically – how the fingers feel the different pitches of each tetrachord. To consider this more closely, let us compare the *santūr* with the *tār/setār* and *'ūd*.

10.5 The advantages of "finger-position awareness"

As described above, the *santūr* is tuned in advance to the *dastgāh* it will be played in. Whichever tetrachords are involved, the player senses no difference in terms of the accompanying physical sensations, since the same strings are struck. This is not the case for instruments like the *tār* or *setār*, where the player uses fingers to determine each pitch within a tetrachord during performance. The somatic sensibility of this action is radically different from simply striking pretuned strings, actively using the fingers to determine the pitches for each tetrachord (or *dastgāh*) played.

As noted, tetrachords are shared by multiple *dastgāhs* and can become opportunities for modulation (*modgardi*). This suggests that the sensations of the fingers while playing a given tetrachord might trigger recollection of other *dastgāhs* containing that tetrachord, which would facilitate natural *modgardi*. This would mean that *modgardi* might come more naturally to players of instruments like the *tār* or *setār*, who experience different physicality of finger-positions specific to each tetrachord while playing, than to players of the pretuned *santūr*, who have the same physical experience of every tetrachord.

Impediments to *modgardi* on the *santūr* are generally explained as arising from the limitations of its construction – specifically, the fact that only seven notes per octave are usually available. However, if we consider the somatic sensibility of the player as well, we might add that the *santūr* player has no physical basis on which to determine which tetrachord is being played, and must determine it from sound alone. This contrasts dramatically with players of the *tār* or *setār* and similar instruments, who also experience tetrachords as sensations of finger positions.

This finger-position awareness is more pronounced in the case of the *'ūd*, a fretless instrument that requires the player to precisely determine each note with exact finger placement. Figure 10.4 shows the fingering positions on the *'ūd* neck to play the simple scale G-A-B-C-D-E-F-G-A-B-C-D-E.

These fingering positions indicate that even the task of playing this simple scale is divided into "open string + two notes separated by a semitone" and "open string + two notes separated by a whole tone" sections (setting aside the fifth string, which is only played open here). These two sections are fingered differently: the first (semitone interval)

Chapter 10

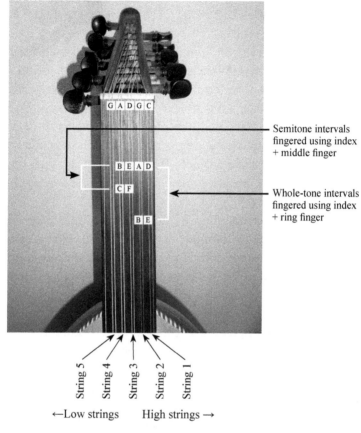

Figure 10.4 Fingering positions on *ʿūd* neck
(after Narīmān 2012: 40. Finger positions are relative.)

with the adjacent index and middle fingers, and the second (whole-tone interval) with the separated index and ring fingers. As a result, whole-tone and semitone intervals (as well as neutral intervals like 3/4 tones) are recognized by *ʿūd* players not just aurally but also through different fingerings (distances between fingers), another decisive difference in somatic sensibility from *santūr* players.

Mode A → ⎡Tetrachord a', as used in Mode A⎤

⎣Tetrachord a', as used in Mode B⎦ → Mode B

Figure 10.5 Basic idea behind *modgardi*

10.6 Conclusion

Awareness of the musical organization, sensed through the finger positions as the music is played, offers more opportunities to players for *modgardi*, a common element in improvised performances of Iranian music. Talā'ī's four tetrachords are, in standard modern fingerings, all played with a combination of open strings and the index, middle, and ring (or little) finger, but each has a unique hand position deriving from how the fingers are placed, and these hand positions are inscribed on the body of the performer. As will be discussed in Chapter 12, if the hand position of a given tetrachord (call it Tetrachord a′) in a given mode (Mode A) is the same for the same tetrachord in Mode B, this also creates opportunities that encourage players to execute more natural forms of *modgardi*.

Santūr players, however, have no access to this finger-position awareness. In that sense, there is a decisive and unbridgeable gap between *santūr* players and *tār/setār* and *'ūd* players in terms of the somatic sensibility of even a short melody they are playing and, moreover, the structure of the *dastgāh* (and its component tetrachords). Similarly, a peculiar "somatic sensibility" surely exists for other instruments as well – for example, wind instruments like the *ney*. Further investigation of this unique form of musical cognition is needed.

Chapter 11
The *santūr*'s new physicality: Toward a geopolitics on the board of the instrument

11.1 Introduction

Musicologists have been discussing the complex of problems of physicality for some time. The excellent 2003 collection *Piano o hiku shintai* [The piano-playing body] presents many papers richly suggestive in this regard, including Ken Ōkubo's "Te no dorama: Shopan sakuhin o hiite taiken suru" [Drama of the hands: Playing and experiencing Chopin's works], which analyzes Chopin's works from perspectives such as the "thrilling left hand," "hand extension and contraction" and "hands clinging to the keyboard." By describing "the way music exists (= raw experience) as felt through performance" (Ōkubo 2003: 165) rather than through scores or sound alone, Ōkubo successfully illuminates areas that traditional music analysis cannot capture. As another contributor to the collection, Nobuhiro Itō points out, we need to develop an appropriate vocabulary and establish the necessary style if we are to describe somatic experience during a performance (Itō 2003: 134), but once this is achieved, researchers should be able to more directly study musical practice.

This was the challenge I had in mind when, in Chapter 10, I examined the different somatic sensibilities of musicians of various specializations – including *āvāz* (vocal), *tonbak*, *tār* (*setār*), *santūr*, *ney*, *kamānche*, and *'ūd* – as they experience the "common ground" of traditional Iranian music. That discussion revolved around comparison of the *santūr* with other string instruments. In this chapter, I will explore how much physicality can differ from player to player of the same instrument. My focus will once more be on the *santūr*, describing first what might be called its generic physicality and then the "new physicality" I encountered during participatory fieldwork at lessons held by *santūr* player Ardavān Kāmkār (hereafter referred to as "Ardavān"), which I have been attending repeatedly since 2014. Through these accounts, I hope to examine the relationship between instrument structure and the player's physical body.

11.2 The new assignment of hands: On the separation of E and F

Let us begin by noting the importance of the choice of left and right hands in *santūr* performance.

When playing the piano, which fingers strike which keys is an issue of great importance. If a score includes fingering instructions provided by the composer or editor, the player must decide how to respond, with options ranging from following the instructions as written to actively ignoring them. Whichever response is chosen makes a major difference for both player and listener, so that the choice of fingering is truly a musical choice in itself.

For *santūr* players who use two mallets (*mezrāb*) to strike the strings instead of their fingers, the situation is similar in that the choice of left or right mallet to play a given note is connected not only to questions of musicality, but also to a group of problems intimately related to virtuosity, as I will explain below.

From this perspective, let us reexamine the physical gap between E and F described in Section 10.3. For *santūr* players, this is an unavoidable technical challenge unique to their instrument (and forced on them by the instrument's structure). Introductory tutors generally contain études designed to help overcome this challenge by smoothly connecting the E and F during performance.

Score 11.1 Etude from *santūr* tutor *Dastūr-e Santūr* (Pāyvar 1961: 18)

The mallet instructions for this étude direct the player to play the ascending sequence C-D-E♭-F with the mallet pattern R-L-R-L. (As is typical for *santūr* notation, notes to be struck with the left mallet are marked with the symbol ∨, while notes to be struck with the right mallet are marked with a ∧ or left unmarked.) Using the string numbering seen in Figure 10.1, the strings to be struck are 15-16-17-20.

Given the positions of the left and right hand, this is quite natural. The E♭ string (17), which is further to the right, is struck with the right mallet; the F string (20), which is further to the left, is struck with the left. This approach to mallet assignment was applied without exception in the

174

santūr lessons I took in Iran in the 1990s, which were chiefly based on the *radīfs* and compositions of Abolhasan Sabā and Farāmarz Pāyvar. It ranked among the simplest fundamentals of playing the *santūr*.

However, Ardavān teaches a different technique, in which the same notes are played with the mallet pattern L-R-R-L.

Score 11.2 Ardavān's mallet technique, in which D and E♭ are both played with the right hand

Not only the E♭ but also the immediately preceding D is played with the right mallet – two notes in sequence. Furthermore, this introduces another unusual feature: the musical figure begins with the left mallet.

What are the benefits of Ardavān's approach to this passage? As described above, since the E and F strings are physically separated, the challenge is to play the E-F sequence exactly like any other two notes, without pause or slowing. If it cannot be done with the traditional mallet assignment, it is often because of the delay in moving from the D string to the F string with the left hand while the right hand plays the intervening note. To rectify this, Ardavān's technique gives the left hand two notes' worth of time to move to the F. When I tried playing the figure this way, playing the D-E♭ sequence with the right hand alone was not as cumbersome as I thought, partly because the right is my dominant hand. Any inconvenience was certainly far outweighed by the benefit of the extra time my left hand had to reach the F – and the faster the tempo, the greater the benefit.

Ardavān's playing is characterized by his unparalleled accuracy and virtuosic technique, and this approach to the mallet assignment is undoubtedly a significant factor. Behind his virtuosity, we see uncompromising pursuit of rationality in mallet assignment.

11.3 Dyad mallet assignment: The pursuit of rationality

Ardavān's rationality is even more apparent when playing dyads (two notes simultaneously).

Chapter 11

Score 11.3 Dyad mallet assignment

Score 11.4 Two dyads

Score 11.5 Conventional dyad mallet assignment

Score 11.6 Dyad mallet assignment by Ardavān

In traditional mallet assignment for playing dyads, it was considered common sense to play the higher note with the left mallet and the lower note with the right, as seen in Score 11.3. The main reason for this was the limitations of the *santūr*'s construction, as described above. If the dyad encompassed the "separated E and F," the lower note was further right on the instrument, so it was struck with the right mallet, while the higher note was further to the left, and therefore struck with the left. This rule was then applied even to dyads that did not encompass the separated E and F – which is to say, dyads where either mallet could strike either note with equal ease. As a result, "Play the lower note with the right mallet, and the higher note with the left" became the basic rule for dyads.

Ardavān's approach to dyads is based on a completely different principle, namely, "Play the string furthest from the player with the right mallet, and the string closest to the player with the left." Like the traditional rule, this is motivated by the problem of the separated E and F. However, Ardavān analyzes this problem in terms of physical distance from the player, and then applies the resulting principle to all other dyads. And this has other benefits.

Score 11.4 has two dyads (Using the string numbering seen in Figure 10.1, the strings to be struck are B (5), D (7), and G (12).). Traditional mallet technique would play this as shown in Score 11.5, requiring both hands to move between the two dyads. (Note that the same note, D, is played first with the left mallet and then with the right.) Ardavān's technique, in Score 11.6, uses the right mallet to play the D in both the first and second dyad, so that only the left hand needs to move.

This is a more rational mallet assignment in that it minimizes the movement of the player's hands. But this is not the only benefit.

The santūr's new physicality

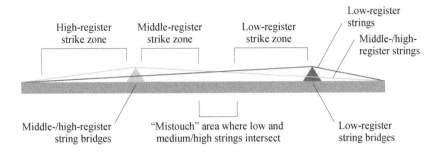

Figure 11.1 Relative positions of low-register and middle-/high-register strings

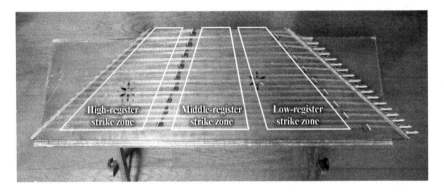

Photo 11.1 Strike zones for each register of *santūr*

As the figures and photographs throughout this book show, the *santūr* is trapezoidal, and so the area in which its high register is played is very awkwardly shaped (see Photo 11.1). Let us take a moment to explain the *santūr*'s "strike zones."

The strings of the *santūr* can be divided into two categories: those that produce the low register, and those that produce the middle and high register. When the *santūr* is viewed from directly above, the two types of strings appear to be mixed in the same area with an alternating pattern. But viewing the instrument horizontally from the front reveals that, due to the different locations of the bridges, the low-register and middle-/high-register strings are strung at different heights.

As Figure 11.1 shows, the bridges that support the low-register strings are on the right-hand side of the instrument from the player's perspective. The bridges that support the middle-/high-register strings are on the left-hand side of the instrument. As a result, on the right-hand side of the

177

instrument, the middle-/high-register strings are physically beneath the low-register strings, which means that only the low-register strings can be struck with the mallets. The opposite holds for the left-hand side of the instrument, where only the middle-/high-register strings can be struck. This gives the *santūr* distinct "strike zones" for each register that are basically as shown in Photo 11.1.

To return to the original point, the high-register strike zone is thus an obtuse trapezoid with its base at the far left of the instrument that "leans" to the right as the notes ascend. When playing a dyad in this register with traditional mallet assignment, the right hand strikes the lower note, closer to the bottom left of the strike zone, while the left hand strikes the higher note, closer to the top right of the strike zone. This brings the hands into close proximity and makes the dyad difficult to play. With Ardavān's technique, however, the right hand plays the string that is furthest from the player. Thus, in the case described above, it will play the high note at the upper right of the strike zone, and the left hand will play the low note at the bottom left, which is a more natural division between the two hands.

What about the low-register strike zone? If traditional mallet technique assigns the right hand to the bottom right of the zone and the left hand to the top left, while Ardavān's technique assigns the hands the opposite way, the same logic gives traditional mallet assignment the advantage here. Therefore, there is no mallet assignment that can be applied to all situations, and in such cases, players strike different parts of the strike zones shown in Photo 11.1. Those differences also reflect different ideas about the ideal place to strike within the long-strung strings.

Let us move beyond mallet assignment for dyads and broaden our perspective to the philosophies underlying these ideas. Where do musicians believe that the *santūr*'s strings should be struck to achieve their ideal sound and technique?

11.4 Philosophy of the striking point

Both Saʿīd Sābet,[1] from whom I took *santūr* lessons in the 1990s, and Farāmarz Pāyvar recommended striking the strings approximately 2 to 3 centimeters from the bridge. Their ideal striking points are visualized in Photo 11.2, connected up into lines.

The *santūr's* new physicality

Photo 11.2 Sābet and Pāyvar's striking points (connected to form lines)[2]

This philosophy has two main points. First is the idea that striking every string at the same distance from the bridge imparts uniformity of tone. Consciousness of tonal uniformity is why, for example, *santūr* player and composer Parvīz Meshkātian told me that both hands should be kept as close together as possible when playing *rīz* (tremolo) on the same string.[3]

Second, "2 to 3 centimeters from the bridge" keeps the striking point safely away from the area where the low-register and middle-/high-register strings intersect, where there is the danger of "mistouch" – accidentally striking the wrong string. Mistouch in this area is a common error among beginners, and so striking the strings near the bridge is an idea widely and thoroughly emphasized in elementary *santūr* pedagogy.

How does Ardavān approach this issue? Rather than recommending individual striking points for each string in terms of distance from the bridge, he teaches his students to imagine strike *lines* across the entire complement of strings, as per Photo 11.3, from the beginning of the lesson. This, too, is based on a distinct philosophy.

Ardavān's strike lines differ from the traditional striking points in one important way: the distance from the bridge varies depending on the string. It can be said that this approach doesn't seem to pay much attention to tonal uniformity between strings. Furthermore, the lower-register strings are struck dangerously close to the area where mistouch becomes more likely.

The benefit of Ardavān's approach, however, is that the three strike lines – one each for the low, middle, and high registers – all stretch out vertically from the player's perspective, rather than following the

179

Chapter 11

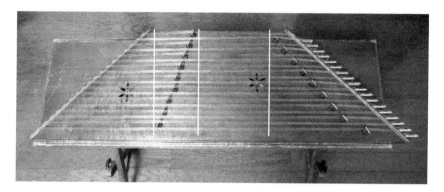

Photo 11.3 Ardavān's recommended strike lines

trapezoidal shape of the instrument and bridge layout. The middle-register line is directly in front of the player, the most convenient place – and Ardavān teaches his pupils to physically move left and right (without twisting their torso) so that whichever line they are playing is always directly in front of them. This allows the low and high register to be played with the same somatic sensibility as the middle register.

On a hammered dulcimer like the *santūr*, depending on the distance and orientation of the hand (striking point) relative to the body's central axis, even techniques that appear to be the same may require a different knack to execute. The idea of aligning the striking line with the body's central axis, and applying this principle to all the registers is, again, the result of the pursuit of rationality – seeking to make the geography of the *santūr*, which tends to be rather complex, as simple as possible. This remains true even if in actual performance the strings are not struck along a perfectly straight line.

How, then, is Ardavān's pursuit of rationality positioned within the history of *santūr* playing technique?

11.5 Standardized difficulty

The modernization of Iranian society after the Constitutional Revolution of 1906 brought the ideas and pedagogic methods of Western music into the country's traditional music in many ways. For example, staff notation was introduced to teach music which had previously been transmitted orally, and the idea of playing études for the purposes of technical refinement was introduced to musical settings which had previously been dedicated to handing down traditional *radīf*s. Elements of Western music itself were also introduced to Iranian music, and – notwithstanding backlash and similar reactions at various times – over the long term these elements became established and are visible in the oeuvres of musicians who viewed themselves as creating "contemporary" Iranian music that was more than just "traditional." One approach that became particularly commonplace was arrangements reflecting the philosophy, also seen in traditional Iranian music, of "reproducing from what already exists" rather than creating something utterly original. For example, a traditional melody might be augmented with harmonic arpeggios or arranged polyphonically.

If such arrangements had been attempted on the *santūr*, the higher voice (which would usually be the melody) would be played with the left hand, and accompaniment in a lower register would be played with the right. This physicality – playing melody with the left hand and accompaniment with the right – was an approach to mallet assignment that did not come naturally to *santūr* players, insofar as it involved playing the melody with the non-dominant hand. From the perspective of musical understanding, it called on the player to conceive of Iranian music, which is fundamentally monophonic, in terms of "melody + harmony (arpeggio)" or "polyphony (two-voice counterpoint)," a difficulty not previously found in Iranian music.

Ardavān's oeuvre, however, includes countless works composed in polyphony or "melody + harmony (arpeggio)" style, using techniques that were not actively adopted before him. Ardavān's playing is generally praised for the flawless accuracy and incredible speed of his mallet technique, but these characteristics can also be explained as an extension of the traditional way of playing. What is more noteworthy is the aspects of his mallet work which were difficult for another player to imagine from experience – aspects that departed from the "common sense" of traditional *santūr* performance, so that the pieces are difficult to play even if they do not contain that many notes – and the fact that he has made even this unique physicality commonplace. Although his oeuvre retains elements unique to *santūr* like tremolo playing and repeated strikes, it could be seen as an attempt to overcome the limitations of the *santūr* on every front, including both construction and technique.[4]

11.6 High notes on the left: Toward a geopolitics on the board of the instrument

As we have seen, playing the *santūr* had certain structural characteristics that rendered it difficult to play due to issues like the separation between E and F and the placement of the higher register on the left side. However, inspired by figures like Ardavān, performers and learners have sought to overcome these difficulties. According to Kourosh Matin, every beginner working through this trial-and-error process thinks to themselves at least once, "This would be much easier if the *santūr*'s design were reversed, so that left were right and vice versa."[5] However, it takes little reflection to realize that while this would resolve some technical issues, it would also create new ones. What is more, countless phrasings considered neutral up until that point would have to change greatly. The technical issues of the *santūr* we have do not exist in isolation as challenges to be overcome – they are inseparable from the benefits and "*santūr*-ness" they also impart. Even the "un-*santūr*-like physicality" of Ardavān is only recognized as such because of how deeply the music and the body of the player is determined by the instrument's construction.

As we consider the idea of an "un-*santūr*-like physicality" from the macro perspective, a question might occur whose apparent frivolity belies its depth: If the piano's keyboard had high notes on the left and low on the right, what would piano playing and piano music be like?

Questions like this are in turn linked to what we might call the "geopolitics on the board of the instrument" – how the geographical relationships between notes on the board of an instrument influences that instrument's music. For players of an instrument, this set of issues has always been felt in a very real way – so much so that it was too obvious to verbalize, or even consciously consider – however, as the geography on the board of the instrument is precisely what the player confronts, it is something that cannot be overlooked.

Chapter 12
What we learn from the *radīf*

12.1 Introduction

As discussed in previous chapters, learning traditional Iranian music involves receiving the teacher's transmission of a *radīf*, which is an aggregation of hundreds of *gūshes*. Through this process, learners come to understand the modal system called *dastgāh* and develop the ability to improvise.

I studied and did fieldwork in Iran in the 1990s, first arriving in the country when I was still in music college in Japan in 1993 and ending in 1998 with my graduation from Dāneshgāh-e Honar, The University of Art in Iran. During this period, improvisation was not something that could be specifically taught. As far as I am aware, there was no conscious instruction in improvisation either at my university or in private teaching arrangements, not even hints as to how it might be carried out. When I began visiting Iran again in 2014, however, I was surprised by the sheer number of classes about improvisation or related material useful for improvisation (setting aside the question of how effective this instruction was). In retrospect, there were a number of students with me at Dāneshgāh-e Honar in the 1990s who grumbled about the lack of concrete information about improvisation in our classes. Two decades later, that generation is now in charge of teaching the new generation, and the situation has changed dramatically.

In this chapter, I will draw on fieldwork conducted at lessons starting in 2014 – and particularly in the latter half of 2019, during my sabbatical at the University of Tehran's College of Fine Arts – to rethink the concrete side of "learning the *radīf*," showing that multiple layers of hints and clues for improvisation exist within the *radīf* itself.

12.2 Paying attention to relationships between *gūshes*

Let us first return to the matter of relationships between *gūshes*.

Figure 12.1 shows the relationships between the chief *gūshes* in *shūr* mode, which are played in progressively higher registers as the

Chapter 12

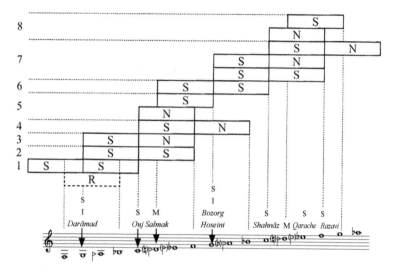

1 Darāmad, Rohāb
2 Ouj
3 Salmak
4 Bozorg, Hoseini
5 'Ozzāl
6 Darāmad-e shūr-e pāyin daste
7 Shahnāz, Qarache, Razavi
8 Ouj dar Shahr-Āshub

Figure 12.1 Temporal structure of *shūr* mode (Talā'ī 2015: 25)

performance progresses.[1] These relationships become clear to learners as they repeatedly play and memorize the *radīf*. But this is not the only aspect of the *radīf* that learners are given to master.

12.3 Understanding the four tetrachords: Bridges to *modgardi* (modulation)

As discussed in Chapter 10, recognizing that the twelve modes of Iranian music are made up of four different tetrachords (Score 12.1) in various arrangements is highly useful when considering degrees of freedom during an improvised performance.

Figure 12.2 presents the temporal structure of *homāyun* mode. Three tetrachords are used at various times: S, C, and N. This indicates that *modgardi* is theoretically possible to (or from) any other mode that includes one of these three tetrachords. The same is true of *māhūr* mode, shown in Figure 12.3, which allows players to visit other modes that

What we learn from the *radīf*

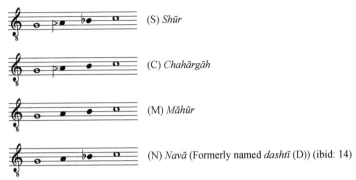

Score 12.1 The four tetrachords (Talā'ī 2015: 14)

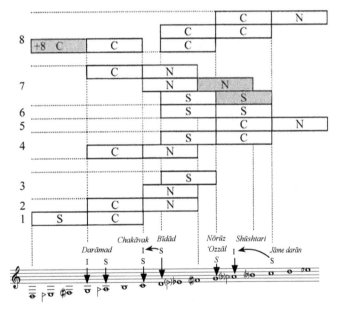

1 Darāmad
2 Chakāvak (*shāhed* C), Bīdād (*shāhed* D)
3 Ouj-e Bīdād
4 Nōrūz-e 'arab
5 Shūshtari, Bakhtiyāri
6 'Ozzāl, Mo'ālef
7 Denāsori
8 Mavāliān

Figure 12.2 Temporal structure of *homāyun* mode (ibid: 31)

include any of the tetrachords M, S, or N (or C). As long as there is a shared tetrachord, *modgardi* is theoretically possible from anywhere. Players of the *tār*, *setār* and *kamānche* understand this not only aurally

185

Chapter 12

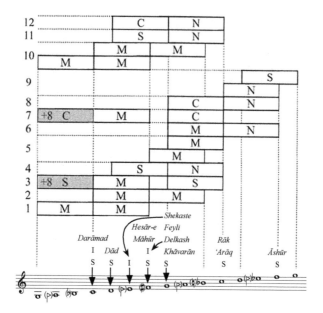

Figure 12.3 Temporal structure of *māhūr* mode (ibid: 34)

1 Darāmad, Dād
2 Hesāre-e Māhūr (*shāhed* F), Feili, Khāvarān (*shāhed* G)
3 Delkash
4 Shekaste
5 Mohayyer
6 'Arāq
7 Rāk
8 Rāk, Esfahānak
9 Safir-e rāk, Āshūr
10 Sāqīnāme, Harbi
11 Koshte
12 Sūfīnāme, Harbi

but also through their fingers. They have perceptual awareness, at the level of finger position, of opportunities for *modgardi* in many places throughout the music. Facility at recognizing tetrachords is thus directly connected to degrees of freedom in improvisation, in that it allows the player to recognize more opportunities for modulation.[2]

The *radīf* contains basically no cases of *modgardi* in the strictest sense of "modulating entirely to a different mode." However, as multiple tetrachords are used in each mode, and these tetrachords change together with the passage of time – as seen in Figures 12.1 to 12.3 – the *radīf* is rich in examples of what we might call "domestic" *modgardi*. Thus, a tetrachord-centric understanding of the *dastgāh* leads to a new kind of freedom, in which *modgardi* is not uncommon in Iranian music and the boundaries between one *dastgāh* and another do not loom larger than necessary.

To deepen our understanding further, let us examine concrete process for *modgardi* using actual improvised performances. Despite the frequency with which *modgardi* occurs, specific methods for effecting it are not theoretically organized in advance. Nor do musicians reflect on or attempt to verbalize its details afterward. By supplementing the above discussion of Talā'ī's four-tetrachord theory and the physicality of their corresponding finger positions with observations of actual cases of *modgardi*, I hope to offer richer insight into the opportunities and factors that facilitate it.

We will begin by reviewing the basic ideas behind *modgardi*, as outlined in Chapter 10. *Modgardi* is basically effected by using a tetrachord shared by different modes.

The shaded areas in Figures 12.4 and 12.5 show the tetrachord structures of, respectively, the *shūr* mode *gūshe* called *hoseini*, and the *darāmad* of *dashtī* mode – the introduction to the mode, which expresses its basic character. Both structures contain the tetrachords S and N.

Scores 12.2 and 12.3 show how these two tetrachords are presented in Sabā's *radīf*.

In Figure 12.4 and Score 12.2, the SN structure appears in the form: C-D *koron*-E♭-F-G-A♭-B♭. (The S tetrachord is C-D koron-E♭-F, the N tetrachord is F-G-A♭-B♭, sharing F note in the middle.) Here, the melodic activities are executed with *shāhed* G, the second lowest note within the N tetrachord.

In Figure 12.5 and Score 12.3, the SN structure appears in the form G-A *koron*-B♭-C-D-E♭-F. (The S tetrachord is G-A koron-B♭-C, the N tetrachord is C-D-E♭-F, sharing C note in the middle.) Here, the melodic activities are executed with *shāhed* D, the second lowest note within the N tetrachord.

If a piece of music moved between these two modes, it would be the simplest *modgardi*, with no need to change in scale. However, as these examples show, the music develops with different phrasing in different modes, even when the component pitches are the same (in relative terms). This is the basic idea of *modgardi*.

Next, let us consider a more typical form of *modgardi*, taken from an actual performance. By "typical," I mean that it is rare for all component pitches to be shared, as they are in the examples above; in actual perfor-

187

Chapter 12

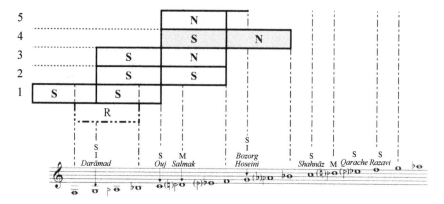

Figure 12.4 Tetrachord structure of *hoseini gūshe* in *shūr* mode (Talā'ī 2015: 25)

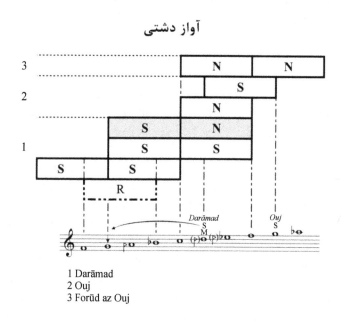

1 Darāmad
2 Ouj
3 Forūd az Ouj

Figure 12.5 Tetrachord structure of *darāmad* in *dashtī* mode (Talā'ī 2015: 26)

mance, it is more realistic to execute *modgardi* to a tetrachord that differs in one component pitch from the originating tetrachord, as depicted in Figure 12.6.

The improvisations transcribed in Scores 12.4 through 12.8 are of a performance on July 30, 2019, in Tehran, at a gathering of semi-professionals (see Chapter 9, note 1). The performers included Mahiyār Moshfeq on *tār* and Sedāqat Jabbārī on vocals.

188

What we learn from the *radīf*

Score 12.2 *Hoseini* in *shūr* mode, from Sabā's *radīf* (Sabā 1991: 30–31)

Score 12.3 *Darāmad* in *dashtī* mode, from Sabā's *radīf* (Sabā 1992: 25)

Mode A → ⎾Tetrachord a' in mode A⏋

⎾Tetrachord b' in mode B, differing in one component pitch from a'⏋ → Mode B

Figure 12.6 A typical form of *modgardi*

During the performance, I observed an example of *modgardi* from *afshārī* mode to *bayāt-e tork* mode. The procedure was as follows: Starting with the *gūshe 'Erāq* in *afshārī* mode, change a single component pitch to modulate to the *darāmad* in *bayāt-e tork* mode. The details are discussed below.

189

Chapter 12

Score 12.4 *Darāmad* in *afshārī* mode (followed by *Qarā'ī*) (transcribed by Masato Tani)

Score 12.5 *'Erāq* in *afshārī* mode (transcribed by Masato Tani)

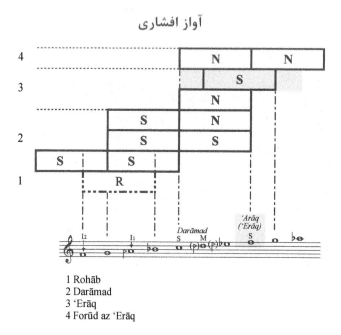

Figure 12.7 Tetrachord structure of *'Erāq* in *afshārī* mode (Talā'ī 2015: 28)

First, the *darāmad* of the *afshārī* mode was played (Score 12.4, whose *shāhed* is C), and then it progresses to *'Erāq* (Score 12.5, whose *shāhed* is F) via a *gūshe* called *Qarā'ī*.

'Erāq in *afshārī* mode has the pitch structure C-D-E *koron*-F-G-A♭. In Talā'ī's tetrachord theory, this is analyzed as "whole tone + S tetrachord (D, E *koron*, F, G) + semitone," as per the shaded area in Figure 12.7. In

190

What we learn from the *radīf*

Score 12.6 *Darāmad* in *bayāt-e tork* mode (transcribed by Masato Tani)

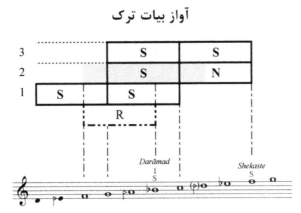

1 Darāmad, Ruh ol-arvāh, Qatār
2 Jāme darān, Mehrabānī
3 Shekaste

Figure 12.8 Tetrachord structure of *darāmad* in *bayāt-e* tork mode (Talā'ī 2015: 27) (example shows a version on B♭, a perfect fifth below)

this performance, as the *gūshe* unfolded, with F as its *shāhed*, it became the point of departure for *modgardi* to the *darāmad* in *bayāt-e tork* mode (with F as *shāhed*).

As Score 12.6 shows, the *darāmad* of *bayāt-e tork* mode (F) develops with F as its *shāhed*, like *'Erāq*. Its pitch structure is C-D-E *koron*-F-G-A, according to Talā'ī's tetrachord theory, is "whole tone + S tetrachord (D, E *koron*, F, G) + whole tone," as per the shaded area in Figure 12.8. The major difference from *'Erāq* is that the pitch structure's A♭ has become an A natural. (In other words, the interval above the S tetrachord is now a whole tone instead of a semitone.) Because of its relationship to the *shāhed* F, this seemingly minor change has a major impact: it changes a minor third to a major third. Let me explain in terms of the emotional impact of the music.

In terms of the *charkh* discussed in Chapter 4, this *gūshe 'Erāq* is played in a higher register as the mood becomes heightened in the latter half of a performance. In this sense, the prolonged F in *'Erāq*, which is expected to be accompanied by sonic gestures and atmosphere that

Chapter 12

sometimes include A♭, can be heard performed with a kind of tension and frequently accompanied by *tahrīr*, as described in Section 6.3.2, performed with an especially strong sense of excitement and urgency.

However, after the move to *bayāt-e tork* mode, the behavior and sound of the extended F changes greatly. Instead of A♭, listeners expect (and hear) sonic gestures and atmosphere that include A natural. This is the "introductory atmosphere" at the beginning of *bayāt-e tork*, introducing the basic feel of the mode. It conveys a sense of calm, and is heard as clearly different from what came before.

From this we see that smooth *modgardi* requires careful attention not only to the component pitches, but also to the gestures and atmosphere around individual notes. In the examples above, the starting mode and the destination mode shared the same S tetrachord, but the approach to prolonging the F within that tetrachord gradually shifted with the *modgardi*, from an initial sense of tension to calm.

After the *modgardi* to *bayāt-e tork* mode, the music returns to *afshārī* mode. To accomplish this, first the singer extends the shared *shāhed*, F, in a richly emotional manner, while making slight changes to it. This method was also used to effect the initial *modgardi* from *'Erāq* in *afshārī* mode. Because both starting point and destination have the same *shāhed*, the performer can begin the *modgardi* smoothly, prolonging the note while gradually changing its timbre and other elements and completing the *modgardi* around it. Here, the singer prolongs an F in a higher register in a way that is not the basic, stable F of *bayāt-e tork* mode but the tenser F of *'Erāq*, and that alone creates the feeling of having returned to that *gūshe*.

The return to *'Erāq* was followed by a *forūd* that brings the music back to its original atmosphere (*darāmad* in *afshārī* mode), which is a typical pattern seen in the *radīf* as well (Score 12.7). To be specific, the music gradually descends, and as it does the E *koron* of *'Erāq* becomes E♭ once more. As the melody repeats its descent, it temporarily stops on A *koron*. A *koron* thus plays the role of *ta'līq* (unresolved note), as will be described later, and this pattern lays the final groundwork for the return to *darāmad* in *afshārī* mode.

Note, however, that the role of "unresolved" is not left entirely to A *koron*. It is also taken up by a *gūshe* called *Rohāb*, which contains gestures and contours that seem designed to play the "unresolved" role as an independent *gūshe*.

What we learn from the *radīf*

Score 12.7 *'Erāq* and returning to original component pitch of *darāmad* (from E *koron* to E♭)in *afshārī* mode (transcribed by Masato Tani)

Score 12.8 *Rohāb* (line 1) and return to *darāmad* in *afshārī* mode (line 2) (transcribed by Masato Tani)

Rohāb has a distinctive melody with an extended final A *koron* that creates an "unresolved" atmosphere. It suggests that the music could go anywhere depending on what the musicians do next, which is why this *gūshe* can be used in many different places during improvised performances. Indeed, it also appears in many places in the *radīf*.

In Score 12.8, the music settles to F in a typical fashion at the end of line 1, which is followed at the beginning of line 2 by the figure F-G-A *koron*-B♭-C. This completes the return to *darāmad* in *afshārī* (whose *shāhed* is C), being a highly typical gesture for that mode.

This example affords us several insights into the opportunities that facilitate *modgardi*. The first point to note is that it was the S tetrachord in particular that provided the opportunity for *modgardi* in the examples above. S is the most commonly used of the four tetrachords and exists as a component of many modes. It is thus easier for the S tetrachord to serve as a "bridge" to *modgardi*. For players of instruments like the *tār* and *setār*, who recognize the tetrachords through finger positions, the habit of "S finger position" itself might be unconsciously associated with *modgardi*.

In a similar way, the *gūshe Rohāb* also appears frequently in various modes, and because of its "unresolved" sonic characteristics, it can be a bridge to other musical destinations.

Taking all of this into consideration, we see that *modgardi* might not be as special as researchers might have imagined from the term.

193

Chapter 12

12.4 Understanding the *gūshe* internal structure and the corresponding melodic development

12.4.1 *Gūshe* internal structure

Learners become aware not only of relationships between *gūshes* but also of their individual internal structures – how the music develops over the course of each *gūshe*. Let us examine this in detail.

Score 12.9, taken from the *radīf* of Abdollah Davāmī (1899–1980), shows the internal structure of the *gūshe* called *darāmad* in *segāh* mode, which is the same as Score 4.2 discussed in Chapter 4. It has four basic sections:

1. *Darāmad* (introduction)
2. *Sh'er* (poetry)
3. *Tahrīr* (passage with melismatic ornamentations derived from vocal technique)
4. *Forūd* (ending phrase)

Score 12.9 Internal structure of a *gūshe* (Pāyvar 1996: 115)

What we learn from the *radīf*

The *gūshe* begins with the introductory section, also called *darāmad*, which expresses the basic character of the *segāh* mode. At line 3, the *shʻer* begins. On line 5, after the end of the poem and a sixteenth-note rest, the *tahrīr* begins and the music becomes more intricate technically. Finally, in the latter half of line 7, the *forūd* section brings the music toward a conclusion.

These divisions are idealized, to some extent. Not every *gūshe* will reveal such a clear internal structure. Nevertheless, as students internalize more and more *gūshes*, they come to grasp not only their structures but also the appropriate atmosphere, feel, and the typical methods of melodic development for each of four sections above. Let us consider these in more detail.

12.4.2 Development in the *darāmad* section: Sequences and added/subtracted notes

Score 12.10, taken from Mirzā Abdollāh's *radīf*, is the *gūshe darāmad* in *shūr* mode. After the opening figure F-G-A *koron*-B♭-A *koron*-G is played, it is followed by a series of variations based on the figure's final two or three notes (A *koron*-G or B♭-A *koron*-G, respectively). Starting in line 2, the B♭-A *koron*-G figure is repeated in sequences (restatements of the same short figure at different pitches; here, it is accompanied by the variant C-B♭-A *koron*, one scale step higher). From line 4, each repetition is preceded by a one-note (C or B♭) or three-note (A *koron*-B♭-C or G-A *koron*-B♭) addition. (Thus, while the initial extraction of the two or three-note figure represented a subtraction of notes, from line 4 we see the addition of notes.) This approach to melodic development, in which sequences of a short figure are accompanied by an increase or decrease in the number of notes, is commonplace throughout the *radīf*.

In the past, these techniques for development were mastered through the process of oral transmission, and musicians did not describe them plainly in words. Today, however, they are recognized and discussed in concrete terms by both teachers and students. This is partly due to the introduction of transcription methods like the one used by Dāryūsh Talā'ī in Score 12.10 (and Scores 12.17–12.19). Instead of filling each line with as many notes as possible, Talā'ī vertically aligns the central musical figures to make their development and variation easier to grasp.

Chapter 12

Score 12.10 The *gūshe darāmad* in *shūr* mode (taken from Mirzā Abdollāh's *radīf*) (Talā'ī 2015: 3 in score section)

12.4.3 Development in the *sh'er* section

Score 12.11 is not an extract from the *radīf* itself, but an example of the diversity that can be found in development of the rhythm "short, short, long, short, long," corresponding to the foot known as *motafā'elon* in classical Persian poetic meter (see Sections 8.5 and 2.3).

Variations like this could be created through manipulation of the *motafā'elon* rhythm alone, without involving poetry.[3] However, in the *radīf*, this method of musical development is learned alongside poetry, as a set.

Score 12.12, taken from the *radīf* of Mahmūd Karīmī (1927–1984), shows the *gūshe Chahārbāgh* in *abū'atā* mode. (This is the same as the *Chahārbāgh* discussed in Section 8.5, except arranged for *santūr*.)

The *sh'er* section normally includes singing a poem. The classical poem recited here has the structure *bahr-e kāmel-e mosamman-e sālem*, in which the *motafā'elon* foot shown in Score 12.11 is repeated.

What we learn from the *radīf*

Score 12.11 Examples of musical development based on *motafāʿelon* foot (Talāʾī 2015: 39)

Score 12.12 *Chahārbāgh* composed by repetition of *motafāʿelon* foot (Atrāʾī 2003: 81)

Chapter 12

Here we see how different words (while repeating the same rhyme) inevitably result in musical variation like that seen in Score 12.11. Furthermore, the fluid shifts in meaning and related emotional peaks that arise from singing the poem (temporal progression) give the generation of these variations additional momentum.

This is among the reasons that playing Iranian music requires a background of classical Persian poetry, as mentioned in this book's introduction. Even in *radīf* scores written for instruments, the words of the poem for the *sh'er* section are always included, and by singing this poetry along with the *radīf* (or learning a vocal *radīf* separately), learners accumulate typical examples of the correspondence between poetic meters and musical rhythms (e.g., the insertion of short *tahrīr* in long notes, such as the parts marked with a box in Score 12.11) and other variations.

Let us take a more detailed look at how classical poetry shapes improvisational performance, based on the teachings of *tār* and *setār* player Bābak Rāhati (1982–). I was able to take classes from Rāhati on the theme of assembling improvisational performances in the latter half of 2019 at the University of Tehran, after which I took private lessons with him as well. At these lessons, he taught me how to assemble an improvisation in *shūr* mode by using the following classical poem by Hāfez, chosen at random:

دوش دیدم که ملایک در میخانه زدند

گل آدم بسرشتند و به پیمانه زدند

dūsh dīdam ke malāyek dar-e meikhāne zadan(d)

gel-e ādam besereshtand o be peimāne zadan(d)

Last night I saw the angels at the door to the winehouse

They were mixing up the clay of Adam and pouring it in the goblet[4]

The first task is to understand this poem's meter. In Table 12.1, row 1 shows syllable length, long (–) or short (⌣); row 2 (shaded) presents the romanized text of the poem; row 3 shows the conjugation of the Arabic verb *fa'ala* (meaning "to do") that corresponds to the rhythmic pattern (foot) in question; and row 4 shows Rāhati's analysis of syllable count, as explained below. Rows 5–7 contain the same information as rows 2–4 for the second line of the couplet.

What we learn from the *radīf*

Table 12.1 Metrical analysis of Hāfez's poetry

long	short	long	long	short	short	long	long	short	short	long	long	short	short	long
dū	sh	dī	dam	ke	ma	lā	yek	da	r-e	mei	khā	ne	za	dan(d)
fā	'e	lā	ton	fa	'a	lā	ton	fa	'a	lā	ton	fa	'a	lon
1		2		3			1	3			1	3		
ge (Short)	l-e	ā	dam	be	se	resh	tan	do	be	pei	mā	ne	za	dan(d)
fa	'a	lā	ton	fa	'a	lā	ton	fa	'a	lā	ton	fa	'a	lon
3		1		3			1	3			1	3		

This couplet, then, has the following syllabic structure:

– ᵕ – – | ᵕ ᵕ – – | ᵕ ᵕ – – | ᵕ ᵕ –

ᵕ ᵕ – – | ᵕ ᵕ – – | ᵕ ᵕ – – | ᵕ ᵕ –

This meter is called *bahr-e ramal-e mosamman-e makhbūn-e mahzūf*: a type of meter (*bahr*) called *ramal* in which the foot *fā'elāton* is repeated eight times (*mosamman*), but with the alterations known as *makhbūn* and *mahzūf*, which respectively mean (1) the foot's initial long syllable is changed to a short one (except for the very first foot), and (2) the final syllable of each line is truncated. Considered in terms of the rules, an improvisatory performance could be completed simply by strictly applying this rhythm to a melody in *shūr* mode, but Rāhati offered a different approach in his lessons.

To begin with, Rāhati did not perform the strict metrical analysis shown above. Instead, he offered a simpler analysis, as shown in rows 4 and 7, breaking the meter down solely by number of syllables. The numbers thus have the following meanings:

♩♪ = 1 (a short syllable at the end of a word is not counted)

♩♩ = 2

♪♪♩ = 3

Of course, this analysis includes not only the number of syllables, but also a certain degree of additional processing performed unconsciously by native Persian speakers. For example, the first rule, "♩♪ = 1," is the result of applying the metrical rule in which the final short syllable in the word *dūsh* is not counted. Alternatively, following the explanation in Section 2.3, the word would still be counted as one extra-long syllable (in

199

Chapter 12

some cases, long + short), but a native speaker processes *dūsh* as a single syllable even without this theoretical underpinning.

Similarly, while the numbers 2 and 3 do correspond to 2- and 3-syllable groupings, the lengths of the syllables involved differ. However, native speakers do not specifically mention the difference because they process this fact "naturally."

To underscore this point, consider the letter-based musical notation once used in Iran and the Arabic world. Score 12.13 shows the correspondence between the letters and staff notation in Iranian music. Note, however, that these letters convey only pitch. The right-hand side of Score 12.14 (which is read right to left) has a number beneath each letter indicating note length (eighth note = 1, quarter note = 2), and the left-hand side has the corresponding musical figure in staff notation. However, there was in fact very little need to write note length in this way. Iran's musical culture was intimately connected to the act of reciting poetry, so note lengths were naturally determined by poetic meter, the rhythm of the language – which, as discussed in Chapter 2, means the various combinations of long and short syllables created by the presence or absence, and type, of the vowel. That is, for native speakers, writing note lengths was simply unnecessary.

Here we can see a point that goes hand in hand with Rāhati's lesson. To a native Persian speaker, syllable length is self-evident. What needs to be consciously remembered is not the lengths of the syllables but their number. For Rāhati, it sufficed for this poem to keep in mind the cycles associated with the poetic feet – which, if grouped together, looked like this:

[1→2]→[3→1]→[3→1]→[3]
[3→1]→[3→1]→[3→1]→[3]

Let us see how these cycles of numbers, along with the melody, were demonstrated in the lesson. Score 12.15 presents a performance Rāhati improvised (Note: The vertical lines separate feet (*fa'ala*) and should not be mistaken for standard bar lines).

According to the rule mentioned earlier about final short syllables not being counted, ♩♪ is counted as 1. In addition, the metric analytical rule in which two short syllables can be counted as one long syllable is also applied to the number of notes, so that ♪♪ is counted as ♩ in the "*dī*" of

What we learn from the *radīf*

Score 12.13 Correspondence between the letters and staff notation (Pūrtorāb et al. 2007: 10)

Score 12.14 Numbers beneath letters to indicate note length (ibid.)

Score 12.15 Demonstration by Rāhati (transcribed by Masato Tani)

the poem. This kind of syllable processing is carried out unconsciously, allowing the musical rhythm to match the poem's meter.

Even more noteworthy than the match with the meter (length and number of syllables) is the alignment with the movement of *shūr* mode, that is, how the meter relates not only to the horizontal movement (rhythm) on the score, but also to the vertical movement. Let us examine the movements of the melody, particularly with respect to G, the *shāhed* and *ist* of the *gūshe darāmad* in *shūr* mode (see Score 12.16).

From this we can see several points regarding the movement of the melody. The following structure can be seen in the couplet (*beit*):

1. Stabilize at the very first foot, establishing the mode's atmosphere
2. Next, create an "unresolved" atmosphere
3. Additionally, introduce a note acting like a "leading tone" to heighten the desire for resolution
4. Complete resolution

Players have a vast stock of phrases for each of the roles 1 through 4 described above, and apply these phrases as necessary from instant to

201

Chapter 12

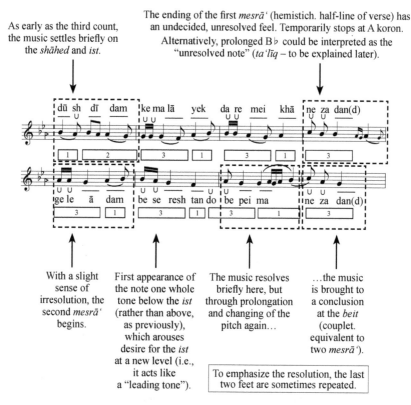

Score 12.16 Analysis of Rāhati's demonstration (transcribed by Masato Tani)

instant during improvisation. Another salient fact is that the important notes mentioned in the above analysis – *ist*, *ta'līq*, and (the note acting like a) leading tone – are assigned to long syllables. Vibrato is also often applied, especially on notes that stir the desire to *ist*.

These various unconscious processes around meter, and the melodic structure corresponding to the couplet (*beit*) are both unobtrusively present in the *radīf*'s "ground" (the parts other than those where the *gūshe*'s character is clearly expressed). Musicians cultivate these internally through the process of playing, mastering, and memorizing more *radīfs*.

12.4.4 Development in the *tahrīr* section

Score 12.17 is, once more, the *gūshe Rohāb* in *shūr* mode, from the *radīf* of Mirzā Abdollāh. The melody of *Rohāb* itself is stated in lines 1–2,

202

What we learn from the *radīf*

Score 12.17 *Rohāb* in *shūr* mode, from *radīf* of Mirzā Abdollāh
(Talā'ī 2015: 7 in score section)

followed by the *tahrīr* beginning from line 3. Here, as in the *darāmad* section, *tahrīr*'s typical tense figures (beginning from the sixteenth notes in line 3) are developed with a mixture of sequences and added/subtracted notes, and partial and full repetitions until it settles down into the following *forūd* section (enclosed in a box at the end of the final line). The entire *radīf* is filled with diverse examples of these *tahrīr* figures and their development, and as students master more and more of them, they gradually become a vocabulary that can be used freely.

12.5 *Gūshe* transfer

Another idea and procedure often seen in improvisation is the "transfer" (*enteqāl*) of *gūshe*. This involves "transferring" a certain *gūshe*'s musical characteristics (particularly its rhythmic characteristics) into a different mode.

Chapter 12

Score 12.18 *Baste negār* (Talā'ī 2015: 79 in score section)

Score 12.18 shows *Baste negār,* a *gūshe* from *bayāt-e kord* mode.[5] Its distinctive rhythmic form, seen in line 1, is developed in sequences (restatements of the same short figure at different pitches). *Baste negār* makes frequent appearances in other modes, and when it does, the same rhythms are played using the component pitches of the target mode. In Score 12.19, which is in *segāh* mode, *Baste negār* appears from line 4 onward. Students thus become aware that transferring or quoting a *gūshe* is a choice available to them during improvisation – an act that improvisers may perform at their discretion. The *gūshe* known as *kereshme*, considered in Chapters 5 and 8, also has distinctive rhythmic forms that are frequently transferred into various modes.

12.6 Grasping the unresolved note *ta'līq*

When analyzing the musical character of a *gūshe*, the notes known as *shāhed* and *ist* require particular attention. *Shāhed* appears frequently throughout the entire *gūshe* and has an emphatic aspect. One meaning of *shāhed* is "evidence" or "proof": the note is repeated and emphasized to "prove" the *gūshe*'s character. Meanwhile, the final note of phrases within the *gūshe* and of the *gūshe* overall is called *ist* (the stem of the verb *īstādan* 'stop'). In many cases, the same note functions as both *shāhed* and *ist*, as in this *gūshe*, *darāmad* (Tani 2007: 140–141).

What we learn from the *radīf*

Score 12.19 *Baste negār* in *segāh* mode (Talā'ī 2015: 182 in score section)

To understand the relationships between *gūshes*, a player must know the *shāhed* and *ist* for each of the main *gūshes* and grasp their temporal progression from a bird's-eye view, so to speak. These two notes, along with *moteghaiyer*,[6] play a vital role in analysis of Iranian music, as previous researchers have noted.[7] However, over the course of an improvisation, it becomes apparent that another note plays a key role as well: *ta'līq*, the "unresolved" note.

Score 12.20 shows the *gūshe Ouj* in *shūr* mode, from the *radīf* of Mahmūd Karīmī. *Ouj* is the sixth *gūshe* in Karīmī's *radīf* and the fifth in Mirzā Abdollāh's. Accordingly, its *shāhed* is on C, the fourth degree above that in *darāmad* (G). It comprises two conjunct S tetrachords, the lower one starting on G. The upper tetrachord starts on C, which functions as *shāhed* as the music develops.

That said, the musical transition from one *gūshe* to the next "is not a matter of completely switching from one to another, but rather of both *gūshes* intermingling as the music progresses" (Tani 2007: 163). Accordingly, a *radīf* "is not a collection of independent and individual *gūshes* with clear boundaries, as is suggested by printed notation with tables of contents," but "a continuous temporal flow that progresses amid mutual co-reference" between the *gūshes* (ibid: 164). As a result, in the *gūshes* after *Ouj*, for some time the music continues to emphasize the C as *shāhed* while returning to the lower G a fourth below at one's discretion (marked with arrows in Score 12.20).

The suspended or "unresolved" note – B♭, in this case – plays an important role in this process. In Score 12.20, from *Ouj* onward, we see the music repeatedly suspending on the B♭ (marked with circles in Score 12.20; the section marked with a dotted line has the same function as a *tahrīr* centered on B♭) a whole tone below C while based on upper S tetrachord with C as the *shāhed* of *Ouj*. This creates a sense that the music has not yet decided where it will go next, which is why this note is also called *mo'allaq*, meaning "suspended" or "undecided." As these names suggest, after using this note in the improvisation, players can choose to either return to the G a third below and end the music, or take the melody higher and continue the music around the C (the *shāhed* of *Ouj*) a whole tone above. The note acts as both a boundary beyond which the player decides on their own destination, and a momentary window of time to make that decision. Although it is less frequently discussed than *shāhed*, *ist*, and *moteghaiyer*, a player's grasp of *ta'līq* and ability to deploy it as they wish is strongly related to the degree of freedom they enjoy in developing the improvisation.

What we learn from the *radīf*

Score 12.20 *Ouj* in *shūr* mode, from *radīf* of Mahmūd Karīmī (Atrā'ī 2003: 23)

12.7 Conclusion

In the early stages of learning Iranian music, the *radīf* is generally played exactly as taught, memorized, or written. Accurately playing something as it was transmitted is no easy task, and takes a great deal of time and effort. At the same time, however, the *radīf* is filled with hints for the student to help develop and improvise the music themselves, pushing them toward new interpretations and devices. This is why there are countless versions of the *radīf* named after the musicians who transmitted them, even if many are ultimately rooted in the *radīf* of Mirzā Abdollāh. Even if they are never published in printed form, musicians always take great pride in creating their own *radīf*, which, surely, is the lifeline of Iranian music.

Notes

Introductions

1. The general definition of *dastgāh* is 'system, organization, or device'. When used as a musical term, it denotes a 'mode'. Traditional Iranian music distinguishes twelve modes, divided into seven major *dastgāh* (*shūr, segāh, homāyun, chahārgāh, māhūr, navā,* and *rāst-panjgāh*) and five secondary modes (*bayāt-e tork, abū'atā, afshārī, dashtī,* and *bayāt-e esfahān*). The first four of the five secondary modes are believed to derive from the *shūr* mode, while the last, *bayāt-e esfahān*, is said to derive from the *homāyun* mode. These five derivative modes are called *naghme* (literally 'melody') or *āvāz* (literally 'voice') in order to distinguish them from the seven major *dastgāh*.

    While *dastgāh* refers to a comprehensive conceptual system regarding rules for traditional Iranian music-making, *radīf* (to be discussed later) can be defined as its concrete manifestation (or as an example of its interpretation by each musician).

2. *Radīf* refers to an aggregate of traditional melody types presented during apprenticeship in Iranian music. Each *radīf* is identified by the name of the musician who promulgated his interpretation (thus, for example, "musician so-and-so's *radīf*") and thus, there exists several versions of *radīf*, according to the master who transmits and interprets *radīf*. *Radīf* comprises smaller melody units or short musical pieces called *gūshe*.

3. A hammered dulcimer with strings stretched over a trapezoidal sound box. The basic type has 72 strings with 18 bridges and is played with two thin mallets, one held in each hand. The sound box is made of walnut wood, the low-register strings are brass or copper, and the middle-/high-register strings are steel. Each bridge supports a course of four strings tuned to the same note, to increase the sound's volume and density. There is no mechanism for silencing strings, so the reverberations and resonances of the many "open strings" mingle and overlap, creating a unique resonance that is rich in overtones. This type of instrument, in which the strings are struck with mallets is seen throughout the Orient.

4. A *tār* and *setār* player born in Shīrāz who became one of the most important figures in Iranian musical history. The various extant *radīf-hā* deriving from different masters (interpreters) can ultimately be traced back to the court music traditions of the Qajar dynasty (1796–1925), but Mirzā Abdollāh's *radīf* is considered the root of them. For that reason, even though this *radīf* was originally for *tār* and *setār*, it is considered essential for performers of other instruments as well, and many transcriptions and recordings for other instruments are in circulation.

5. *Tār* means "string" in Farsi; the *tār* is a representative Iranian instrument plucked with a plectrum. It has a long neck and a mulberry sound box with a membrane of fetal lambskin covering the top. Three courses of double strings are plucked with a brass pick. It has a distinctive sharp-edged timbre.
6. "*Se*" means "three" in Farsi, and thus, *setār* means three strings. However, a fourth string has been added since the nineteenth century. The *setār* is a long-necked plucked lute with a wooden sound box which is smaller than that of the *tār*. A plectrum is not used; the strings are plucked with the nail of the index finger. The *setār* is quieter than the *tār*, with a distinctively sweet, "murmuring" timbre.
7. Also called the *barbat* (although, strictly speaking, this is a different instrument), this is a plucked instrument with pear-shaped body played from the Arab countries of Northern Africa to the Middle East. It normally has eleven strings in six courses (with all strings except the lowest doubled), and is played today with a plastic pick. It has no frets, and because its neck is bent toward the player, it is thought to be the ancestor of the Japanese four-stringed biwa.
8. Ardavān Kāmkār is a Kurdish musician born in 1968 in Sanandaj, Iran. As a member of the famous musical family, Kāmkār Ensemble, he began learning *santūr* from his father at the age of 4, and shot to fame upon the release of his first album *Dariyā*, both for his compositional style – which retains the essence of Iranian and Kurdish traditional music while still exhibiting strong influence from Western music – and his dazzling technique, using both hands in exactly the same way (giving no indication which is non-dominant). He remains at the forefront of contemporary Iranian music.

Chapter 1

1. Another statement from the same paragraph: "The teacher who was doubtful about the effects of staff notation forbade transcribing into notation," suggests that transcription may not have been used for teaching the *radīf* here.
2. Hereafter, I will quote Scores 1.1–1.7 from Ma'rūfī (1995): 1, 3, 6, 9, 16, 21, 23, in that order.
3. The core tone (*shāhed.* see Chapter 5) is shown in parentheses next to the name of each *gūshe*. However, I would like to remark that a sense of this note as a core tone is felt only after passing beyond this stage of exercises. "*Koron*" indicates lowering a pitch by a quarter tone (see note 7 below).
4. This indicates that the core tone or emphasizing note is not a single note, but are multiple notes: in this case, between G and B flat.
5. The arrow indicates movement of the core tone from the first note to the second – here, from C to E *koron*.
6. Hereafter, I will cite scores 1a, 3a, 4a, 5a, and 7a, from Mas'ūdie (1995): 127, 129, 130, 133, and 134, respectively.

7. One of the microtones (an interval smaller than a half tone) in traditional Iranian music. *Koron* (𝄭) lowers the pitch a quarter tone, whereas *sori* (𝄰) raises it a quarter tone.
8. I entered the Music Department of Art University in September 1996, and graduated in August 1998. Besides classes at the University, I studied *santūr* individually with Sa'īd Sābet (1959-) and Farāmarz Pāyvar (1933–2009).
9. From this perspective, general descriptions of Iranian music, exemplified by that in the *New Grove Dictionary of Music and Musicians*, in which each *dastgāh* is described as a scale having an octave, do not capture the reality of Iranian music at all, even for convenience sake. The temporal disposition of *gūshes* will be discussed in Chapter 4.
10. In contrast, *gūshes* such as *kereshme* (see Scores 1.2 and 1.6) which characteristically have fixed rhythm or melody, are performed in various tessituras without altering their musical characteristics, regardless of the kind of *radīf* or performance. In this sense, these are interpolating *gūshes*, not directly involved in the temporal progression of the *gūshes*.

Chapter 2

1. *Āvāz* is a term that has a wide variety of meanings, and is largely used in the following senses:

    1. Song; vocal music

    2. Non-metric rhythmic form

    3. Five secondary modes among the twelve Persian musical modes

    Among the above, there are quite a few cases in which 1 and 2 are intertwined and become inseparable. In the discussion in Chapters 2 and 8, I limit my use of the term primarily to its second meaning.
2. Scores 2.1 and 2.2 have bar lines (or quasi-bar lines shown with a dotted line). These are exceptional cases in which lines are deliberately added considering phrasal or metrical breaks in classical poetry, as discussed later. Hence, my discussion disregards those bar lines and the time signatures in Score 2.2.
3. However, the actual pitch of the microtones varies slightly from person to person.
4. Abolhasan Sabā (1902–1958) was a Tehran-born composer, violinist and *setār* player. He was also known for his ability to play piano and many other traditional Iranian instruments. For students of the *santūr*, he is known as the author of the *santūr radīfs Doure-ye Avval, Dovvom, Sevvom*, and *Chahārom-e Santūr*, originally published in four volumes, and as the teacher of the *santūr* player Farāmarz Pāyvar.

Traditional Iranian Music

5. To note further, the prosody of classical Persian poetry in the pre-Islamic period is called *hejā'ī*, while subsequent poetry is called *'arūzī*. *Taqtī'* refers to "scansion."
6. Romanization of the Persian language in this study follows that presented in Table 2.1 (by Kuroyanagi 1998: III).
7. Tsuge (1985: 64; 1990:150) calls these eight foot patterns *joz'*, but *rokn* and *afā'īl* seem to be the more commonly-used terms in the field of classical Persian poetry.
8. For more information about the circular figures, see "Khalīl's Five Metrical Feet" by Horiuchi (1985: 32–33, Figure 2).

Chapter 3

1. Authors frequently reveal this tendency in their speculation on improvisation by first citing the examples of individual musicians, as in the following example:

   > The music of Banān is a good example of improvisation. He would first choose a poem, basing the choice on his mood and his assessment of the audience's mood and desires. He would also choose [sic] the *dastgāh* to go with that poem. (Caton 2002: 141)

   Here, the author attributes improvisation to the musician's talent, rather than looking into improvisation *per se*. This is manifest in her use of words like "choose" or "choice" with their nuance of autonomy. We find a similar tendency in descriptions of musicians' behavior deviating from tradition, as in the next paragraph:

   > An instrumental rendition would involve similar choices. The musicians chose the *dastgāh* as well as the individual *gūshe*. Although the order of *gūshe-hā* in a *radīf* begins with the *darāmad* and progresses according to a traditional arrangement, <u>in actuality a performer might begin in the middle of the *dastgāh* and play only one section</u>. The more experience and expertise a musician had, <u>the more freedom he had in performance.</u> (ibid.; underlining added)

   The implication here is that "individual" musicians "deviate" from what is presumed to be the ordinary practice of performance. In other words, the word "improvisation" typically invokes a notion of "individual diversity" generated through deviation or exceptional acts, and the "creativity" which makes those acts possible.

2. Since there is a negative valuation of playing existing phrases as they are, it is crucial to clarify the concepts behind the perception of "same/different" in order to logically explain the contradictions outlined in Section 3.1.
3. Here, the *segāh* mode has been presented as an example, but this structure occurs in all twelve modes. I will discuss the structure in detail in Chapter 4.

4. Farāmarz Pāyvar was a Tehran-born composer and *santūr* player. Through the publication of his two *santūr radīfs Doure-ye Ebtedā'ī / Doure-ye 'Ālī* (*Radīf-e Chap Kuk*) and numerous *santūr* works, as well as his recordings and performances with many well-known musicians, he has dramatically increased the awareness of the *santūr* as an instrument in traditional music and has laid the foundation for the modern *santūr* technique.
5. This is a point which often confuses interviewers. When the researcher asks the performer the identity of "the creator" of the performed music, the researcher probably means something approximating "the composer." But the musician would often reply that it is his music, answering according to the sense above.
6. Although Iranian musicians often mention that they can improvise in one thousand ways, the number one thousand is commonly used in Persian as a metaphor for "countless," that is, an "infinite" rather than a finite number of times.
7. The fact that the *radifhā* of various teachers differ somewhat is due in part to the fact that each musician, once he has learned his master's *radif*, may <u>set out to create his own version, making changes and innovations</u>, and also in part because many musicians studied, successively or simultaneously, with two or more teachers and <u>created their own *radifhā*</u> by combining their teachers' versions. (Nettl 1972: 19; underlining added)

If, for example, there were only a scale taught to the student and he were asked to improvise on this, his task would be very different and probably difficult. But the teacher says, in effect, 'play something similar to what I'm playing,' not, 'improvise something on this model.' Thus the student has the opportunity of <u>departing</u> very gradually <u>from the teaching version</u>, at first perhaps doing little beyond adding ornaments, repetitions, and brief extensions later <u>striking out more on his own.</u> As will be seen later, <u>performers devise melodic turns and formulate characteristic of their own improvisation</u> but not found in teaching versions... (ibid.: 20; underlining added)

8. This tendency is observed in a variety of topics indirectly, as seen in the following description:

The art of improvisation was usually not taught separately. Instead, in the process of aural transmission of the *gūshe-hā* the musician internalized a pool of melodic figures as well as the underlying structures that he was <u>intuitively</u> able to draw on during performance. In listening to master musicians, the student was able to comprehend the possibilities and limits of improvisation. In developing a rapport with his audience, he also learned to match his choices to his own mood and the mood of his audience, <u>according to the inspiration of the moment.</u> (Caton 2002: 141; underlining added)

The description above ostensibly touches upon the learning process for improvisational performance, but it merely relegates what the musician does during the performance into a mysterious realm. Expressions such as "intuitively" or "inspiration of the moment" do not explicate anything after all without further elucidation of those terms. (In the first place, the question, "whether or not it is teachable" represents the perspective of modern education in text-centered culture. Details are discussed in Section 6.2 and Section 7.1.)

9. In the quotations below, for instance, we can understand that there is always the *radīf* located at the center of the variations in improvisational performance. In other words, the *radīf* is interpreted here as an absolutely fixed text, and the problem revolves around how one will treat it.

> The primary variable in Persian improvisation is the degree or extent to which it is grounded in the *radif*... The criterion of *radif* reliance goes a long way in defining an individual artist's style... [T]he diverse style of individuals...vary and each is defined to a large degree by his use of the *radif*. (Simms 1996: 124–25)

> [T]he degree of adherence to the teaching version differs with the performer. (Nettl 1972: 20)

10. Of course, I am not suggesting that all the oral-centered cultures share this attitude toward improvisation. For example, if we compare improvisation in Iranian music to that in Indian music, another oral-based culture, the degree of personal freedom in improvisation in Indian music may be higher than that in Iranian music, considering the fact that studies of improvisation in Indian music have largely dealt with the subject of individual uniqueness (Nettl 1998: 4). In fact, Nettl treats Indian music as having a higher degree of freedom than Iranian music in his discussion comparing the rules and degrees of constraint in improvisational performance in various musical cultures, such as Baroque music, jazz, Iranian music, Indian music, etc., by using the term "density" (Nettl 1974: 13). I agree with him to a certain degree, but, if Nettl views such difference in terms of a gradation of density of constraints and rules for the models, I would think it should rather be interpreted as a qualitative difference in the mental attitude of the musician who deals with the model and the ways he uses the model, as I discuss as the theme of the present work. Examining the nature of "arbitrariness" itself in each musical culture will make it possible to highlight the difference in the concept of improvisation not only between orality-centered cultures and literacy-centered cultures, but also between and within various oral cultures.

This chapter does not claim that there is no individuality in Iranian music, nor is it claiming that Iranians do not place value on the new creation of beauty. They certainly do see worth in those things. However, we must bear in mind that Iranians first find joy in their repetitive remembrance of what they share. Only after having that experience does it become an issue that someone's performance has a unique quality which is different from anyone else's. In other words, I don't think Iranian music's reality and characteristics would reveal themselves if we were to think about the problem of individuality first.

Of course, as we will see in Chapter 6, the concept of improvisation – which is not paraphrasing but instead a conscious creation of something new – is emerging today, through the influence of the text-centered perspective. Or, as Nettl points out (2001: 95), there are performers who memorize their own improvisations and perform those variants. This is a natural phenomenon in contemporary Iranian society which is replete with sound recordings and music notation.

Nevertheless, I have consciously avoided too hasty a discussion of the current status of Iranian music, because I believe that the recognition of Iran as belonging to an oral-centered culture should form the basic stance for the study of improvisation in Iranian music. Iranian culture has numerous characteristics that are specific to oral-centered cultures, as Ong points out. The meter of classical Persian poetry is closely related to its memorability, and the Iranian educational system emphasizes memorization above all (Morita 2008). We observe that verbose compliments or flattering words, called *ta'ārof*, function as a ritualized pattern of behavior. All of these are testimony to the fact that Iran belongs to an oral-centered culture. Such attributes of the oral-centered culture should be discussed independently; otherwise, they are likely to be overlooked in the view of a text-centered mentality, just as scholars unconsciously tried to find individual creativity first in improvisation.

Chapter 4

1. The original is as follws:.

مرحوم استاد
محمدکریم پیرنیا به ما معماری ایرانی می‌آموخت. پیر معماری ایرانی می‌گفت: (تا حد امکان قریب به مضمون) «.. آنهایی که با موسیقی ایرانی آشنا هستند، خوب درک می‌کنند، از سردر قیصریه که وارد شویم، گویی که در گوشمان دستگاه شور را زمزمه می‌کنند، اول «درآمد شور»، یکنواخت و آرام که در طاقنماها نیز تجلی می‌یابد، بعد در عالی‌قاپو به «شهناز» می‌رسیم و در مسجد امام (شاه) به «سلمک» و پس از آن در مسجد شیخ‌لطف‌الله به «زیرافکن» که اوج زیبایی است و از آنجا نغمه به «فرود» می‌رسد و به «درآمد» بازمی‌گردد و میدان نیز به سردر قیصریه و این خود یک موسیقی دلنشین است...»

2. The structure of *charkh* presented in this chapter applies to all 12 modes of Iranian music, as mentioned in Chapter 3, note 3. I will use the *shūr* mode for this discussion, based on the description by Jihānī (2003: 9). The original liner notes are reproduced below. In Figure 4.1, I changed the layout of Pāyvar's performance list to vertical in order to make it correspond to the arrangement of the other two lists.

```
Zākerī. 2004.                                        (Bahārī n.d.)
        روی الف:                                    دستگاه شور
○ مقدمه و پیش درآمد شور                              ۱- درآمد
○ درآمد - پنجه شعری - کرشمه - فرود                   ۲- پیش درآمد
○ چهار مضراب - شور مرکب                              ۳- چهار مضراب
○ شهناز - قرچه                                       ٤- شهناز - رضوی
○ چهار مضراب شهناز از حبیب سماعی                     ٥- رهاب
○ رضوی - حسینی - دوبیتی - نغمه و فرود به شور         ٦- حسینی
○ رنگ شور                                            ۷- کرد، بیات
                                                     ۸- رنگ شور
```

```
Pāyvar. 1978.
روی دوم: شور: پیش درآمد، چهارمضراب، درآمد خارا، درآمد اول، درآمد دوم، جمله معترضه
و تحریر ابوعطائی، درآمد اوج، چهارمضراب، شهناز، رضوی، ضربی حسینی حسینی و فرود.
```

3. For example, the D natural on the fourth staff line in the *darāmad* section changes to the D *koron* in *shahnāz*, and the higher A in *hoseini* is employed only as a flat note whereas all the A notes in the middle and lower registers up to that point were *koron*. See Chapter 5, note 5 and Chapter 12, note 6 for more information.

4. The *moteghaiyer* notes mentioned in note 3 return to the original sound in the *forūd* movement.

5. However, if a specific *gūshe* name is added to the musical form, such as *chahārmezrāb-e razavi*, then the *chahārmezrāb* is composed upon the characteristics of that *gūshe* and may not have a complete *charkh* structure.

6. Here, *darāmad* is not the name of a *gūshe* but instead refers to the introductory part of a *gūshe*.

Chapter 5

1. Showing *radīfs* in notation may tend to highlight the individual differences between them, but as stated in Chapter 3, this view originates in the perspective of a text-centered culture. While in the present work I must adopt transcriptions as methodological tools, the music to which they refer is not a static one. Instead, we should treat this as a non-literal art which exists only while the sound is being produced. In this sense, the notation

Notes

used here should be viewed in the same light as the transcriptions of improvised performances.

2. The first column lists the names of the six inheritors of the *radīfs,* while column headings indicate the temporal progression of *gūshes* that establishes the *charkh* cycle. I have also indicated, using shaded cells, the *gūshes* that play an important role in the progression of the music.

3. In the actual transcription, *zang-e shotor* of Davāmī's *radīf* shown in Score 5.45 is presented immediately before *maghlūb*.

4. According to the performance by Talā'ī (1993), a simile mark to indicate repetition of the third and fourth notes on the first stave is missing from the transcription.

5. *Shekaste* in other modes, such as *māhūr* or *bayāt-e tork*, is achieved by altering the tone a third above *shāhed* of *darāmad* (or of a *gūshe* equivalent to it) to *koron*. This kind of altered tone is called *moteghaiyer*.

6. The E flat that had been used in the *gūshes* before *mokhālef* is now altered to E *koron*, which is a neutral second below *shāhed*, while the A *koron* that was introduced in *darāmad* is altered to A flat an octave higher in *mokhālef*. Such modifications of notes in *mokhālef* can be observed in other *radīfs* as well, as shown in Scores 5.38 (A *koron* to A flat; E flat to E *koron*) and 5.39 (E flat to E *koron*. Although not shown in this example, the higher A appears as A flat as well instead of A *koron* later in the score.).

7. In Chapter 4, I stated that there were *gūshes* in Sabā's *radīf* that have a melodic movement which incorporates elements of subsequent *gūshe* even before the new *gūshe* officially takes over under its own name. The example below presents the ending part of *mūye* immediately before *mokhālef*, which illustrates this point.

Score 5.n.7: The ending part of *gūshe mūye* from Sabā's *radīf* (Sabā 1991: 16)

In this score, we can observe that after the melody ends temporarily on A *koron* – the *shāhed* of this mode – it heads toward F, which is the sixth degree above, even with the alteration of the note E flat to E *koron*, to prepare for the next *gūshe* to come – *mokhālef*.

8. The B flat having been used until immediately before *mokhālef* now changes to B *koron*, which is a neutral second below *shāhed*, while the E *koron* that had been introduced in *darāmad* is altered to E flat an octave higher here in *mokhālef*. Similar alterations occur in other *radīfs*, as shown in Score 5.41 in which the B flat is altered to B *koron*. Later in the score (but not shown in this example), the higher E appears as E flat instead of E *koron*.

9. The F natural that had been used in the *gūshes* before *mokhālef* is now altered to F *sori*, which is a neutral second below *shāhed*, while the B *koron* that was introduced in *darāmad* is altered to B flat an octave higher here in *mokhālef* (not shown in this score because it appears in the later part of this *gūshe*.)
10. According to Rūhafzā's performance (1998), the transcription in this example is missing a flat symbol on the second circled B.
11. According to Talā'ī's performance (1993), the transcription in this example is missing a flat symbol on the circled note E.
12. The key signature here indicates a *sori* on the higher F and a natural on the lower F. Thus, a characteristic *forūd* movement there – a return from F *sori* to F natural – can essentially be achieved by simply descending from the higher to lower echelons.
13. The "fixed melodies" in *maghlūb* and *hoddī o pahlavī* have some relationship with their position in *charkh* as well. In that sense, they have characteristics of both *gūshe* types.
14. As pointed out in Section 4.4, "Small *charkh*," there are other musical forms that display the features of major *gūshes* in the order of performance. These include *chahārmezrāb* (lit., "four plectrums;" a relatively fast-tempo piece for solo instrument), *moqaddameh* (lit., "prelude;" a piece for instrumental ensemble in calm tempo), and *pishdarāmad* (lit., "before *darāmad*;" a calm, musical piece for instrumental ensemble which is longer than *moqaddameh*).

Chapter 6

1. In the following discussion, I will assume that the dominant hand is the right hand, and thus, the non-dominant hand is the left hand.
2. Parvīz Meshkātian (1955–2009) was a composer and *santūr* player born in Neishābūr, Iran. He has given numerous performances and recordings in his country and abroad, including managing the 'Ālef Ensemble *Gorūh-e 'Ālef* in 1977. He is also well versed in the art of *setār* and is highly regarded in Iran both for his fluid tone and technique on the *santūr*, and his compositional excellence.
3. The score was not transcribed by Meshkātian himself, and there is some debate as to whether the "repeated strikes with the left hand" are actually played as transcribed, especially in this piece. Nevertheless, there is no doubt that this is a frequently used technique in recent *santūr* playing.
4. Dāryūsh Talā'ī (1952–) is a Tehran-born *tār-setār* player. He is a well-known scholar on *radīf*, and his *Tahlīl-e Radīf* (Nashr-e Ney 2015), which is referenced extensively in this book, was Iran's Book of the Year for 2016. He has taught at the University of Tehran for a long time.

Chapter 9

1. Improvisation in a group of different instruments and vocalist is a common way of performing Iranian music, and Moshfeq organizes such sessions regularly.
2. Generally speaking, the *santūr* can only play seven notes per octave, although the standard nine-bridge instrument can be tuned to include an altered E and F as well. However, when the music moves to a different *dastgāh* due to *modgardi*, the *santūr* has difficulty following, as it cannot play any notes it was not tuned to in advance.
3. One benefit of this string placement is that shifting by an octave is a simple matter of moving left or right.
4. The notes in classical Indian music are named, from lowest to highest, *sa, ri (re), ga, ma, pa, da, ni*. Sharma tuned the strings in the *chikari* course to *sa*, which plays the role of core tone; *pa*, a perfect fifth above *sa*; and *ga*, the third between *sa* and *pa*, the interval of which depends on the raga.
5. Older Iranian playing styles also used a pair of mallets of bare wood, but this is not the standard today.
6. Conversely, the Iranian *santūr*'s felt-tipped mallets do not rebound with enough force to use this technique.
7. Because the Iranian *santūr* mallet is much lighter than its Indian counterpart, it can be used for a rapid and fine tremolo technique called *rīz* (fine).
8. When the vertical column of bridges includes a note not to be played, its course can be muted with the fingers of the left hand to allow the *ghaseet* technique to pass on and continue to the next note.
9. At present, the standard Iranian mallet's striking edge is covered in felt or similar material, as seen on the mallet marked A. The mallet marked B is sold at the school of Majid Kiyāni (1941–), who is known for playing with mallets of bare wood. Because players are expected to use the mallet "as-is," its handle and tip are thicker than A.

Chapter 10

1. The cent is a unit for measuring pitch devised by Alexander John Ellis. A semitone is defined as 100 cents, allowing variations in pitch smaller than a semitone to be quantified.
2. Strictly speaking, there are slight numerical differences between the two explanations. Modarresi's "2," theoretically 100 cents, corresponds to intervals ranging from 80 to 120 cents in Talā'ī's diagram in Figure 10.3. His "3" is theoretically 150 cents but corresponds to 140 cents, and his "4" is theoretically 200 cents but corresponds to 180 to 220 cents. Additionally, Modarresi analyzes the *shūr* tetrachord by starting from what is in Figure 10.3 the middle finger (thus, the interval proportions are 220:140:140).

3. In Talā'ī (2015), this tetrachord is renamed *navā*. Accordingly, in Chapter 12 of this book, it is represented with the initial "N."

Chapter 11

1. Sa'īd Sābet (1959–) is a Tehran-born *santūr* player. A pupil of Farāmarz Pāyvar, he has produced many recordings of both his teacher's *radīf* and the *radīf* of Abolhasan Sabā.
2. Note that the lines in Photos 11.2 and 11.3 express general principles or ideals rather than actual striking points in performance.
3. From a July 1998 interview with Meshkātian.
4. This difference in physicality is recognizable even before the first sound is produced, simply from his hand posture as he prepares to play. For example, different musicians use their wrists in widely varying ways when striking a string – different angles, different heights – which leaves beginners quite lost at times. Most teachers treat this as an important topic to provide guidance on, as the seal of their musicality and performance philosophy.

    For example, as a basic rule, Farāmarz Pāyvar (and his pupil, Sa'īd Sābet) only move their hands from the wrist to strike notes, while Ardavān Kāmkār and his older brother Pashang Kāmkār advocate rotating the forearm "like turning a doorknob." Regarding wrist height, Pāyvar and Sābet tend to hold their hands angled downward at the wrist, with the wrist itself "floating" above, while the Kāmkār brothers, especially Ardavān, keep the wrist low and hold their hand angled upward from it. This results in audible differences: Pāyvar and Sābet produce a finer, lighter sound, while Ardavān's sound is stronger and more robust.
5. From a January 2014 interview with *santūr* player Kourosh Matin.

Chapter 12

1. In the list below the figure, the names of the *gūshes* are listed in a temporal order and numbered for ease of reference. Figures 12.2, 12.3, 12.5, 12.7 and 12.8 are organized in the same way.
2. In that sense, improvisation is much more intuitive on instruments like the *tār* and *setār* than on the *santūr* or similar, on which tetrachords can only be recognized aurally. What is more, as described in the introduction, *radīfs* for the *santūr* (excepting Mirzā Abdollāh's *radīf*, prepared under the supervision of Majid Kiyāni) exclude certain *gūshes* due to tuning limitations. For example, the *gūshe* with the S tetrachord (*'Ozzāl*) is excluded from *homāyun* mode. As a result, the possibilities and choices for *modgardi* that occur naturally to *tār* and *setār* players are not revealed to *santūr* players.

3. For example, when *tār* player Qāsem Rahīmzādeh (1983–) taught, he had his students take the F-G-A *koron*-B♭-A *koron*-G figure at the beginning of Score 12.10 and create countless variations on it, fleshing it out with other phrases before and after and expanding it with internal repetition and ornamentation. He then evaluated their work, and had the students memorize and practice the best until they could use them freely in improvisation. In other words, he had students create many "drawers" of musical material in advance and trained them to open these drawers unconsciously as necessary.

4. The English translation is from:

https://peaceformeandtheworld.ning.com/group/poetry-lounge/forum/topics/hafez-translated-from-persian-into-english-by-alan-godlas?commentId=5143044%3AComment%3A202421&groupId=5143044%3AGroup%3A10638 (accessed on February 29, 2024).

5. *Bayāt-e kord* is not usually counted among the "twelve modes" due to its similarity to *dashtī* mode.

6. *Moteghaiyer* refers to altered notes. This is traditionally explained as cases in which, during the progression from *gūshe* to *gūshe*, the E♭ (for example) used earlier in the mode "changes" to E *koron*. However, this change comes from implicitly viewing each *dastgāh* as a scale fixed in the octave and comparing them on that basis. When the modes of Iranian music are conceptualized as constructed of four different tetrachords, it can be said that the traditional concept of *moteghaiyer* has little meaning.

7. In Figures 12.1–12.3, 12.5, 12.7 and 12.8, each has S (*shāhed*), I (*ist*) or M (*moteghaiyer*) directly above the corresponding notes.

Bibliography

Atrā'ī, Arfa'e. 1990. *Davāzdah Maqām-e Mūsīqī-ye Mellī-ye Irān barāye Rāst kuk-e Santūr bar pāye-ye Radīf-e Ostād Mahmūd Karīmī.* Esfahān: Enteshārāt-e Vāhed-e Sorūd va Mūsīqī. Edāre-ye Koll-e Farhang va Ershād-e Eslāmī-ye Esfahān.

اطرایی، ارفع، (۱۳۶۹)، دوازده مقام موسیقی ملّی ایران برای راست کوک سنتور برپایه ردیف استاد محمود کریمی، انتشارات واحد سرود و موسیقی، ادارهٔ کل فرهنگ و ارشاد اسلامی اصفهان، اصفهان.

_____. 2003. *Haft Dastgāh va Panj Āvāz-e Mūsīqī-ye Irānī barāye Santūr.* Tehran: Moassese-ye Farhangī – Honarī-ye Māhūr.

اطرایی، ارفع، (۱۳۸۲)، هفت‌دستگاه و پنج آواز موسیقی ایرانی برای سنتور، مؤسسه فرهنگی هنری ماهور، تهران.

Caton, Margaret. 2002. "Performance Practice in Iran: *Radīf* and Improvisation" In *The Garland Encyclopedia of World Music.* Vol. 6, *The Middle East*, edited by Virginia Danielson, Scott Marcus, and Dwight Reynolds. New York and London: Routledge, pp. 129–143.

During, Jean. 1995. *Radīf-e Sāzī-ye Mūsīqī-ye Sonnatī-ye Irān, Radīf-e Tār va Setār-e Mirzā Abdollāh be ravāyat-e Nūr'alī Borūmand.* Tehran: Soroush Press. 2nd ed.

دورینگ، ژان (۱۳۷۴)، ردیف سازی موسیقی سنتی ایران، ردیف تار و سه تار میرزا عبدالله به روایت نورعلی برومند، ترجمهٔ پیروز سیار، چ۲، انتشارات سروش،تهران.

Farhat, Hormoz. 1965. *The Dastgāh Concept in Persian Music.* Los Angeles: Ph. D. Diss. at University of California.

Farhat, Hormoz et al. 1980. "Iran." In *The New Grove Dictionary of Music and Musicians.* Vol. 9, edited by Stanley Sadie et al., London: Macmillan, pp. 292–309.

Horiuchi, Masaru. 1985. "Arabu no rizumu-kan: Nishi Ajia yūboku seikatsu kara no hassō" [The Arabic sense of rhythm: An idea from western Asian pastoral lifestyles]. In *Kōtō denshō no hikaku kenkyū* [Comparative studies in oral traditions] Vol. 2, edited by Junzō Kawada and Gen'ichi Tsuge. Tokyo: Kōbundo, pp. 26–58.

Ikuta, Kumiko. 2001. "Shokunin no 'waza' no denshō katei ni okeru 'oshieru' to 'manabu': Dokuji no 'chishikikan,' 'kyōikukan' o megutte" ["Teaching" and "learning" in the process of transmitting artisanal "waza": On unique views of knowledge and education]. In *Jissen no esunogurafī* [Ethnography in practice], Jōkyōrontekī apurōchi [A situation theory approach], edited by Yūji Moro. Tokyo: Kaneko Shobō, pp. 230–246.

Itō, Nobuhiro. 2003. "Oto no 'miburi' o kijutsu suru: Haidon no piano sonata to gakkyoku bunseki" [Describing "gestures" of sound: Haydn's piano sonatas and musical analysis]. In *Piano o hiku shintai* [The piano-playing body], supervised by Akeo Okada. Tokyo: Shunjūsha, pp. 113–136.

Jairazbhoy, Nazir, A. 1980. "Improvisation." In *The New Grove Dictionary of Music and Musicians*. Vol. 9, edited by Stanley Sadie et al., London: Macmillan Publishers Limited, pp. 52–56.

Javāherī, ʿAlīrezā. 1997. *Gol-e Āʾīn Hejdah Qatʿe barāye Santūr az Parvīz Meshkātian*. Tehran.

جواهری، علیرضا (۱۳۷۶)، گل آئین ۱۸ قطعه برای سنتور از پرویز مشکاتیان، تهران

Jihānī, Hamidrezā. 2003. "Yek Jahān va Naghsh-e Jahān," *Īrān*. 23 June 2003, p. 9.

جیحانی، حمید رضا (۱۳۸۲)، یک جهان و نقش جهان، روزنامه ایران (۲ تیر ۱۳۸۲)، ص۹.

Kāmkār, Ardavān. 2016. *Majmūʿe-ye Qataʿāt-e Ardavān Kāmkār*. Tehran: Nashr-e nāy o ney.

کامکار، اردوان (۱۳۹۵)، مجموعه قطعات اردوان کامکار، نشر نای و نی، تهران.

Kāmkār, Pashang. 1996. *Āsārī az Pashang Kāmkār barāye Santūr*. Tehran. Entehārāt-e Āmūzesh.

کامکار، پشنگ (۱۳۷۵)، آثاری از پشنگ کامکار برای سنتور، انتشارات آموزش، تهران.

Khāleqī, Rūhollah. 2012. *Dastūr-e Moqaddamātī-ye Tar va Setār-e Honarestān, Book 1*. Tehran: Nashr-e nāy o ney.

خالقی، روح الله (۱۳۹۱)، دستور مقدماتی تار و سه تار هنرستان (کتاب اول)، نشر نای و نی، تهران.

Kiyāni, Majid. 1990. *Radīf-e Mirzā Abdollāh (1) Dastgāh-e Shūr*. Tehran: Nashr-e Ney.

کیانی، مجید (۱۳۶۹)، ردیف میرزا عبدالله (۱) دستگاه شور، نشر نی، تهران.

Koizumi, Fumio. 1978. "Chūtō ongaku no sankyoku" [The three poles of Middle Eastern music]. In *Chūtō handobukku* [Middle East handbook], edited by Yūzō Itagaki. Tokyo: Kōdansha, pp. 358–360.

Kuroyanagi, Tsuneo. 1998. *Gendai Perushiago jiten* [A dictionary of contemporary Persian]. Tokyo: Daigaku Syorin.

Maʿrūfī, Mūsā. 1995 (1963). *Radīf-e Haft Dastgāh-e Mūsīqī-ye Irānī*. Tehran: Anjoman-e Mūsīqī-ye Irān. 3rd ed.

معروفی، موسی (۱۳۷۴)، ردیف هفت دستگاه موسیقی ایرانی، انجمن موسیقی ایران، چ ۳، تهران.

Mas'ūdie, Mohammad, Taqī. 1995 (1978). *Radīf-e Āvāzī-ye Mūsīqī-ye Sonnatī-ye Irān be ravāyat-e Mahmūd Karīmī*. Tehran: Anjoman-e Mūsīqī-ye Irān. 3rd ed.

مسعودیه، محمدتقی (۱۳۷۴)، ردیف آوازی موسیقی سنتی ایران به روایت محمود کریمی، انجمن موسیقی ایران، چ ۳، تهران.

Miller, Lloyd Clifton. 1999. *Music and Song in Persia: The Art of Āvāz*. Richmond: Curzon Press.

Mizuno, Nobuo. 1992. "Shominzoku no ongaku yōshiki" [The musical forms of various peoples]. In *Minzoku ongaku gairon* [Ethnic music in outline], edited by Tomoaki Fujii et al. Tokyo: Tokyo Shoseki, pp. 30–48.

Modir, Hafez. 1986. "Research models in ethnomusicology applied to the *radif* phenomenon in Iranian classical music" *Pacific Review of Ethnomusicology*, Vol. 3, pp. 63–78.

Morita, Toyoko. 2008. "Iran to Nihon no gakkō kyōiku ni okeru kyōiku hōhō no hikaku: Koe no bunka to moji no bunka" [Comparing the Iran with Japan in teaching method in school education: Orality and literacy], *Iran kenkyū* [Journal of Iranian Studies], Vol. 4, pp. 217–230.

Narimān, Mansūr. 2012. *Shīve-ye Barbat Navāzī*. Tehran: Entehārāt-e Soroush.

نریمان، منصور (۱۳۹۱)، شیوهٔ بربط نوازی، انتشارات سروش، تهران.

Nettl, Bruno. 1974. "Thoughts on improvisation: A comparative approach" *Musical Quarterly*, Vol. LX, No. 1, pp. 1–19.

_____. 1998. "Introduction: An art neglected in scholarship" In *In the Course of Performance: Studies in the World of Musical Improvisation*, edited by Bruno Nettl with Melinda Russell. Chicago: University of Chicago Press, pp. 1–23.

_____. 2001 "Improvisation." In *The New Grove Dictionary of Musical Instrument 2nd. ed.* Vol. 12, edited by Stanley Sadie et al., London: Macmillan, pp. 94–98.

Nettl, Bruno with Bela Foltin, Jr. 1972. *Daramad of chahargah: A study in the performance practice of Persian music*. Detroit Monographs in Musicology. Detroit: Information Coordinators.

Okada, Emiko. 1981. *Iranjin no kokoro* [The Iranian soul], NHK Bukkusu [NHK Books]. Tokyo: NHK Publishing.

Ōkubo, Ken. 2003. "Te no dorama: Shopan sakuhin o hiite taiken suru" [Drama of the hands: Playing and experiencing Chopin's works]. In *Piano o hiku shintai* [The piano-playing body], supervised by Akeo Okada. Tokyo: Shunjūsha, pp. 165–188.

Ong, Walter. 1982. *Orality and Literacy: The Technologizing of the Word.* London: Methuen.

Pacholczyk, Jozef M. 1996. *Sufyana Musiqi: The classical music of Kashmir.* Berlin: VWB.

Pāyvar, Farāmarz. 1961. *Dastūr-e Santūr.* Esfahān: Entshārāt-e Vāhed-e Sorūd va Mūsīqī, Edāre-ye koll-e farhang va Ershād-e Eslāmī-ye Esfahān.

پایور، فرامرز(۱۳۴۰)، دستور سنتور، انتشارات واحد سرود و موسیقی، ادارۀ کل فرهنگ و ارشاد اسلامی اصفهان، اصفهان.

_____. 1982. *Qata'āt-e Mūsīqī-ye Majlesī barāye Santūr.* Esfahān: Entesharāt-e Vāhed-e Sorūd va Mūsīqī, Edāre-ye koll-e farhang va Ershād-e Eslāmī-ye Esfahān.

پایور، فرامرز(۱۳۶۱)، قطعات موسیقی مجلسی برای سنتور، انتشارات واحد سرود و موسیقی، ادارۀ کل فرهنگ و ارشاد اسلامی اصفهان، اصفهان.

_____. 1988. *Doure-ye Ebtedā'ī barāye Santūr.* Tehran.

پایور، فرامرز(۱۳۶۷)، دورۀ ابتدایی برای سنتور، تهران.

_____. 1996. *Radīf-e Āvāzī va Tasnīfhā-ye Qadīmī be ravāyat-e Ostād Abdollāh Davāmī.* Tehran: Moassese-ye Farhangī – Honarī-ye Māhūr.

پایور، فرامرز(۱۳۷۵)، ردیف آوازی و تصنیف‌های قدیمی به روایت عبدالله دوامی، مؤسسه فرهنگی هنری ماهور، تهران.

_____. 2019 (1972). *Sī Qat'e Chahārmezrāb barāye Santūr 9th.ed.* Tehran: Moassese-ye Farhangī – Honarī-ye Māhūr.

پایور، فرامرز(۱۳۵۱)، سی قطعه چهارمضراب برای سنتور، مؤسسه فرهنگی هنری ماهور، چ ۹، تهران.

Peabody, Berkley. 1975. *The Winged Word: A Study in the Technique of Ancient Greek Oral Composition as seen Principally through Hesiod's Works and Days.* Albany: State University of New York Press.

Powers, Harold S. 1980. "Kashmir." In *The New Grove Dictionary of Music and Musicians.* Vol. 9, edited by Stanley Sadie et al., 1980. London: Macmillan, pp. 817–819.

Pūrtorāb, Mostafa Kamāl et al. 2007. *Mabānī-ye Nazarī va Sākhtār-e Mūsīqī-ye Irānī,* Tehran: Sāzmān-e Chap va Entesharāt-e Vezārat-e Farhang va Ershād-e Eslāmī.

پورتراب، مصطفی کمال و دیگران (۱۳۸۶)، مبانی نظری و ساختار موسیقی ایرانی، سازمان چاپ و انتشارات وزارت فرهنگ و ارشاد اسلامی، تهران.

Sabā, Abolhasan. 1991 (1950). *Doure-ye Avval-e Santūr 10th ed.* Tehran: Entshārāt-e Montakhab-e Sabā.

صبا، ابوالحسن (۱۳۷۰)، دورهٔ اول سنتور، انتشارات منتخب صبا، چ ۱۰، تهران.

_____. 1992 (1956). *Doure-ye Dovvom-e Santūr 4th.ed.* Tehran: Entshārāt-e Montakhab-e Sabā.

صبا، ابوالحسن (۱۳۷۱)، دورهٔ دوم سنتور، انتشارات منتخب صبا، چ ۴، تهران.

_____. 1990 (1958). *Doure-ye Sevvom-e Santūr 4th ed.* Tehran: Entshārāt-e Montakhab-e Sabā.

صبا، ابوالحسن (۱۳۶۹)، دورهٔ سوم سنتور، انتشارات منتخب صبا، چ ۴، تهران.

Sharma, Shivkumar. 2002. A *Journey with a One Hundred Strings*. Penguin India.

Simms, Robert. 1996. *Avaz in the Recording of Mohammed Reza Shajarian*. Ph.D. Diss. University of Toronto.

Talā'ī, Dāryūsh. 1993. *Negareshī Nou be Te'ory-ye Mūsīqī-ye Irānī.* Tehran: Moassese-ye Farhangī – Honarī-ye Māhūr.

طلایی، داریوش (۱۳۷۲)، نگرشی نو به تئوری موسیقی ایرانی، مؤسسه فرهنگی هنری ماهور، تهران.

_____. 1997 (1995). *Radīf-e Mirzā Abdollāh*. Tehran: Moassese-ye Farhangī – Honarī-ye Māhūr. 2nd ed.

طلایی، داریوش (۱۳۷۶)، ردیف میرزا عبدالله، مؤسسه فرهنگی هنری ماهور، چ ۲، تهران.

_____. 2002. "A new approach to the theory of Persian art music: The *radif* and the modal system." In *The Garland Encyclopedia of World Music*. Vol. 6, *The Middle East*, edited by Virginia Danielson, Scott Marcus, and Dwight Reynolds. New York and London: Routledge, pp. 865–874.

_____. 2015. *Tahlīl-e Radīf.* Tehran: Nashr-e Ney.

طلایی، داریوش (۱۳۹۴)، تحلیل ردیف، نشر نی، تهران.

Tani, Masato. 2016. "Santūru ensō no atarashii shintaisei: 'Gakki banmen no chiseigaku' e mukete" [The new physicality of *santūr* performance: Toward a "geopolitics on the board of the instrument"]. In *Chūtō sekai no ongaku bunka: Umarekawaru dentō* [Music cultures of the Middle Eastern world: Traditions reborn], edited by Tetsuo Nishio and Nobuo Mizuno. Tokyo: Stylenote, pp. 98–115.

Tsuge, Gen'ichi. 1970. "Rhythmic Aspects of the *Āvāz* in Persian Music", *Ethnomusicology*, Vol. 14, pp. 205–27.

———. 1985. "Perusha no rizumu: Nishi Ajia, inritsu to hakusetsu" [Rhythms of Persia: Poetic and musical meter of western Asia]. In *Kōtō denshō no hikaku kenkyū* [Comparative studies in oral traditions] Vol. 2, edited by Junzō Kawada and Gen'ichi Tsuge. Tokyo: Kōbundō, pp. 59–80.

———. 1989. "Iran koten ongaku no riron to jissen" [Iranian classical music in theory and practice]. In *Ongaku no kōzō* [Musical structure], Iwanami Kōza: Nihon no Ongaku, Ajia no Ongaku [Iwanami Lectures: Music of Japan, Music of Asia] Vol. 5, edited by Satoaki Gamō. Tokyo: Iwanami Shoten, pp. 270–288.

———. 1990. "Perushia ongaku ni okeru āvāzu no rizumu" [Rhythmic Aspects of the *Āvāz* in Persian Music]. In *Minzoku to rizumu* [Ethnicity and rhythm], Minzoku Ongaku Sōsho [Ethnic music series] Vol. 8, edited by Tetsuo Sakurai et al. Tokyo: Tokyo Shoseki, pp. 144–172.

———. 1997. "Iran ongaku e no shōtai (dai 8-kai): Futari no shishō" [Invitation to Iranian music, Vol. 8: Two teachers], *Chashm* [Bulletin of the Japan–Iran Society), No. 69, pp. 48–53.

———. 1998. "Iran ongaku e no shōtai (dai 18-kai): Bārubado no 'Sanjū no rahan' o megutte" [Invitation to Iranian music, Vol. 18: On *bārbad* and the "thirty *lahn*"], *Chashm* [Bulletin of the Japan–Iran Society), No. 80, pp. 26–32.

———. 1999. "Iran ongaku e no shōtai (dai 22-kai): Tasunīfu o megutte" [Invitation to Iranian music, Vol. 22: On *tasnīf*], *Chashm* [Bulletin of the Japan–Iran Society), No. 84, pp. 29–35.

Zonis, Ella. 1973. *Classical Persian Music: An Introduction*. Cambridge: Harvard University Press.

Video and audio materials

Bahārī, 'Alī, Asghar. n.d. *Kamānche*. Tehran: Iran Sedā.
بهاری، علی اصغر، (بی تا)، کمانچه، ایران صدا، تهران.

Davāmī, Abdollāh. 1997. *Radīf-e Āvāzī-ye Ostād Abdollāh Davāmī*. Tehran: Moassese-ye Farhangī – Honarī-ye Māhūr.
دوامی، عبدالله (۱۳۷۶)، ردیف آوازی استاد عبدالله دوامی، مؤسسه فرهنگی هنری ماهور، تهران.

Patel, Jabbar. 2007. *Antardhwani: A film on Pandit Shiv Kumar Sharma*. Films Division of India.

Pāyvar, Farāmarz. 1978. *Chahārgāh-Shūr*. Tehran: Kānūn-e Parvaresh-e Fekrī-ye Kūdakān va Noujavānān.
پایور، فرامرز (۱۳۵۷)، چهارگاه – شور، کانون پرورش فکری کودکان و نوجوانان، تهران.

Rūhafzā, Soleiman. 1998. *Radīf-e Mūsā Ma'rūfī*. Tehran: Moassese-ye Farhangī – Honarī-ye Māhūr.
روح افزا، سلیمان (۱۳۷۷)، ردیف موسی معروفی، مؤسسه فرهنگی هنری ماهور، تهران.

Talā'ī, Dāryūsh. 1993. *Radīf-e Sāzī-ye Mūsīqī-ye Irān*. Tehran: Moassese-ye Farhangī – Honarī-ye Māhūr.
طلایی، داریوش (۱۳۷۲)، ردیف سازی موسیقی ایران (ردیف میرزا عبدالله)، مؤسسه فرهنگی هنری ماهور، تهران.

Zākerī, Behnāz. 2004. *Shūr-Navā*. Tehran: Kārgāh-e Mūsīqī.
ذاکری، بهناز (۱۳۸۳)، شور و نوا، کارگاه موسیقی، تهران.

Index

People

'Alīzādeh, Hosein حسین علیزاده 116–117
'Abdollāh, Mirzā میرزا عبدالله فراهانی 9, 53, 56–57, 73–76, 80, 82, 84–86, 89, 92–93, 97, 99–102, 104–105, 107–108, 112, 121, 126, 134, 195–196, 202–203, 206, 208–209, 220
al-Khalīl, Ibn, Ahmad خلیل بن احمد فراهیدی 40–41
Atrā'ī, Arfa'e ارفع اطرایی 137, 197, 207
Bahārī, 'Alī, Asghar علی اصغر بهاری 63, 67–68, 216
Davāmī, 'Abdollāh عبدالله دوامی 69–70, 74–76, 79, 87, 91, 95, 98, 100, 104, 107–108, 124–125, 194, 217
During, Jean, 126
Ellis, Alexander John, 219
Esfahānī, Hātef هاتف اصفهانی 38, 147–148
Farāhānī, 'Alī, Akbar علی اکبر فراهانی 73
Farhat, Hormoz هرمز فرهت 21, 143
Hāfez حافظ 12, 83, 143–146, 198–199
Hoseinqolī, Āqā آقا حسینقلی 73
Ikuta, Kumiko, 7, 117–118
Kāmkār, Ardavān اردوان کامکار 11, 121, 123, 140, 154, 161, 173, 175–176, 178–182, 210, 220
Kāmkār, Pashang پشنگ کامکار 139, 220
Karīmī, Mahmūd محمود کریمی 26, 31, 39, 50, 74–79, 87, 91, 95, 98, 103, 106, 110, 137, 146, 148, 196, 206–207
Kiyāni, Majid مجید کیانی 121–123, 219–220
Koizumi, Fumio, 1
Lotfi, Mohammadreza محمدرضا لطفی 123
Ma'rūfī, Mūsā موسی معروفی 23, 26, 31, 53, 56–58, 74–75, 79–80, 82, 84–85, 87, 89, 91, 98–99, 101–103, 105–106, 112, 210
Mas'ūdie, Mohammad Taghī محمدتقی مسعودیه 39, 50, 74, 76, 78, 87, 91, 95, 98, 103, 106, 110, 137, 146, 148, 210

Matin, Kourosh کورش متین 164, 182, 220
Meshkātian, Parvīz پرویز مشکاتیان 121–122, 154, 179, 218, 220
Mizuno, Nobuo, 14–15, 63, 77, 144
Modarresi, Bābak بابک مدرسی 167–168, 219
Moshfeq, Mahiyār مهیار مشفق 154, 157, 188, 219
Nettl, Bruno, 2–5, 31–32, 45, 47, 58–59, 71, 113, 128, 136, 213–215
Okada, Emiko, 61
Ong, Walter, 4, 7, 51, 56, 60, 116, 215
Pāyvar, Farāmarz فرامرز پایور 26, 53, 63, 65–68, 70, 74–76, 79–80, 86–87, 91, 95, 97–98, 100, 104, 107–108, 112, 120, 139, 149–151, 154, 160, 166, 174–175, 178–179, 194, 211, 213, 216, 220
Pīrniyā, Mohammad Karīm محمد کریم پیرنیا 62
Rahīmzādeh, Qāsem قاسم رحیم زاده 221
Rūhafzā, Soleiman روح افزا سلیمان 218
Sabā, Abolhasan ابوالحسن صبا 26, 37–38, 41–42, 52, 64, 68, 74–75, 78–79, 83–84, 86, 92–94, 97, 99–100, 103, 107, 110, 134, 145, 175, 187, 189, 211, 217, 220
Sābet, Sa'īd سعید ثابت 178–179, 211, 220
Sharma, Shiv Kumar, 154–159, 161, 219
Sopori, Bhajan, 161
Talā'ī, Dāryūsh داریوش طلایی 21, 53, 57, 74, 76, 80, 82, 84–86, 89, 92–93, 97, 100–102, 104–105, 107–108, 112–113, 126–127, 134, 167–168, 171, 184–185, 187–188, 190–191, 195–197, 203–205, 217–220
Tsuge, Gen'ichi, 19–21, 38, 40, 43, 56, 118, 143, 145, 149, 212
Vazīrī, 'Alīnaqī علینقی وزیری 36, 115
Zākerī, Behnāz بهناز ذاکری 63, 67–68, 216
Zarrinpanje, Nasrollāh نصرالله زرین پنجه 56
Zonis, Ella, 21, 83, 143–145

Modes (*dastgāh/āvāz*)

abū'atā آواز ابوعطا 37, 63, 67–68, 93, 147–148, 196, 209
afshārī آواز افشاری 93–94, 189–190, 192–193, 209

bayāt-e esfahān آواز بیات اصفهان 209
bayāt-e kord بیات کرد 63, 68, 204, 221
bayāt-e tork آواز بیات ترک 93, 148–151, 189, 191–192, 209, 217

231

Traditional Iranian Music

chahārgāh دستگاه چهارگاه 41, 209
dashtī آواز دشتی 93, 187–189, 209, 221
homāyun دستگاه همایون 83–84, 145, 184–185, 209, 220
māhūr دستگاه ماهور 146, 184, 186, 209, 217
navā دستگاه نوا 93, 209
rāst-panjgāh دستگاه راست‌پنجگاه 209

segāh دستگاه سه‌گاه 23, 26, 50, 52, 69–70, 74, 76–77, 80–82, 84–85, 87, 89–96, 98–99, 101–103, 105–107, 109, 111–112, 133, 135, 194–195, 204–205, 209, 212
shūr دستگاه شور 12, 56, 62–63, 68, 92–93, 183–184, 187–189, 195–196, 198–199, 201–203, 206–207, 209, 216

Gūshes

baste negār بسته نگار 75, 88–90, 100, 111, 204–205
chahārbāgh چهار باغ 37–39, 148, 196–197
chahārpāre چهارپاره 144, 147–148, 150
darāmad درآمد 24, 26, 28, 30, 50, 52, 56, 62–70, 75–82, 84–86, 88, 90, 92–94, 96, 99–100, 102, 104–107, 109, 111–112, 133–135, 184–196, 201, 204, 206, 212, 216–218
forūd فرود 25–30, 49–50, 62–71, 75, 81, 88, 104, 106–111, 113, 188, 190, 192, 194–195, 203, 216, 218
hājī-hasanī حاجی حسنی 75, 101, 104, 111
hazin حزین 75, 104, –107, 109, 111
hoddī o pahlavī حدی و پهلوی 75, 109, 218
hoseini حسینی 63–68, 184, 187–189, 216
hozān حزان 106
kereshme کرشمه 24–25, 28, 30, 63, 67–68, 75, 81, 83–85, 88, 96, 99–100, 111, 144–145, 204, 211
maghlūb مغلوب 75, 102–104, 108, 217–218
mansūrī منصوری 41–42
masnavī-ye mokhālef مثنوی مخالف 107–108
mehrabānī مهربانی 148–151, 191

mokhālef مخالف 25–28, 30, 50, 75, 96, 99–102, 104–107, 109, 111, 113, 217–218
mokhālef be maghlūb مخالف به مغلوب 106
moqaddameh مقدمه 218
mūye مویه 24, 26–28, 30, 50, 75, 90, 92–95, 105, 108–109, 111, 113, 217
naghme نغمه 63, 68, 75, 81–83, 85, 100, 111
ouj اوج 63, 68, 96, 184–185, 188, 206–207
razavi رضوی 63–68, 184, 188, 216
reng-e delgoshā رنگ دلگشا 75, 111
rohāb رهاب 63, 68, 184, 190, 192–193, 202–203
salmak سلمک 62, 184, 188
sāqīnāme ساقی نامه 144–146, 186
shahnāz شهناز 62–68, 184, 188, 216
shekaste شکسته 95–96, 186, 191, 217
shekaste mūye شکسته مویه 75, 95, 109
tasnīf-e dogāh تصنیف دوگاه 148–149
zābol زابل 24, 26–28, 30, 50, 75, 86, 88, 90, 92, 96, 99–100, 105, 111–112
zang-e shotor زنگ شتر 75, 81, 85, 99–100, 111, 217
zīr afkan زیرافکن 62

Subjects

'ūd عود 11, 153, 163–164, 168–171, 173
āvāz آواز (Five secondary modes among the twelve Persian musical modes), 166–167, 209
āvāz (Non-metric rhythmic form), 2, 36–38, 41–43, 45, 143, 147, 151
āvāz (Song; vocal music), 9, 37, 43–44, 119–120, 137–138, 154, 163–165, 173
barbat بربط 210
bi-zarbi بی ضربی 143, 147, 151
chahārgāh (tetrachord), 168, 185
chahārmezrāb چهارمضراب 63–68, 216, 218

charkh چرخ 7–8, 61–62, 64–74, 77, 80–81, 88, 90–92, 95, 100–102, 104–106, 109–111, 113, 117–119, 124–125, 128, 191, 216–218
darāmad (as the internal structure of a gūshe), 69, 88, 194–195, 203, 216
dashtī (tetrachord), 168, 185
dastgāh دستگاه (mode), 1, 3–4, 8–9, 11–13, 19, 23, 29–30, 45–50, 54–55, 58, 63, 91, 111, 131, 133–135, 143–144, 154, 166–167, 169, 171, 183, 186–187, 209, 211–212, 219, 221

Index

enteqāl انتقال 203
gūshe گوشه (melody type), 7, 9, 19–23, 26, 28–33, 35, 37, 41, 45–46, 48–52, 54–56, 62–65, 68–77, 79–86, 88, 90–96, 99–112, 115–117, 119, 124–125, 128, 131, 133–135, 144–145, 147–148, 183, 187–196, 201–206, 209–213, 216–218, 220–221
ist ایست 75–76, 82, 92, 94, 96, 150, 152, 201–202, 204–206, 221
kamānche کمانچه 9, 44, 124, 153, 163–165, 173, 185
koron کرن 24–27, 29, 36, 65–66, 76–80, 82, 84–85, 90, 92–96, 102–108, 110, 112–113, 135, 138, 165, 168, 187, 190–193, 195, 202, 210–211, 216–218, 221
māhūr (tetrachord), 168, 185
maqām مقام 133
mezrāb مضراب (mallet), 42, 122, 174
mo'allaq معلق 206
modgardi مدگردی 9, 11, 169, 171, 184–189, 191–193, 219–220
moteghaiyer متغیر 64, 107, 205–206, 216–217, 221
naghme نغمه 209
navā (tetrachord), 185, 220
ney نی 44, 124, 163–165, 171, 173
pāye پایه 112
pishdarāmad پیش درآمد 63–68, 218
radīf ردیف 6–9, 11–14, 19–23, 26, 28–29, 31–33, 35, 37–38, 41, 46, 48–50, 52–53, 56–57, 59, 65, 68–70, 73–80, 82–87, 89, 91–95, 97–112, 115–119, 121–122, 124–128, 133–137, 140, 145–146, 148, 175, 181, 183–184, 186–187, 189, 192–196, 198, 202–203, 206–214, 216–218, 220

radīfdān ردیف دان 127–128
reng رنگ 63–68, 75, 111–112
rīz ریز 42–43, 179, 219
santūr سنتور 8–11, 15, 41–42, 44, 74, 118–124, 137–140, 153–161, 163–166, 168–171, 173–182, 196, 210–211, 213, 218–220
setār سه تار 9–12, 56, 74, 116, 118, 121, 138–139, 153–154, 163–165, 167–169, 171, 173, 185, 193, 198, 209–211, 218, 220
sh'er شعر 69, 81, 88, 194–196, 198
shāhed شاهد 75–82, 85–86, 88, 90, 92–96, 102, 104–105, 111, 135, 149–152, 185–187, 190–193, 201–202, 204–206, 210, 217–218, 221
shūr (tetrachord), 168, 185, 219
sori سری 36, 93, 108, 211, 218
ta'līq تعلیق 192, 202, 204–206
tahrīr تحریر 63, 68–70, 81–82, 109, 120, 122, 147, 152, 159–160, 190, 192, 198, 203, 206
tahrīr (as the internal structure of a gūshe), 69, 81, 88, 194–195, 202–203
takie تکیه 120, 122, 160
tār تار 9–10, 12, 23, 36, 41, 74, 115–116, 118, 121, 123, 138–139, 153–154, 163, 165, 168–169, 171, 173, 185, 188, 193, 198, 209–210, 218, 220–221
tetrachord دانگ (dāng), 9, 11, 165, 167–169, 171, 184–193, 206, 219–221
tonbak تنبک 161, 163, 173
zarbi ضربی 143–149, 151

India related

alaap, 158–159
chikari, 158, 219
drone, 139, 158
ghaseet, 159, 219

Hindustani music, 153–159, 161
Kashmiri *santūr*, 154–157, 159, 161
meend, 158–159

233

Poetry Prosody Related

'arūzī عروضی   38, 40, 212
anapaest (short-short-long) pattern,   43
bahr بحر   40–41, 199
bahr-e kāmel-e mosamman-e sālem
   بحر کامل مثمن سالم   196
fā'elāton فاعلاتن   41, 83, 145, 199
fa'ūlon فعولن   41, 109–110, 146
iambic (short-long) pattern,   37, 43

kāmel کامل   41, 148
mojtass-e makhbūn مجتث مخبون   83, 145
mostaf'alon مستفعلن   41, 83
motafā'elon متفاعلن   41, 148, 196
motaqāreb متقارب   146
sālem سالم   41
taqtī'-e hejā'ī تقطیع هجائی   38